Stellium in Scorpio

Second in the Richfield & Rivers Mystery Series

What Reviewers Say About Bold Strokes Authors

Kim Baldwin

"*Force of Nature* is filled with nonstop, fast paced action. Tornadoes, raging fire blazes, heroic and daring rescues…Baldwin does a fine job of describing the fast-paced scenes and inspiring the reader to keep on turning the pages." – L-word.comLiterature

Rose Beecham

"…her characters seem fully capable of walking away from the particulars of whodunit and engaging the reader in other aspects of their lives." – *Lambda Book Report*

Georgia Beers

"Beers weaves a tale of yearning, love, lust, and conflict resolution. She has constructed a believable plot, with strong characters in a charming setting." – *JustAboutWrite*

Ronica Black

"*Wild Abandon* tells how these two women come to realize that 'life was too precious to be ruled by…fears, by…demons.' While these two women struggle with their issues, there is some very, very hot sex. If you enjoy complex characters and passionate sex scenes, you'll love *Wild Abandon*." – *MegaScene*

Gun Brooke

"*Course of Action* is a romance…populated with a host of captivating and amiable characters. The glimpses into the lifestyles of the rich and beautiful people are rather like guilty pleasures…a most satisfying and entertaining reading experience." – *Midwest Book Review*

Cate Culpepper

"…an exceptional storyteller who has taken on a very difficult subject …and turned it into a spellbinding novel. As an author, she understands well that fiction can teach us our own history." – *JustAboutWrite*

Jane Fletcher

"*The Exile and the Sorcerer* is a mesmerizing read, a tour-de-force packed with adventure, ordeals, complex twists and turns, and the internal introspection of appealing characters." – *Midwest Book Review*

JD Glass

"*Punk Like Me*...is different. It is engaging. It is life-affirming. Frankly, it is genius. This is a rare book in that it has a soul; one that is laid bare for all to see." – *JustAboutWrite*

Grace Lennox

"Chance is refreshing...Every nuance is powerful and succinct. *Chance* is not a novel about the music industry; it is about a woman discovering herself as she muddles through all the trappings of fame." – *Midwest Book Review*

Lee Lynch

"Lynch, with a dozen novels to her credit dating back to the early days of Naiad Press, has earned her stripes as a writerly elder. She was contributing stories to the lesbian magazine *The Ladder* four decades ago. But this latest is sublimely in tune with the times." – *Q-Syndicate*

JLee Meyer

"*Forever Found*...neatly combines hot sex scenes, humor, engaging characters, and an exciting story." – *MegaScene*

Radclyffe

"...well-plotted...lovely romance...I couldn't turn the pages fast enough!" – Ann Bannon, author of *The Beebo Brinker Chronicles*

Susan Smith

"This disparate duo's lush rush of a romance - which incorporates reincarnation, a grounded transman and his peppy daughter, and the dark moods of a troubled witch - pays wonderful homage to Leslie Feinberg's classic gender-bending novel, *Stone Butch Blues*." – *Q-Syndicate*

Ali Vali

"Rich in character portrayal, *The Devil Inside* by Ali Vali is an unusual, unpredictable, and thought-provoking love story that will have the reader questioning the definition of right and wrong long after she finishes the book." – *JustAboutWrite*

Stellium in Scorpio

Second in the Richfield & Rivers Mystery Series

by

ANDREWS & AUSTIN

2007

STELLIUM IN SCORPIO

ISBN 10: 1-933110-65-1
ISBN 13: 978-1-933110-65-3

This Trade Paperback Original Is Published By
Bold Strokes Books, Inc.,
New York, USA

First Edition January 2007

.

Credits
Editors: Cindy Cresap and Stacia Seaman
Production Design: Stacia Seaman
Cover Design By Sheri (GRAPHICARTIST2020@HOTMAIL.COM)

By the Authors

Richfield & Rivers Mystery Series

Combust The Sun

Acknowledgments

We are extremely proud to be working with Bold Strokes Books and its award-winning publisher and author, Radclyffe. Many thanks to the BSB team: editor Cindy Cresap, cover artist Sheri, and technical editor Stacia Seaman. Special thanks to Shelley and Connie for general hand-holding.

Dedication

To Billie Jean King
Women's champion on and off the court

Prologue

It was at once the most prestigious and whispered-about evening in Las Vegas, replete with drag queens, mafia dons, and upscale hookers, all of whom, having had enough alcohol and drugs to sufficiently numb the senses, displayed no remorse as they bet on who in this gambler's paradise would most likely die in the next twelve months: a macabre game for the rich and bored.

Gypsy Rose Ross, a twenty-three-year-old Las Vegas showgirl with the requisite long legs and cover girl complexion, followed the flickering black candles held aloft by the beautiful bronze chorus boys in feathered masks and leather breastplates as they wafted through the marble arches and down a long tunnel where the walls parted, revealing a small but dramatic theater-in-the-round.

The processional formed a circle around the stage, a forty-foot metal disk, a polished steel mechanical masterpiece, a series of precisely engineered circles within circles, each able to spin at varying speeds to create theatrical illusion—for this was a town of illusion. Tonight, its highly polished metal surface reflected the ring of costumed guests, as if they'd fallen face up into a large silver pond.

Marlena, a particularly striking drag queen, yelped as she hit her foot on the edge of the metal circle. "Ouch, this thing is hard!"

"You never complained before," Joanie Burr, another drag queen, said slyly as fog began to seep out below the disk, enveloping the guests' legs in a mysterious mist.

A deep, disembodied voice welcomed the guests to this All Hallows' Eve Ghoul Pool.

"I'm into the ghost," Marlena purred.

"I heard he's into you about twice a week," a chorus boy sniped, and Elliot Traugh, an erudite gay man, looked away, obviously pained.

A Latin chant arose, and the mirror-like disk turned slowly at their feet; its inner circle spun faster, hypnotically, and then separated and rose into the air as the chanting reached a crescendo. The swarthy ghost arose from the Underworld beneath the disk—bare-chested, black-booted, leather-strapped, spike-balled—an apparent denizen of West Hollywood.

Elliot Traugh held the silver bowl aloft as the ghost drew thirteen names, reading each one slowly before tossing it into the cauldron of flames that skirted the stage.

The redheaded young Gypsy Rose Ross leaned into Sophia, a tall, brashly handsome Italian woman. "Do people on the list ever really die?"

"Don't worry about the list. It's just a stupid game," Sophia said, keeping her eye on Elliot Traugh. Rose gasped as two male dancers coupled in a shadowed corner, one having mounted the other from behind. "It's a hologram, an illusion. Faux-fucking," Sophia whispered very close to Rose's ear. "Personally, I like real fucking."

"Rose Ross!" the ghost intoned. Sophia's wineglass slipped from her hands and shattered on the floor. Rose's eyes darted away from the ghostly lovers, and she stared at her host in disbelief.

All heads swung to observe the statuesque showgirl, and the room raised its collective glass, their voices like thunder. "The ghost has got us, the ghost has hung us, and now we toast the ghosts among us!"

CHAPTER ONE

The large, ninety-pound, tricolored basset hound was approaching at warp speed across the backyard, past the lemon tree, over the flagstone patio, ears spread wide like the wings of a 747, going airborne three feet from me and belly flopping into my lap, snatching half of the ice cream bar out of my hand and gulping it down in one joyous swallow.

"Damn it, Elmo! You've wrecked my suit! What in the hell am I going to wear?"

Elmo licked the side of my face to remove the chocolate he'd splashed there and then gave me two more licks out of sheer gratitude. I had thought he was safely in his wicker basket in the living room taking a nap, otherwise I would never have sat down on the back steps to indulge in Elmo's one uncontrollable addiction. He gave me one more lick, this one decidedly a kiss for my not having berated him further, and he buried his head under my arm, smearing more ice cream onto my suit. I sighed in resignation of the disaster he had wrought and patted his head in sympathy. "I completely understand a craving you can't control," I said, thinking of Callie and how I hadn't heard from her in more than a week and how every time the phone rang I dove on it like Elmo on ice cream.

I pulled myself to my feet, shrugged out of my Ralph Lauren suit, tossed it into the dry-cleaning bag, and rummaged through the closet for something else that matched. I settled on a double-breasted blazer with a matching vest and a starched pair of jeans.

"This is the last clean outfit I have, so stay away from me with those chocolate-covered jowls," I warned the large hound, who merely belched in reply and closed his eyes, having reached some basset nirvana brought on by dairy products.

I grabbed the folder labeled *Midnight Rodeo*, picked up my car keys, and headed for the door. I couldn't concentrate on anything these days, not even the network movie I was about to pitch in an hour.

Elmo watched me with furrowed basset brow as I breezed past him, gave him a quick pat on the head, and said, "Back by noon. Guard the joint and stay out of the freezer."

Having set the burglar alarm, I dashed out the door, jumped into the Jeep, and backed up at high speed, narrowly missing the lilac bush with the left side mirror and the side of the house with the right side mirror as I maneuvered down a driveway the width of a bike path. No scrapes. Pretty good depth perception for a person who never slept. My nights, and a good part of my days, were spent obsessing over Callie Rivers. Our final lovemaking had been nothing short of spectacular. If we had been tires, we would have been treadbare from the friction. We fell asleep only to awaken a few hours later, wet and wired to make love again, as if our bodies, without any help from our minds, were magnetically drawn to repeating the orgasmic sensation again and again. How, after that, could she have postponed our meeting in Las Vegas? First a week, then two, now ten weeks had passed, all due, so she claimed, to her work. *Maybe for her it was just great sex. Wham, bam, thank you, ma'am. Maybe she's seeing someone else. Maybe psychics are basically crazy. Maybe I'm going insane from thinking about it. I've got to stay focused on this pitch to the network...and not wreck the car!* I thought as a man swerved, narrowly missing me, and shouted, "Fuck you, lady!" I almost smiled at the oddity of "fuck you" and "lady" in the same sentence. *Fuck you, bitch, maybe. But fuck you, lady must mean that, basically, he likes women, unless they're trying to crush him with their cars.*

The Hollywood Bowl marquee flashed news of last night's Halloween Concert as I drove by, heading over the hill.

I recited my pitch notes that lay on the seat of the car. "Bobby Jo was a raw-boned girl from Alabama whose horses often exhibited more sense than she did." I said the line again into the air, more casually this time, as if I were just formulating the thought. The light turned red at the corner of Sunset and Highland, trapping me alongside a transient wearing a propeller beanie on his head. He leaned into the passenger side of my car and waved a ragged piece of cardboard at me:

Will work for food. I waved him off, having seen the recent exposé on L.A.'s transient population who apparently collected ten bucks from people like me, headed for a pay phone and dialed their "junk dealer," and within twenty minutes, a beat-up car would cruise by with a dirty needle full of forget.

Minutes later I rolled through the Fairfax District where two elderly Jewish men, wearing yarmulkes on their heads, were entering Cantor's Deli for a morning bagel. It dawned on me that society drew a very fine line between a beanie that was acceptable and one that wasn't. It apparently had to do with the propeller.

Turning left on Beverly Boulevard, I pulled onto the CBS lot, found a parking space along the narrow alleyway that faced the executive offices, and entered the main lobby. Unlike the vaulted ceilings of the ABC lobby or the more horizontal quarters of NBC, the CBS lobby felt genteel even if, on this particular day, the huge windows could have used a good bath. I reported to the receptionist that I was waiting for Nan Connors, vice president of Mitafilms, and director Granger Goodman, who would be joining me at ten o'clock, and then we would all be seeing Marshall Tevachney.

"Your name, please?" the receptionist asked.

"Teague Richfield," I replied.

"I'll ring Mr. Tevachney when you're ready."

I stared out the window and continued rehearsing my pitch. "Bobby Jo had no idea that the cowboys she'd befriended that night would turn on her. She'd known one of them for years. He was like a brother. But the heat and the alcohol changed all that."

I tapped my foot nervously.

My cell phone rang. It was Barrett Silvers, the tall, handsome, androgynous motion picture executive who held the distinction of being the only Hollywood executive to have both physically and psychologically fucked me. We hadn't spoken since midsummer, when she'd admitted to planting a little artifact on me that had endangered my life, and Callie's. Hearing her voice brought that up again.

"Hi, Teague, Barrett. Where are you?"

"I'm at CBS getting ready to go into a pitch."

"I thought you only pitched to me." Her voice sounded seductive.

"Not lately," I said with an edge to my voice.

"I'm back at work now, and I'm feeling better. I was pretty out of my head on drugs when we last spoke. Anyway, I'm figuring I owe you one." She paused, and I said nothing to let her off the hook. She sure as hell did owe me one. In fact, what she owed me would overflow Yankee Stadium. The silence between us was palpable. She finally continued, "There's a big director friend of mine who's bankable, and he's looking for material. I told him about you. I want to get the three of us together."

"And do what?" I tried to sound disinterested, but I was already mentally whoring out. Bankable directors could get movies made.

"Make one of your theatricals, if all goes well." She kept her voice silky smooth.

"And what do you get out of this?" I asked with unveiled sarcasm.

"I'd like to say a weekend with you, but from the look in your eye when I saw you at Il Faccio's with the pretty blonde, I'd say you look…taken."

I didn't know if I was taken or not. Barrett Silvers's voice had more urgency in it than Callie's these days. At least Barrett wanted to see me soon. I had no idea if or when Callie would finally decide the same.

"*Are* you taken?" Barrett probed seductively.

My mind slid back to Barrett on top of me in bed, inside me with the same kind of urgency she had in her voice right now. I had to remind myself that while she was technically brilliant in bed, she was also emotionally heartless and had slept with every female writer in L.A.

"I'm not up for games, Barrett. If you've got someone who wants to make a movie, great, but that has nothing to do with my personal life."

Through the tall CBS plate glass windows, I spotted Nan clacking along the concrete walkway in her spike heels. Granger, in ragged blue jeans, trailed her with the studied nonchalance of one who has a studio deal and is loved by the networks. His presence at this pitch was purely sales insurance.

"I gotta go," I said to Barrett. "My guys are here for the pitch."

"We'll talk soon," she said and hung up.

I straightened the collar on my starched white shirt, buttoned my blue blazer, and dusted off my starched jeans before shaking my head vigorously, much like Elmo when he wants to get rid of a bad conversation.

Nan came through the big double doors, looking tense, crisp, and businesslike. Granger was tall, wiry, bushy-haired, and looked distracted. We said our hellos and gave each other Hollywood air-kisses.

"So are we ready?" Nan addressed me using the collective pronoun. I assured her *we* were. Nan asked Granger if he remembered the story well enough to "do the character arc," describing the dramatic change a character has undergone by the end of the movie.

"I've been thinking about the story," Granger said, crossing his arms, shifting his weight, and staring up at the ceiling. "I think this girl…Bobby Sue—"

"Bobby Jo," I corrected with a smile.

"I think this girl needs a greater handicap in life than the psychological abuse she carries with her from her childhood."

"What do you mean?" I asked pleasantly.

"I think she should have something like—" He broke off, musing.

"Like?"

"I don't know…like…one leg." He pursed his lips pensively.

I burst out laughing. "Why not put her in an iron lung for the entire movie?"

"I think it makes her need for love that much greater," Granger said, ignoring me the way one would an unruly child.

"Interesting," Nan said in a manner that would have me believe she really thought he'd come up with a provocative idea.

"I hope you're kidding!" I blurted out. "At one point, the woman becomes a bareback rider!"

"That ties in. People expect circus people to be odd." Nan nodded her head pensively.

"She's not in the circus. She's on the *circuit*—the rodeo circuit! Look, a girl with a wooden leg…" I tried to sound calm.

"No leg," he corrected me. "She's too poor to afford a wooden leg, so we have a sort of…Tiny Tim empathy working for us."

I bent over at the waist and did a ninety-degree pirouette on one heel, trying to release tension and avoid thrashing Granger, who as far as I was concerned had just gone nuclear.

"A girl with *no* leg? How does that work in the scene where she *runs* a mile after being raped to escape being killed by her torturers?" I felt my voice rising.

"You can talk around that," Nan said confidently, letting me know that she too was experiencing a meltdown.

This was why everything on television looked the same. Projects were autopsied before they were even declared dead. *Why do I feel compelled to develop and write stories for morons? Why do I ever believe anything I write will ever reach the viewing audience in any form I would want to claim as my own? Why the hell am I even here with these people?* I began to sweat from the sheer heat of holding in my emotions.

"Look, I have nothing against doing a movie about a girl with one leg but it's not *this* movie, and we can't rewrite this movie here in the lobby in ten minutes!" I checked my watch. "Make that five minutes. We've had four months to make this decision…"

"The best creative decisions don't always come on schedule." Granger smiled indulgently.

"This isn't the best creative decision," I said firmly. "The girl is raped—"

"That's something that's always bothered me," Nan said in a Prozac drawl. "I think we should avoid the use of the word *rape* in this pitch. I would say she was aggressively attacked."

I was losing control of the situation. In minutes I would be standing before Marshall Tevachney, Vice President of Movies and Mini Series for one of the major television networks in the United States, trying to tell a story I was making up as I went along.

"Aggressively attacked is with hammers. Raped is with penises!" I shouted into the lobby, which was filling up with other writers and producers who had appointments. It's odd how one can be forgiven the public utterance of almost any word, save the anatomical name for the male member.

Granger and Nan stared at me in utter shock as the receptionist, her eyebrow arched all the way into her hairline, said, "Mr. Tevachney will see you now."

The receptionist punched the button to a set of doors that let us into the CBS inner sanctum as Nan and Granger eyed me warily. It was apparent they perceived me to be dangerous.

"Nuts," I said to no one as our feet sank into the plush hallway carpet and the lobby doors closed behind us.

❖

An hour later I was back home, where I nuked a cup of old coffee in the microwave, shrugged off my jacket, kicked off my shoes, and sagged into a chair. Elmo strolled over and rested his heavy basset jowls on my leg by way of condolence.

"The whole town's nuts," I told him as the doorbell rang.

I opened the door to find Mary Beth Engle standing there with a Tupperware container and a big smile on her pert, thirtysomething face. Mary Beth and I had been paired on a blind date only two nights before by a well-meaning friend wanting to end my extended mourning over Callie Rivers.

"Thought you might enjoy lunch," Mary Beth said in a way that made me think she envisioned herself as lunch, and whatever was in the Tupperware as merely bait. I was horrible at situations like this, and I avoided them like the proverbial plague. I had considered our blind date a disaster. First, I didn't know I was on a blind date—you might say I was blind to that fact. I just thought I was meeting friends for a drink. They surprised me with Mary Beth, who they said they'd brought along to cheer me up and to make me forget Callie, a woman seemingly uninterested in seeing me anytime soon. Mary Beth's round, cherubic face was cute, but not sexy. She tried very hard to please, laughing at all my jokes, staring into my eyes, and never offering up a thought of her own, and now, here she was serving herself up with lunch. In short, Mary Beth should have been straight, because there were a hundred guys who wanted nothing more than exactly what Mary Beth had to offer: vapid attentiveness and a potluck meal. Unfortunately, Mary Beth just wasn't doing it for me. She set the container on my kitchen countertop in a proprietary way and gave the kitchen a once-over as if sizing up something she thought she might soon own.

"I have a special floor wax that will get those scuff marks right off this floor," she said and spun on her toes to face me, taking two steps forward and sliding her arms around my waist.

"I had such a super time with you the other night. You are so funny." She giggled to accent the word *funny*. "I would love to spend more time with you."

Elmo moaned and flopped to the ground, one ear landing squarely over both of his eyes, as if he couldn't bear the idea of my infidelity to Callie. His moaning gave me an excuse to pull away.

"Sorry, when he makes that sound, it means his collar's too tight,"

I lied and leaned over to fake-adjust Elmo's collar. When I stood up, she was standing in front of me with her shirt unbuttoned, revealing bare breasts. I had to give her points for speed. She took my hands in hers, yanked them forward, and placed them on her breasts.

"What I'm saying"— she drawled the words—"is that I'd like to see more of you. A lot more of you," and she reached for the zipper on my jeans, deftly unzipping them and sliding her hand inside. I knew if I didn't move quickly I was a dead woman. I could easily do this because it was easy, not because I had any feelings for Mary Beth. It might even have been an exciting diversion because it was unexpected and uncharted, but I was old enough to know that if I took a moment of my life to fuck Mary Beth, Mary Beth would fuck every moment of my life thereafter: calling, visiting, crying, and showing up with Tupper-suppers! I pulled back suddenly, aching a bit from the effort it took, just as the phone rang.

"Sorry," I said and grabbed the phone.

"Teague?" It was Callie calling from Tulsa, and she sounded upbeat.

"Hello," I breathed, feeling my heart leap to higher ground somewhere in my upper chest, where the beating just stopped, as if it had been put on pause. While I struggled to breathe, I was aware that love could actually kill me.

"What are you up to, darling?" she asked as I zipped my pants back up.

"I just got back from a network pitch, and if you'll permit me a negative word," I said, mocking Callie's dislike of my swearing, "it was a fucking disaster!"

"Why don't you meet me in Las Vegas and tell me all about it?" Her voice had a silvery ring to it that had an instant sensual effect on me.

"When, two weeks from Thursday?" I asked sarcastically.

"You need a break. My client is one of the original owners of the Desert Star Casino. He's given me a two-week stay, and there's no one I'd rather stay with. How about tonight?"

"Tonight?" I breathed, my whole body coming alive. Mary Beth took this unguarded moment to wrap her arms around me from behind and nibble my ear. I yanked my shoulder up to my neck so quickly I nearly dislocated it, and I groaned in pain.

"Are you with someone?" Callie asked suddenly.

"No! A friend stopped by to have lunch, that's all," I said, and Mary Beth retreated sullenly.

"There's a seven o'clock flight…" Callie's voice trailed off.

It was true that a plane flight would put me in Vegas in about forty-five minutes, but today had been harrowing enough without adding to it an opportunity for high-altitude free fall.

"Okay, so drive," she said, reading my thoughts, "but be very careful. See you in the hotel lounge at nine." She hung up on me in her standard form of good-bye.

I pretended she was still on the line for Mary Beth's sake. "All right then, I'll leave now. No, sure, I can be there." I checked my watch. "No problem." I hung up and shrugged happily at Mary Beth. "Sorry, I've got to leave town suddenly."

"Oh." Mary Beth looked hurt as I put my hand on her shoulder and walked her to the door. "Can I call you when you get back?" she asked.

"Actually," I said, "I'm…getting married." I had no idea where that remark came from, but it just popped out and, having heard it out loud, I figured it was as good as any lie I could have conjured.

"Were you getting married forty-eight hours ago when you and I went out?" Mary Beth asked tersely, exhibiting the first signs of real life I'd seen in her.

"No, I wasn't. It just came up."

Mary Beth paused, tapped her little foot three times on the hardwood floor, huffed loudly, and left. Elmo rose up on his back legs, leaving his front legs plastered to the floor, stretched, and passed gas, blowing Mary Beth down the road.

"You really like Callie, don't you? Me too."

❖

Every nerve ending in my body was tingling with excitement. I would see Callie tonight. "You care if I go to Vegas, Elmo? I'll call Wanda and she'll come and play with you…and give you rice with your dinner…and some chips…and a huge Milk-Bone before bedtime."

Elmo's expression never changed as he lifted his muscular behind off the floor and ambled out of the room. He was a Hollywood dog. He knew a snow job when he saw one.

I jumped up, pulled a small suitcase and suit bag out of my closet, and began flinging clothes into them without regard for what matched. I was so happily nervous that I couldn't think straight, and I couldn't locate the simplest of items like the number for Wanda, Elmo's dog-sitter. I rummaged through drawers trying desperately to find it. That was one thing I hated about Vegas: there were no dogs allowed in any of the hotels. No one could tell me that a dog would pee on their fancy hotel carpet any more frequently than the drunks who inhabited the rooms.

I looked over at Elmo, his large brown eyes rolled up in his head as if he were preparing to be beamed up by aliens. Dropping to my knees, I lifted his head up and looked into his big, soft face.

"You know what?" I said, "Screw those Vegas hotels. I'm taking you with me." His ears elevated off his head a full inch, and he became alert.

"You'd like to see Callie too, wouldn't you?" He stood up and shook his huge fur suit in that way he had of getting physically ready for something important.

"But here's the deal: we have to smuggle you in, and you have to be quiet in the room, and sometimes, I might have to leave you for a couple of hours in the car with the windows cracked, but it's pretty cool now, so I think you'll be fine. Still want to go?" He wagged his entire body. "Great!" I said. "Let's get you packed. And remember, once we're with Callie, NFL—No Farting or Licking."

Elmo let out a long, loud belch and I laughed. "You always have to have the last word," I said.

CHAPTER TWO

I tossed the suitcases and a thermos of coffee into the Jeep, loaded up Elmo, and we were on our way by four o'clock in the afternoon.

Once through the maze of traffic on I-5, heading east on the 14, I felt the cool, high desert wind wash away the tension in my chest and shoulders and I relaxed enough to suck in a deep breath of fresh air. The drop-down seat in the back allowed Elmo to lie down on his tummy and place his head and shoulders on the console between the front seats so he was hound-happy himself, until I punched the CD button on the dash and the first mournful notes from k.d. lang enveloped us. Elmo whipped his head left and glared at me.

"Relax, I didn't even *bring* 'Constant Craving,'" I assured him. "How about 'Big Boned Gal'?" I asked the big-boned dog who was always there for me. I cued it up and we bobbed our heads in unison to the bouncy country beat as we drove across the sand.

Slowing down to round the bend toward Barstow, I passed the coveted triangle of sand occupied by itinerant vendors. Today an elderly man had lined the roadside with an overwhelming array of pink plastic flamingos. The sight of the plastic lawn ornaments bobbing in the wind cheered me up. If this guy thought he could sell lawn ornaments in the desert, I should be able to sell a movie to CBS!

I cranked up the radio and stepped on the gas, whipping past scraggly sage and Joshua trees, singing the auction song about falling in love with a lady in the second row. By the time I hit the Nevada line, I was wired on coffee and country music.

Four and a half hours and three hundred and fifty miles later, I rounded the bend on I-15 and exited onto the avenue of strange geometric shapes that made up the Vegas skyline: lions, pyramids, castles, Roman amphitheaters, and lights as far as the eye could see. They flashed and spun and spelled out messages. Giant spotlights that fanned the sky, beckoning us to look where they pointed, lights of every size and color and description, setting the anachronistic landscape of pyramids and palaces aflame in an over-the-top electrical outburst that appeared to have been designed by aliens on acid.

"Okay, Elmo, we're here. Check it out." Elmo stood up and looked left to right through the front windshield at the bright lights on the horizon. "You know how you like to gnaw on a bone or play ball when you're bored? Well, Vegas is what people do when they're bored." Elmo let out a long, low groan and flopped back down on the leather upholstery. "You're right. It wears you out just looking at it."

I was chatting with Elmo to keep from focusing on my churning stomach, not wanting to admit what a wreck I was over seeing Callie again. It had been so long, I could barely remember the small things about her features. I could picture her ethereal blue eyes, but not her ears, her beautiful big smile, but not her hands, her body nude, but not in specific detail, just in its small, exquisite entirety. When I thought of her, I had feelings rather than visuals, which was odd because she was so smashingly beautiful. I remembered the first night I'd laid eyes on her in Tulsa. She'd kissed me so passionately I'd almost had a physical meltdown. Nonetheless, she insisted at the outset that she wasn't going to sleep with me. It was odd, in one minute, to be kissed with such obvious longing and then to be summarily rejected for any further pleasure the next. Because she was so fabulous looking, I assumed she must have slept with a lot of people and was suffering an elegant ennui, a disinterest in yet another love affair. Persistence being my strong suit, I finally got her into bed with me. We were wild for each other, but at the moment of surrender, Callie pulled away, admitting the reason she didn't want to sleep with me was her fear that she wouldn't be able to give herself to someone after so many years of determining not to. Our romance, which lasted only a few weeks, was erotic but erratic, certainly not the traditional gay relationship to which I was accustomed. This one was different, but then Callie Rivers was completely different from anyone I'd ever known. She had an assuredness about her that emanated from her total belief in spirituality and the cosmos and a vulnerability about her that sprang from a childlike innocence.

I don't want to admit it, but I'm, well, might be, at least I could see myself—definitely with her, I thought, confusing even myself.

"There's a possibility that we won't even connect like we did in L.A.," I said to Elmo. "That happens, you know. If that's the case, well then, you and I will just go home." Elmo let out a long, loud sob.

"That's right, and cry!" I laughed at his vocalizing. "Don't worry. Deep down, I know that you and I and Callie Rivers belong together," I said to reassure myself.

❖

Winding down the avenue, past the Tropicana and the MGM Grand, alongside the gargantuan statues in front of Caesar's Palace, and beyond the hoopla of Circus Circus, I inched my way through bumper-to-bumper traffic until I eased into the valet parking circle in front of the Desert Star. A valet parker wearing a large purple turban and billowing knee-high pants swept open my car door with a bow and tried to usher me out onto the pavement. I took the parking stub and insisted on parking my own car. I found a parking space in the shade about a hundred feet from the hotel, fluffed up the pillow I'd brought Elmo, gave him a dog bone, and cracked the windows.

"You're safe here. I'm paying the guy in the weird hat to keep an eye on the car, and if anyone does try to open the door, you have my permission to bite him. I'll be back for you in a little while. Wish me luck, buddy." I gave him a kiss on his head. I could feel his soft brown eyes on me as I crossed the parking lot to the hotel entrance, where another turbaned employee ushered me through the large gold and glass hotel doors. A blast of cold air hit me along with the sounds of slot machines and happy revelers creating a comforting background walla that beckoned me to forget my other life.

I scanned the horizon: Million Dollar Slots, Star Roulette, Keno Desert Star Style, Free Buffet, Star Poker, Blackjack, and Craps. I was looking for something a little more mundane, like the ladies' room and a bar girl. I found the former and ducked inside to freshen up, staring at my ashen face in the mirror. I definitely needed a break. *Fatigue and no rouge are a bad combination*, I thought. I dipped my fingertips under the faucet and flipped the droplets vertically through my punked auburn hair with its newly highlighted blond streaks and commanded the spikes to stand at attention. I washed my hands, took out my sage eyeliner, and gave my green eyes a little color, adding mascara to my already long eyelashes. My eyes were one of my best features. I knew that because people constantly complimented me on them. The glint of gold was back in them now. After all, they were about to see my future. Finally, I put on lip liner, lipstick, and a touch of rouge, noted that my jeans had a chocolate stain on one leg and that my white shirt looked a bit used from lifting Elmo in and out of the car, but after all, I'd been traveling. I flipped the shirt collar up slightly and noted that I was looking taller than my 5'7" only because I'd lost ten pounds, thanks again to Callie Rivers. *Here goes,* I thought and headed back out into the hubbub in search of the lounge. A friendly change girl pointed the way.

The lounge was nestled back in the far corner of the hotel. I spotted Callie seated across the room on a red velvet-tufted ottoman and wearing what looked like a white Chanel suit. I had to remind myself to breathe. She was literally breathtaking. I was certain it was no accident that she'd picked a location where the overhead lights would bounce off her swept-back, Norwegian-blond hair, making her look like a movie star from some long-forgotten era. My entire body went weak when I saw her. The connection I felt for her was inexplicable. It was as if I'd been hypnotized by her. I moved toward her as if reeled in on a magnetic wire, unaware of people parting to get out of my way. She turned and looked over her shoulder, catching my eye as if she'd sensed my presence. Her smile was electric. I had never felt such heat from so far away, as if a piece of the sun had broken off and landed at my feet: a gift from the gods.

A slightly tipsy fiftyish man who was about my height stood beside her trying to strike up a conversation. She leapt to her feet and said breathlessly, "I'm so glad you're here!" I fell into her arms, swept away in her sheer sensual warmth, like that first blast of heat as one stands in front of a fire on a cold winter's night. I could have stayed there, warming myself in her for hours. When she tried to pull away, I refused to let her go. Gone was any thought of being reserved because of her having put off our reunion.

"Don't you look great," I whispered, as my eyes met hers.

"Do you think you should let go of me?" she asked. "Before you singe my suit?" Her mouth brushed my lips, sending seismic waves of heat rippling through my body.

"Are we checked in? Let's check in," I breathed as the inebriated man wedged himself between us.

"You gonna introduce me to your friend?" the man asked Callie, his stale breath hitting me full in the face.

"Fella, I've had a bad day in L.A., so how about leaving us alone?" I said in my friendliest and most tolerant manner.

"Maybe you meet my friend Paco." He slid his hand into the pocket of his baggy silk pants. His fingers moved up and down inside the loose pocket like a hand puppet straining to escape. "Paco, say hello to the nice lady." The bobbing cloth lunged at my thigh and suddenly pinched me. I took a step backward, shocked at having my skin mashed in a public place by a total stranger pretending to have a friend in his pocket. Callie couldn't suppress a giggle as she told the drunken man he should leave us alone.

"Oh, I get it." He dragged the words out. "You two are dykes."

It was bad timing on his part. As we say in Oklahoma, I'd "had an ass-full" for one day. I spun my body around, keeping my arm bent at waist level, and buried my elbow under his left rib. He doubled over and groaned. Callie grimaced, and I realized once again that knowing how to defend myself had always been a two-edged sword. I signaled for the bartender to come over and give me a hand, explaining that a man had just suffered an accident.

The young bartender bounded around the brass-studded leather bar and got the man by the arm, asking how he'd injured himself.

"With his mouth," I replied.

The bartender grinned at me and said it happened a lot around here. He led the half-drunk man away explaining that he was an old-time club performer, a regular at the hotel, and sometimes he drank a little too much and lost his manners.

Callie studied the pattern on the carpet. "You've got Mars square Mars today. It means you could get into a fight with someone, most likely a man."

"Men only know three labels: bitch, whore, dyke."

"You need to unwind," Callie said. "I ordered you a drink, because our room's not ready. In fact, no rooms are ready." As I began to moan, Callie interrupted, taking my hand. "I've missed you, and I can't wait to get into bed with you. I intend to ravage you," she said, barely moving her lips, her facial expression as serene as Grace Kelly's. I burst out laughing.

"Well, now that I know your intentions, I can relax."

"Tell me about your meeting," she said.

I told her about Granger and Nan trying to rewrite the movie in the CBS lobby five minutes before the pitch and how I'd made the silent decision on the walk to Marshall Tevachney's office to pitch the show as I'd developed and written it.

"So we said our hellos to Marshall and I started the pitch. Bobby Jo was a raw-boned girl from Alabama. The director interrupted and said, 'Who has one leg?' Then I said, Bobby Jo had no idea that the cowboys she'd befriended that night would turn on her. She'd known one of them for years. The director added, 'They knew each other in the veterans' hospital where Bobby Jo was fitted for her prosthesis!'" Callie giggled as my voice rose. "Now she's not only one-legged, but she's in a veterans' hospital, for God's sake! What the hell's she doing in a veterans' hospital! Did she go there for a sex change right after she served as a colonel in the war? Tevachney's head was whipping back and forth between the two of us like he was watching a ping-pong match. At the end of the pitch, he couldn't have repeated the storyline if I'd paid him a million bucks."

Callie insisted that he actually liked it. I protested loudly, saying he didn't even know what the movie was about. She smiled and said it didn't matter because it had excited him, and that seemed to ignite Callie. "Let's go see if we can get into our room." Callie gave me a seductive smile, as if my animated pitch had somehow turned her on.

❖

I carried my drink with me to the registration desk, where a friendly young girl dressed in a silky bejeweled costume beamed at us from behind a large name tag that said Harem Girl Gloria. She took our names and located us in the vast computer system, informing us that we were in room 712 and it was ready. When I asked if that was a nonsmoking room, she said no. Callie insisted she'd requested nonsmoking. Gloria said she hadn't. We argued back and forth with her, and the vibes became less pleasant with every passing second. Life in Vegas was becoming as difficult as life in L.A. Finally, Callie stepped in front of me, partially blocking my view of Gloria, and addressed her directly.

"My friend has had a very trying day, and I wanted this experience to be relaxing for her. So far it's not turning out that way."

"I can't help that." Gloria's harem veil sucked in and out with each breath.

"I really need a nonsmoking room." Callie's tone remained even. Gloria paused and locked eyes with Callie. There was silence, and then Harem Girl Gloria's fingers smashed down on the computer keys as if she were cutting the heads off chickens.

"I will be happy to upgrade you to a suite free of charge, and the hotel is sorry you've experienced this inconvenience," she said in a decidedly unsorry tone.

Callie thanked her. Harem Girl Gloria yanked the printout off the machine, slapped two room key cards down on the desk, and rang for the bellman. We were headed to suite 1142.

"Gotta get one more piece of luggage," I said.

"What's in it? Can't we get it later?"

"Elmo." I grinned.

"You brought Elmo?" She lit up. "How are you going to get him in here?"

"Can't tell you or I'd have to kill you!" I teased.

"Don't say things like that. Words have power," she said, somewhat shocked.

"Sorry, meant to say that information is classified," I replied. "Be right back."

Borrowing a luggage cart from the lobby, I wheeled it out to the Jeep, opened the empty suitcase with the air holes I'd cut in it and said, "Okay, guy, hop in." Elmo jumped in just like I'd taught him. I carefully removed the suitcase from the Jeep and lifted it onto the cart. "No barking, no moaning," I ordered as I pushed the cart across the parking lot, handed the doorman my car keys, and asked him to have someone get the remainder of my luggage from the Jeep and bring it to my room before valet-parking my vehicle.

I joined Callie and the bellman and the three of us, plus the incognito canine, stepped into the elevator. Two golden rams on the elevator doors came together butting heads, and the elevator swept us silently up eleven floors.

Elmo got wind of Callie's perfume and began to wiggle and make a very tiny sound of excitement. I coughed to cover it, but Elmo moaned incessantly and Callie giggled uncontrollably.

The bellman unlocked the door to 1142. It was a gorgeous bedroom with two king-sized beds and off to one side a sitting room with swag curtains pulled back on either side of a huge chaise lounge. Everything was desert brothel motif. Callie and I moved through the room, grinning at our good luck. A wonderfully stocked refrigerator, the mattresses were so new you could bounce a quarter off them, and the view of the Strip was breathtaking. The bellman started to lift Elmo in his suitcase from the cart.

"Whoa, leave that one, please. I'll take care of it in a minute, and I'll push the cart outside." He paused, but I tipped him generously and to the point that he left not caring what I had in the bag.

I closed the door on the world and put my arms around Callie Rivers and felt her soft, warm, full lips slide effortlessly over and around my mouth. We held each other gently, just our fingertips touching each other's waists, a space between our bodies, so that only our lips met, only the softness of our mouths greeted one another as if any other pressure might take away from this most sensual of hellos. It was hypnotic, and I swayed slightly from the amazing heat that spread down my neck, across my chest, and into my groin. It was the unquenchable hunger of ten weeks. It was the insatiable lust of ten weeks. It was the moment I had envisioned endlessly—for ten weeks!

"My God, I just want to devour you," I whispered.

Suddenly the suitcase began to move and Elmo whined, battering at its sides to get out.

"Elmo, sorry, here, honey." I unzipped the bag and he escaped into Callie's arms, his tail wagging furiously. He let out a large bark and we both tensed and shouted, "Shh!" at the same time, giggling like teenagers.

"How will we disguise him to get him up and down stairs to walk him?" Callie asked.

"He can wear your clothes. You won't be needing them." I grabbed her and began unbuttoning her shirt, burying my face in her breasts.

"Stay right where you are. I'm going into the bathroom for just a moment…"

"Based on the size of this room, there may be a swimming pool in the bathroom." I kissed her again, unable to let her go.

Callie disappeared into the bathroom for only a second and then, shrieking, backed out of the room and crashed into me. “Call security!” She slammed the bathroom door shut. “There’s a dead man in the tub!”

CHAPTER THREE

I pushed the bathroom door open and saw the man lying there, wearing a tuxedo, his head jammed back under the faucets, his arm dangling over the side of the tub. On his little finger a gold signet ring bore the image of a bird, its leg poised in the air, its claw extended to do battle.

"Teague, close the door, please. I don't want to look at him," Callie whispered, and Elmo growled in agreement, seemingly ready to attack the corpse for the intrusion.

Security had said they'd be right up. We stood outside in the hallway, waiting. A maid scurried up to us with a load of linens on her arm.

"I forgot the towels, sorry." She reached around me to put her master key in the lock.

"Don't go in there!" I nearly shouted.

The maid jumped back, apparently startled. I took the towels from her, saying we'd put them inside for her. I laid them on the floor as Callie fidgeted. We were both in a state of shock. There's something about seeing a dead body, even if it's only for a few seconds, that imprints on your mind. A gray, thick-skinned, rubbery corpse lying in state at the local funeral parlor is upsetting enough, but freshly killed bodies, stiff but still pink, blood still oozing, are enough to give you the creeps for months. I'd seen a lot of bodies during my brief stint as a police officer, and like snakes, I was okay with them as long as I wasn't surprised by them. If I went to a crime scene, I expected to find bodies, but finding one in the bathroom of our luxury hotel room was an entirely different matter.

Like a kid wanting to cut and run, I told Callie we could speed this whole process up if we went down to security ourselves. Callie said maybe we should guard the hotel room door. I assured her that the dead guy didn't need guarding, and the two of us headed down the long corridor toward the elevators with Elmo in tow. We quickly spotted two hotel employees in bright red jackets heading back in our direction. The older, shorter man had his sparse white hair sheared into a flattop and moved in the strained way of a pudgy person in a hurry—his creased pants tugging with each step. His jacket had the word Security emblazoned over the left pocket. I was comforted that his name tag simply stated Roy. Not Harem Guard Roy or Tent Tender Roy, just Roy. The younger man looked like he could lift an SUV with one arm on any given afternoon and wore the name tag Ted. I skipped the introductions and told them to follow us.

"You say he was in your room when you got back?" Roy asked.

"We weren't back from anywhere," Callie said. "We'd just checked in."

Roy let me know how seriously the hotel was taking our call when he drew his gun, popped the lock with his master key, and he and brick-shit-house-Ted slipped inside alone. Seconds later, Roy pushed the door open and beckoned us to enter. The bathroom door was open, the tub clearly visible. There was no body in it.

"The guy was in the tub, you say?" Roy sagged into an adrenaline low.

Callie and I stared at the pristine bathroom. Nothing out of place, certainly no dead guy lounging under the faucets. I went into action opening closets, looking under beds, checking balconies. There was no one there.

"Wearing a tuxedo," I said. Ted shot Roy a look that said *these ladies may just be bonkers*.

"Could be some drunk stumbled in here while the maid was cleaning, you know, behind her back and fell into the tub. We've had stranger things happen." Roy let out a sigh of relief on behalf of hotel security, legal, and public relations.

"This man was dead," Callie said.

"You seen a lot of dead people, miss? I mean, excuse me for saying so, but when you're upset, you know…"

Roy was giving her the dumb-blonde dismissal.

"The guy was dead," I said, backing her up. "And we weren't out of this room two minutes. Just the time it took us to walk down the corridor to the elevators and meet you. So somebody's been rehearsing a two-minute drill on removing dead guys."

Roy decided not to argue. He said he'd fill out a report and file it with the hotel and with the LVPD so there would be an official record. There wasn't much else to be done. Having been a cop, I knew—no body, no crime.

"We'd like to move you to another room. You know, so we can keep an eye on this one and to let you get on with your vacationing. Ted, help the ladies with their luggage, and by the way, no dogs allowed in the hotel," Roy said.

"What do you think, Roy? Would the maid rather deal with a decomposing body in the bathtub or a little dog hair on the porcelain? We're not talking psychological damage and suing the hotel. All we're asking for is dispensation for our…police-trained drug-sniffing dog." It was a stretch, but I did have some interaction with drug-sniffing dogs in my former line of work. Granted, drug-sniffing dogs usually had longer legs and came when you called them, but other than that, Elmo could fill the bill.

Security guard Ted chose not to press the point and scooped up our luggage, putting it under one arm as he held the door for us with the other, while large sweat droplets fell off his forehead, landed on his jutting chin, and plummeted onto his shirt front. We followed him to the elevator. He used his free hand to radio the front desk. There was a great deal of static as he spoke into the radio.

"I got 1142 moving to 611, over," Ted said in a businesslike manner.

Someone on the other end okayed 611 and we were back in the rams' head elevator heading down to the sixth floor. Ted opened the door to 611 with his master key and said someone from the front desk would bring us new electronic keys right away. We thanked him and he hulked off.

"Not as nice as our upgrade," Callie said.

"Yeah, but the bathroom's not being used as a morgue," I said, checking to be certain.

Callie and I plopped down on the bed in a heap. The events of the evening had taken some of the wind out of our desert sails. I wanted to know if someone put that guy in the tub for our benefit, but then, why would someone do that and how would it even be possible? After all, we didn't know what room we'd be in until minutes before we got on the elevator. Nonetheless, it just seemed uncanny that out of 126,000 hotel rooms in Las Vegas, ours was the one with the dead body.

"Must be our energy together," Callie mused, somewhat unconcerned. "Very high sexual energy draws other energy to it."

"Like dead guys who miss having sex?" I asked.

"I try to explain and you start that negative humor. Are you going to stop it?" Callie's voice had a playful lilt to it.

I swore I would. Of course, I was swearing to anything these days to make Callie happy. She was unquestionably the center of my universe.

I kissed her and her mouth radiated heat and longing, and I felt myself about to dissolve. Elmo shook himself loudly, jangling his dog tags, and I paused just momentarily to tell him to "settle." The mere mention of Elmo sent Callie into swoons of adoration toward my large satchel-shaped companion.

"I'm so glad you brought him." She recited our agenda for the next few days, telling it directly to Elmo. "I see lots of good food, short walks and"—she looked up at me—"hours of mad, passionate lovemaking." She slid into my arms and kissed me. It was almost physically impossible for a human mouth to be that hot. I dropped all interest in what happened to the dead and focused entirely on what could happen to the living. She ran her hands up my sides and let them travel down the curve of my waist, and the sensation it created on my skin disconnected my mind from my body. I was floating against my will, the way one floats in heavy salt water, happily unable to sink to the bottom. My body was shaking slightly and involuntarily as if it had been exposed to extreme cold, and yet, I was so molten hot that I was about to erupt. The anticipation of falling into her silken breasts and cupping her small buttocks in my hands, and being inside her, had created a laserlike focus on my senses, driving me through ten weeks of wanting, to this moment, and now that I was here, I was almost immobilized by the intensity of the sensation.

She stopped kissing me long enough to lock eyes with me, those celestial blue eyes that saw through me to my very core. "I have ached night after night wanting you," she said.

"Then what in the world took you so long…"

"Anticipation isn't always a bad thing." She teased me with her mouth, starting to kiss me but pulling back, brushing my throat with her lips, then pulling away.

I placed my hands on her waist and in a move that surprised even me, I lifted her up and sailed her backward onto the bed as she gasped, her eyebrow raised in amused surprise.

"I will not be toyed with," I said in mock-macho fashion.

"You're very strong." She laughed. "You don't look that strong."

"I didn't know I was." I laughed. "Maybe you're just little."

"The best gifts come in—"

"Small packages," I completed the well-worn phrase and slid her suit jacket off her shoulders and pushed aside her silk blouse. As if on cue, Elmo put his nose to the lock on the suitcase and sniffed and squeaked.

I decided to ignore him, and I focused on Callie's phenomenally soft breasts, putting my face in them and breathing in her perfume, loving the sounds of pleasure she emitted. Elmo's high-pitched squealing continued. "Elmo, be quiet!" I demanded, but Elmo was unusually disobedient. Moments later, he moved up an octave and let out a sustained violin sound. Callie giggled.

"Elmo!" I barked. "Quit it!" He glared at me and then deliberately punched the suitcase with his nose, backed away from it, glared at me again, and threatened to go up yet another octave.

"He's unhappy. Maybe he's a neatness freak. You have to unpack anyway, or your clothes are going to look like they were pressed in an accordion," Callie took up for him. I was less enthused since I had no desire to ever put my clothes on again. However, I crawled out of bed and tossed the luggage up on the spare bed and clicked open the latch. Inside, right on top, was a small manila folder with the hotel logo in the upper left-hand corner. Elmo sniffed at it as if it contained a bomb. As I wondered aloud how this had gotten into my luggage, Callie tore into it and removed a scrap of yellowed paper torn from some larger document. She flipped the delicate, faded piece of paper over and stared at it intently, her mind seeming to wander. She placed the scrap of paper on the writing desk and sank down into the straight-backed, elaborately scrolled chair and gently rubbed her hands back and forth across the symbols on the page as if transporting herself into them. I watched her without making any sound, wondering what this gorgeous woman was thinking, or doing, and why this scrap of paper seemed to mesmerize her. When she spoke it was quietly and from a faraway place, as if by speaking softly she could keep the details of that place in her mind and not scare them away.

"How did you get this?" she asked.

"I didn't put this in here. Someone's been in my luggage!" I rummaged through the suitcase and then opened the other bags to make sure there wasn't more than just an envelope stashed in my belongings. "It had to have been put there by the bellman or someone who helped unload them in valet parking."

"But how would they know to put something astrological in your bag, when it's meant for me?" Callie asked.

"Someone must have seen us together in the bar and knew we'd be sharing a room," I replied.

"I pulled up this astrological chart almost two decades ago for the builder of this hotel," Callie said, fixated on the yellowed piece of paper.

"You were here with the builder? How did that happen?" I held my shirts up to the light and checked the pockets, for what I wasn't sure.

"I was in my early twenties at the time, and I had just met Robert Isaacs. He brought me to Las Vegas to impress me."

I hated any sentence with Robert Isaacs's name in it, the smarmy Marathon Studio executive who had married Callie Rivers years ago. Their marriage according to Callie lasted roughly "ten minutes" and went something like I do, I did, I'm done. She'd tried to explain the reasons she'd accepted his proposal, and the lessons it had taught her, and the fact that marrying him was somehow in her personal growth chart, but I still could not grasp the idea that Callie, who was so in tune with the cosmos, could have tuned out and married a creep like Robert Isaacs.

"I was this young, blond psychic telling the builder about the stars. I remember that I had just begun to think about everything in the world as having a birth chart, because a birth is nothing more than a beginning. Everything has a beginning, middle, and an end—a life span, in essence—and of course I believe lives recycle," she continued a dialogue with herself. "I told the owner that this hotel had a birth chart. This is a piece of that chart..." Her voice trailed off.

"How do you know it's from the same chart?" I asked, leaning over her chair and kissing her shoulders, not really caring all that much about the chart.

Callie smiled at me as if I'd asked how she'd recognized one of her own children. "I know where the planets were…right down to the minute. It's a birth. You don't forget a birth."

A piece of the birth chart of a hotel and casino, I thought in my usual jaded fashion. *I am absolutely mad about a woman who creates birth charts for buildings.*

"I know what you're thinking." She focused on me for the first time. "He felt the same way. He asked what kind of hotel it would be, and I told him the hotel would be an overly sexual place, even for a hotel, with Scorpio being ruled by Pluto, and Mars in Scorpio in the Eighth House. It would attract money to it, perhaps money from the Underworld, another Plutonian connection. Of course I had no idea that Mo Black had mafia connections. I was so naïve, and that amused him."

She pointed to the chart she had created, her finger tracing the symbols for the six planets that had found their way into the Eighth House at that exact moment in time. Then she fired up her laptop, plugging in numbers and data, tapping on the keyboard and watching the planets change position on the screen, finally announcing decidedly, "October thirty-first, Halloween, Las Vegas, three p.m., with a new Moon, and Mars at 29 critical degrees, the day of the groundbreaking, part of an Eighth House Stellium in Scorpio!" Callie explained how she'd told him that kind of power, particularly in the Eighth House, could be used for good or for evil, depending on one's intent, so he would have to watch carefully to avoid the darker side of the hotel business.

"He laughed and said, 'Tell you what, Blondie, if this joint ever gets into trouble growing up, I'll send for you.' I asked how I would know it was he, and he smirked, 'I'll give ya a little clue,' and in a mock whisper, as if he were saying *Rosebud*, he uttered, 'Stellium in Scorpio,' and then laughed, shouting to Robert, 'Like your girlfriend, Isaacs. Very entertaining little broad.' And then, I'll never forget it, he looked at me seriously and said under his breath, 'That guy ain't no good for you.'"

"Meaning Isaacs?" I asked, and Callie nodded. "I like the guy already. Who is he?"

"Mo Black," Callie said.

"So what's on this little torn piece of paper?"

"Just the Eighth House—with the Stellium in Scorpio," she said quietly.

"Sounds like he's trying to tell you something about the hotel. Right after I make love to you," I said, pulling her into me, "we'll give Mo Black a call and hear what he has to say."

"Mo Black is dead," Callie said.

CHAPTER FOUR

I picked up the phone and explained in detail to the woman at the front desk that I'd found a manila folder bearing a hotel logo in my suitcase and I had not put it there, so someone had rifled my luggage. The woman apologized, but she wasn't too concerned beyond that. After all, a manila folder hadn't ever harmed anyone to her knowledge. I didn't tell her about the astrological chart, which would have taken me all day to explain. I decided to wait and see if whoever put it there would follow up. My focus was on Callie and just being as close to her as was physically possible.

"What did she say?" Callie asked when I hung up the phone.

"She wants me to bring it down to the front desk. We'll do that later," I said, pulling her down on the bed and kissing her, going instantly hot.

"We'd better do that now." Callie pulled away and slipped her jacket back on. "We might be busy later." She kissed me again.

"Thanks, Elmo." I shot him a look. "Your sussing out this folder in my suitcase has derailed my evening. Try to remember that you're a basset hound, not a bloodhound, okay? You're cramping my style."

Elmo snorted as I headed out the door.

I bolted across the lobby and slapped the folder onto the counter at the front desk, more out of sexual frustration than anger over my luggage being invaded. The young woman behind the desk gave the folder the once-over and asked if there was anything in it. I hesitated before replying that there wasn't. She then exhibited true managerial finesse by inquiring if the folder had damaged any of my clothes, or if the ink had rubbed off on my luggage, or if it had caused any other issue for which she could reimburse me, thus diverting me from the real issue of my luggage having been opened. I mentally applauded her polished handling of my circumstance and went back to Callie with the news that there was no news about the envelope.

"As long as we're downstairs, there's someone here I have to meet, a client's daughter. Will you go with me?" Callie asked. "Her last show ended at 11:00 p.m. We might catch her at the theater."

I was miffed to say the least. I hadn't seen Callie in weeks, we were here to be together, and our reunion was feeling like two sorority sisters away for a weekend. Self-doubt was my psychological Samsonite. I tried not to take it on every trip, but I had to admit to myself that it did appear that Callie Rivers wasn't exactly unable to stand it until we made love. *Here we are visiting showgirls, for God's sake!* I thought as I followed her along the trail of posters and banners that heralded the *Boy Review* as the oldest, biggest, and best nightclub act in Las Vegas!

"You look smashing, those strong legs, and your great ass," Callie said and leaned in, kissing me on the lips before veering off toward the hotel theater. I perked right up. *I am so easy!* I thought.

The *Review* was a staple with visitors to the fabulous Strip because it had just the right combination of exotic costumes, death-defying feats, and blatant sexuality that appealed to everyone—a blend of male and female and a challenge to determine which was which.

"Why do you have to go see a showgirl?" I asked.

"My client is worried about her. She's young. There are a lot of things you can get into here."

"Yeah." I put my hand down the waistband of her pants. "Gotta watch yourself all the time."

She jumped and batted my hand away as we walked hurriedly along the concourse beneath the wide expanse of massive marble that reached to the sky, then arched and crisscrossed the heavens in graceful arcs that ran as far as the eye could see. The hotel was stunning.

The in-hotel theater was a city block's distance from the main lobby. In fact, no two places were conveniently together. Just getting from the gift shop to the front desk was a feat. People left the lobby for the elevators and while still in sight shrank to half their size due to the distance between each destination, and if you weren't tired when you checked in, you would be by the time you walked to your room. Mo Black obviously loved Italian grandeur, because the Desert Star was, sans gambling machinery, an architectural homage to the spacious and dramatic cathedrals of Rome. I couldn't imagine what a structure like this cost, or what people paid to sleep in this cathedral. I was just glad our rooms were comped.

A young boy with a name tag that read Desert Greeter Joey opened the theater door for us, revealing a tiered seating arrangement for at least a thousand people. It was theater on a grand scale and completely unexpected. How could a theater this large be inside a hotel?

The theater's interior was irretrievably overdone in that gay-man-gone-mad fashion that characterized the entire city. One couldn't blame the theater for trying to keep up.

"I love empty theaters. They seemed to capture the essence of what we do in life: prepare, execute, take a final bow, and exit stage left," I said with a bit of melancholy.

"Too confining," Callie said. "Life in a box."

I couldn't help but laugh. Callie was obviously not a person who indulged in melancholia or sentimentality, while I partook of it routinely.

Callie asked Joey to let Rose Ross know that we were here. He radioed another man who came over and escorted us up a staircase to a set of dressing rooms where the cast got ready for their show every night. Beyond the dressing room was a greenroom, the theatrical name for a private area where stars await their cues and their family and friends are entertained.

"So is the theater owned by the hotel?" I asked the man, thinking that if they filled all one thousand seats, six shows a week, at a hundred bucks a pop, they'd gross thirty million annually. Even if they only netted a third of that, it would be a nice payday for the hotel.

"Uh, I think it's leased out to the theater company that does the *Boy Review,* but I could be wrong," the man replied. "It's a great place for theater kids to work because every job in the hotel is treated like a part in a play. When you're not in a production, you can be a bellman, or a desk clerk, or a valet parker and still be performing. Theater people fill in for regular staff wherever needed and the idea is to play your offstage role so perfectly that everyone believes you're part of the core staff."

"So who are you really?" I asked playfully.

"Today, I'm your guide to the greenroom. Who knows tomorrow what I'll be for you," he said with a twinkle.

"What happened to your name tag?" I asked him, by now hooked on the ridiculous hotel titles and missing an opportunity to grin over something like Camel Boy Kevin.

"Forgot it this morning. My name is Rob," he said, depositing us on a couch in the clubby setting, opening a fridge and offering us wine. The tables were already laden with fresh cheese and crackers, and on the wall, a flat screen TV was muted. "I'll get Ms. Ross for you."

"Nice manners," I said to Callie.

Moments later, a long-legged, redheaded twenty-three-year-old showgirl strode into the room.

"Are you Ms. Rivers?" she asked, extending her hand to Callie.

"I'm Callie Rivers, and this is Teague Richfield," Callie said.

"I'm so silly! I freaked out that night at the party. I realize worrying my father, and now you, was a mistake." Her stance, and her movements, and everything about her communicated that she felt her own importance.

"It's wonderful to meet you. You look a lot like your handsome father," Callie said.

I didn't particularly like the fact that Callie thought meeting this young girl was wonderful, or that her father was handsome, or that she was handsome by proxy. I wanted all Callie's admiration reserved for me. *Childish of me,* I thought.

Rose Ross didn't duck her head in shyness, as most young girls would with a compliment. Instead she jutted her jaw forward in a striking pose and said with a big smile, "Thank you!"

A tall, glamorous, brunette drag queen swept into the greenroom and kissed Rose on the cheek. "Hello, darling," she said, "Excusez-moi! I didn't realize you had guests."

"Joanie Burr, this is—"

"Callie and Teague," Callie interrupted.

"I'm Joanie Burr, Rose's best and only friend because, of course, she's from Oklahoma and no one in Las Vegas even speaks to anyone from Oklahoma," she teased. "Where are you from?"

"Oklahoma," Callie enjoyed saying.

"Oops." She put her long slender fingers to her electric-red lips in mock embarrassment and slid gracefully onto the couch next to Rose. She took Rose's hand, and the light bounced off the huge amethyst on Joanie's ring finger and off the gold piping of her white silk lounging pajamas. While no one in her right mind could deny that a young woman like Rose was attractive, she paled in comparison to the exceptionally well-made-up Joanie, whose facial features and body parts were sheer elegance on a grand scale—femininity embellished and enhanced. Her moves were practiced and fluid, with a casual sensuality. She was a fascinating experiment in gender bending, her every waking hour obviously occupied with the way she looked, and dressed, and moved. She was the glamorous woman who was not woman—a genetic mirage in the desert, and I could not take my eyes off her, despite knowing that she wasn't really there.

Rose spoke openly in front of her, telling Callie that she'd become frightened when she'd made the ghost's ghoul pool list.

"Because she's a baby girl, aren't you, precious? And she didn't know that it's an honor to make the list," Joanie said, and with one long, slender, manicured hand, she tossed her short hair back out of her eyes where it remained for only a second and then slid seductively back where it originally hung, half concealing the long lashes of one perfectly mascara-lined eye.

"What's the ghoul pool list about?" I asked.

"Just a spook night for every spook in town…at midnight they draw names and everybody on the list freaks," Joanie said with even more dramatic flair.

"It's a list of people you think will die in Las Vegas in the next twelve months," Rose managed to say and glanced sideways at her friend to make sure it was okay to say it.

"I'd rather make worst dressed," I quipped. "So does the ghost actually show up?"

"Giovanni Gratini does," Joanie said, gesturing with her hands and whispering to Rose. "He loves wearing that toga. If his skirt gets any shorter, the entire front row can gobble his baubles, instead of just Marlena."

"Anyone on the list ever die?" I asked

"Just their hair, honey," Joanie said raucously.

"Do you have the list?" I asked.

"Every queen in the city has been on the damned thing at one time or another. I think Rose is the only one who ever remembered she was on the list! Everybody else was too freaking drunk!"

"Your father asked that we check on you and make sure that you're okay." Callie gave Rose a meaningful look that seemed to say this was her chance to tell us if she needed help.

"Perfectly okay. Really." She shrugged and smiled, but an underlying nervousness belied her cavalier attitude.

"We had a weird thing happen to us, actually a couple of weird things," I said, deciding as I spoke to skip the one about the dead body in our tub. "When we checked in, someone had put an astrological chart in my luggage." I watched them both for even a twitch of a reaction.

"Did it say you would meet someone exciting?" Joanie gave me a knowing smile, and I wondered if my feelings for Callie were flashing across my forehead like images on the Times Square JumboTron.

Callie quickly changed the subject. "We're headed over to the buffet. Would you like to join us?"

Rose looked as if she were about to accept our invitation.

"Gotta run through that scene we blew tonight, honey," Joanie reminded her with just the appropriate note of regret in her tone.

"Thanks for coming to my rescue. Sorry it was a false alarm. It was nice meeting you both," Rose said.

We said our good-byes and they departed, leaving my mind bouncing around in my head performing its own lie detector test—and Rose was failing. *Was Joanie hanging around to report our conversation to someone, or to protect her friend Rose, or was she trying to derail our interest in the ghoul pool by trivializing the game?*

We exited the theater and walked back to the lobby. I slung my arm around Callie's waist, walking slowly beside her, enjoying the feeling of her body against mine, our hips moving in sync as we walked.

"So what do you make of that?" Callie asked.

"Lying. What do you make of it?"

"Same."

"You see? I could have been the psychic and you could have been the cop; we both got the same vibe. So what are you going to do next?" I asked.

"Eat," she said, already heading toward the buffet line in the open-air restaurant. She filled two plates with food that she first examined as if it were loaded with explosives, carefully lifting the edge of a pastry, tilting a slice of ham toward the light to see its true color, asking the chef behind the chafing dishes if he knew how long the sausage had been sitting out under the lights. After tedious selection techniques had been applied, she Saran-Wrapped the plates and handed them to me to carry so that she could juggle our drinks, asking the waiter where the water for the ice had come from. I was starting to fidget, patience not being my particular virtue. I wondered if this was her ongoing modus operandi.

Perhaps, at the end of the river of love, there's silt: that which is left to wade through after the waves of ecstasy have washed over us. I was on the lookout for silt. Would Callie turn out to be too good to be true: a sexually passionate, exciting woman of insane beliefs and annoying little habits?

Callie unwrapped the plate to have one more look at the condition of the ham, just to make my point. Fairly certain we would not be poisoned during this particular meal, she smiled at me. "My mom and dad are flying in."

"Really, when?" I was caught off guard, still focused on the ham pat-down.

"In a couple of days, I think. They'll let me know. You'll love them. I've told them all about you. I want them to meet you. We'll all go out."

We're visiting your client's kid on our time together, we have barely had a moment to ourselves, and now you're flying in your parents. What in the hell are you doing?

"They're not staying in our room, are they?" I asked, my inner child turning nuclear.

"Adjoining," she said, unintentionally rubbing it in.

"Adjoining. Not across the hall or on another floor?"

"That way we can be…"

"…together!" I finished her sentence with an upbeat sarcasm. "Is there going to be any personal time for you and me, or is it just going to be dead folks and old folks?"

Callie gave me a look that said she might want to reevaluate having a relationship with someone as callous as me, and then gave me a rather lengthy dissertation on the meaning of family. Callie's family were her friends: her father, Palmer, and her mother, Paige. She'd apparently told Paige and Palmer about us, much in the way one would talk to a girlfriend.

"I told them that you and I are having a relationship and that I wanted them to meet you. That's perfectly reasonable, since we are lovers."

"You told them we're sleeping together?" I asked, slightly alarmed.

"What does a relationship mean between two women over forty?" Callie leaned in and kissed me somewhere between the sausage patties and the fruit bowl. "I'm going to set you free, Teague. You're way too uptight."

Callie picked up a tiny piece of steak, held it between her fingers, and fed me as if I were no more than an exceedingly loud baby bird. My mouth wrapped around her fingertips and gently pulled the meat from them, caressing her fingers with my tongue. "There are even better things to eat in our room," she said and I swooned, completely forgetting the issue about her family. They could all show up as far as I was concerned. Then she wrapped a few small steak bites and some boiled potatoes in a large napkin and rolled it up.

"Elmo has to eat too," she reminded me. "He's getting anxious to see us, I can feel it."

"Oh, my gosh, I forgot," I said, taking the food from her and thinking she might just be a better mom to Elmo than I was.

Callie furrowed her brow and shook her head as if to shake out loose thoughts and keep only those that were tightly anchored. "The paper left in your suitcase with the Stellium in Scorpio keeps flashing through my head, and the whole ghoul pool thing, everything's connected, you know," Callie said.

I, of course, couldn't see the connection. I *could* see, however, as we got on the elevator, that there was something about 29 critical degrees in the Eighth House that seemed to lock up her mental hard drive. She repeated again and again that in Scorpio, those 29 degrees meant something was imminent, perhaps something sexual or secretive.

"Something that's already happened, or is about to happen, in or to this hotel; that's what I feel, but that should only apply to the past when this chart was created, so I don't know…" Callie mused.

I assured her that the imminent sexual event involved the two of us. I slid the electronic card into its metal slot, and our hotel room door clicked open. I immediately dumped the plates onto the dining room table and turned to greet Elmo. His cage door was open, his toys were scattered around the room, but Elmo was nowhere to be seen.

"He's gone! Oh, God, he's gone!" I wailed.

Callie was on her knees looking under the bed and into cramped spaces where we both knew Elmo was far too big to hide, and furthermore, would never think of hiding. I ran into the bathroom and looked around. No Elmo. Callie grabbed the phone and rang the front desk, telling the clerk on duty that our dog had been stolen. In other circumstances, I would have taken time to savor her having called him "our dog," but right now, he was my missing puppy, the guy who took road trips with me, listened to me, even slept with me, and someone had taken him.

CHAPTER FIVE

The desk clerk told Callie she'd check with the front office, and maid service, and security, and see what she could find out, reminding us that no dogs were allowed in the hotel. Callie hung up and hurried out into the hallway and banged on the adjacent hotel room doors. I heard a door open and Callie interrogating someone in a slightly elevated voice.

A man said loudly, "Never saw him. Didn't know dogs were allowed."

The thought crossed my mind that since dogs weren't allowed maybe they'd discovered him and confiscated him, hauling him off to the pound.

After talking to half a dozen people in the hallway, Callie returned to the room, plopped down on the bed, took a deep breath, and closed her eyes, rubbing her forehead with her small, pale hands. My heart was pounding, and I felt like I might burst out crying.

I picked up the room phone and called maid service myself. I asked for the supervisor, quickly told her what had occurred, and said that if her entire crew would search all the hotel rooms, I would gladly pay several hundred dollars to whoever located my dog. The women on the phone said she would contact the maids right away.

"I'm feeling we should find that woman—at the front desk—I see her face when I close my eyes—dark hair—older, trim, well dressed."

I headed for the door, willing to follow any lead, do anything to see Elmo again. We were in the elevators in no time, not saying a word to one another as we rode, afraid we might voice our fears that Elmo was gone forever.

Is there some hideous group working at the hotel who eats dogs, or sacrifices dogs, or maybe it's just some horrible guy who steals them and sells them to biology labs or...

"Stop that!" Callie said as if reading my mind. "We're going to get him back."

Fear was turning to anger in me, a male trait, my mother often reminded me. Regardless, it had the advantage of turning a passive emotion that caused weakness and trembling into an active one that produced results.

"I'm fully capable of killing anyone who hurts Elmo," I admitted out loud, my jaw clamped shut.

"I know," Callie said, and I heard no condemnation in her voice.

I launched myself from the elevator across the sun, moon, and stars of the lobby floor like a meteor headed for the front desk. The stars were aligned. The tense and impeccably dressed front desk manager, wearing a name tag that said Ms. Loomis, was standing at attention in conversation with another guest. She looked exactly like the dark-haired woman Callie described. I interrupted. "My dog is missing from my room. Someone has taken him!"

"Just let me finish with this guest and—" she began.

"No, this is an emergency. My dog has been stolen from my room, and I want this entire hotel to begin a search and find him!"

The woman guest whom Ms. Loomis was helping stepped back out of reverence for an animal in distress and for fear of being trampled by an out-of-control pet owner.

"If you'll just step over there to the concierge, she will help you." Ms. Loomis tilted her thin, black-rimmed glasses down her long, narrow nose and waved to the small, silky-haired Asian woman at the concierge desk.

"Did I hear you say you lost your dog?" the Asian woman asked as I dashed toward her, fear making it difficult for me to breathe.

"I didn't lose him. He was taken from my room—stolen! Who had access to my room today? Who has a master key? I want to see those people."

"We can't, of course, let our guests interrogate staff for legal reasons. It would be inappropriate—"

"Get everyone who has a key to my room out here now, or I'm calling the police and my attorney!"

Ms. Loomis realized that the concierge didn't have me under control. She darted out from behind the marble counter, waved her off, and personally herded me back to the front desk.

"Ms. Richfield, we want to help you, but you must keep your voice down—" Her sentence snapped like a twig when I grabbed her by both forearms and held her in my grasp so that she could feel my agony.

"Find my dog!" My voice cracked, and I could feel tears falling over the edge of my eyes.

"Let go of me or I will call security."

"Call security, that's who in hell I want to see!"

As she moved a few yards down to pick up the phone, Callie, who had remained silent and removed from the dialogue, suddenly dashed behind the desk, pushed the door open, and shouted loudly, "Elmo! Elmoooo!"

"You can't go back there!" Ms. Loomis called after us, but I was already through the door, following Callie down the rabbit hole of the hotel's interior offices.

There was a low, muffled bark. I whirled. Ms. Loomis froze. People in the corridor turned and stared. It was an EF Hutton moment. Callie was moving rapidly past row after row of offices shouting Elmo's name. His barking had become louder and incessant. At the very last office, she flung open the door, and there was Elmo standing in the middle of the room. Callie fell to her knees as he rose up on his hind legs and put his short, stubby front paws on her shoulders. She threw her arms around his big middle and tears ran down her cheeks.

"Who took this dog and put him back here?" I demanded loudly of the staff at large.

One of the clerks seated behind a mound of paperwork said, "A guest complained that he was howling, so the assistant manager brought him in here to avoid any conflict and to keep him safe until you arrived back in your room."

"We just had a shift change. I assure you, Ms. Richfield, that we had only his, and your, best interest at heart," Ms. Loomis apologized. "Our assistant manager should have left a note in your room, or a message on your phone. He will be reprimanded. It seems you've had a very difficult stay, what with the situation in your bathtub, and now, thinking your dog had been kidnapped. We would like to comp your meals and bar tab for the remainder of your stay and offer you complimentary show tickets, and of course, Mr. Elmo is more than welcome to complete his stay with us, although, in the future, he might be more comfortable at home."

It was that last comment that set me off. "I'm going to give you my cell phone number. If anyone feels compelled to put anyone *in* my room or to remove anyone *from* my room, I highly recommend that they phone me first."

"Of course," she said with a polite bow that, in contrast to my own explosive anger, made me appear to be a maniac.

I leaned over and gave Elmo a big kiss on the snout and rubbed his head. "Let's get him out of here," I said, ignoring Ms. Loomis, who was standing in the doorway.

We talked, and cooed, and patted Elmo during the entire elevator ride up to our room. Several guests who'd been caught up in the drama said nice things to him as we walked past. By the time we got to our room, I felt weak and exhausted from the realization that I could have lost Elmo for good.

"You found him, Callie. If it hadn't been for you, I don't know what would have happened," I said, my voice shaking.

Callie held me in her arms and kissed me without saying a word, seeing that I was getting more upset after the fact. Elmo nudged the plates of what was now limp and uninviting food. We plopped down on the bed, unwrapped the food, and quickly handed it over to him. He gobbled it down voraciously. We both agreed that what we all needed was a good night's sleep.

The front desk's explanation of why they took Elmo bothered me almost as much as their having taken him. They said he was howling and someone had reported it, and they'd removed him until they could find us. I knew for a fact that Elmo didn't howl at just anything. It made no sense.

"Somebody wanted him," Callie said. "At least that's what I'm getting."

"You mean like a hotel employee who just wants to own a basset hound? That means he's not safe here at all. I wish I'd taught him to bite the hell out of people!" Elmo let out a low growl as if to assure me that should the need arise, he was up for the challenge.

"They won't bother him again," she said. "Too many people in the hotel have been alerted."

"How did you know to go back there?" I asked.

"I knew that's where Loomis's office must be," Callie said.

"But why Loomis?"

"It was her face I saw when I meditated. She called you Ms. Richfield. She knew your face. How? She wasn't there when we checked in."

I was silent for a moment, thinking about that. "You're right. She said, 'Ms. Richfield, I want to help you…'"

There was a knock at the door. The front desk had sent a bellman up to our room to move us. Callie balked, saying she was too exhausted to pack, but I wasn't spending another night in a room from which someone had tried to steal my dog. I packed everything and helped the bellman load it up.

We followed him down the hallway with all of our belongings hanging off the side of his clanking metal cart. I thought about the bag lady who lived in L.A. and pushed her metal grocery cart filled with bags of clothing from street corner to street corner. Now our metal cart filled with bags of clothing was being pushed from room to room. And I realized that the only difference between a bag lady and a lady with bags is the person pushing the cart.

Room 1250 was a newer version of our last room. Every room in the hotel had a different theme. This room was snowy white from top to bottom, and fit Callie to a T. She swooned over it. All the furnishings were Italian Provincial, which was really French Provincial with improved posture, the delicately curved chair legs having been replaced by straighter chair legs exhibiting slight thigh muscles. The bed was covered in white quilted brocade, and I made a mental note to pull back the bedspread on Elmo's bed since, when stressed, he was capable of sleeping in a drool state. The bathroom was done up in rich browns, and the TV was the finishing touch that gave it the look and feel of a small den sporting a tub and shower.

I tipped the bellman, slung our luggage onto the racks, and set up Elmo's wire playpen.

"I've been in more rooms than a hooker," I groused.

Callie cocked her eyebrow at me and yanked my shirt out of my pants, kissing me on the back, derailing the task at hand. I turned and wrapped my arms around her, returning her kisses.

She pushed me away playfully in favor of getting ready for bed and I wondered if Callie's sex drive had been impaired by so many years of abstinence or if there was something else she wasn't telling me. Spontaneous lovemaking didn't seem to be on her agenda, just spontaneous foreplay. We were in dress rehearsal with absolutely no opening night in sight.

Callie's idea of getting ready for bed was far more complicated than mine. Hers involved face scrubbings that bordered on Rolfing, and vigorous brushings of the head to stimulate hair growth, not to mention the slathering of face creams and body lotions. Then there was the issue of getting the blinds drawn just right and creating subdued lighting, but not total darkness, assessing the direction in which the heat or air was blowing, and examining the bedclothes for possible vermin. It made me realize that for forty-odd years I had never really "gotten ready" for bed but had merely fallen into it.

Callie disappeared into the bathroom. After a few minutes I heard the water shut off as she no doubt toweled off and dried her hair before peering around the corner at me and Elmo, just to see if we were both still there. She didn't want to admit it, but Elmo's disappearance had upset her, evidenced by the fact that she insisted we lift Elmo up on the bed and allow him to wedge himself between us.

"Could you move over, Elmo? You're getting all the soft spots that, frankly, I consider mine. I can't believe a woman of your overwhelming fastidiousness is allowing this!" I said as he burrowed down into the covers.

She laughed good-naturedly. "He was traumatized, so we have to make an exception."

"I was traumatized too," I replied, "and I'm getting nothing."

"Not true," she said and leaned across his body to kiss me warmly on the lips, pressing up against Elmo in doing it. Elmo let out a couple of short grunts, flopped over, put his big nose in Callie's cleavage and his paws against her chest, let out a sigh, and went fast asleep.

"I am going to need another bath," she whispered, giggling.

"He loves the way you smell. I have to say, I agree." I draped my arms over Elmo to reach Callie. "This wasn't what I had in mind for tonight," I muttered.

"We'll let him stay for a little while longer, and then we'll get up and—"

"Hose off!" I finished her sentence. "Do you think it's true that someone complained about him?"

"They could have," Callie said.

"But did they?" I pressed.

"No," she said softly. "Ms. Loomis said the assistant manager should have left us a note or a message. How did she know that he hadn't?" Callie asked.

"She assumed he hadn't because we were in the lobby screaming at her," I offered.

"Maybe," Callie replied, more suspicious than I.

I sat up in bed unable to take another close-up whiff of Elmo, whose basset glands had been working overtime due to the stress of his harrowing ordeal. He'd secreted enough basset oil in his skin to make him as shiny as a seal and as smelly as one. Callie sat up and asked Elmo to hop onto his bed, giving him one last pat. He let out a disgruntled groan. Callie got up to strip the bedcovers and shake them before disappearing into the bathroom again. I could hear the valves in the showerheads squeal as she turned the water on.

"I'm so happy about sweet Elmo," she called out.

"Me too," I said, and surprised her by stepping into the shower with her. "These hotel rooms have more surprises in the bathrooms than you ever thought possible, don't they? We have Elmo to thank for this opportune moment. You don't want to sleep with someone who's slept with Elmo, unless she's showered." I wrapped my left arm around her soapy, slick waist and held her steadily as I slid my hand down her tight little buttocks, letting the warm water pound her breasts as I gently massaged between her legs and sighed over the softness.

"That feels so good," she moaned.

Suddenly the TV in the bathroom turned on, apparently the result of a preset timer, startling us and giving us an unasked-for late-night recap of the local evening news. The news anchor's voice was blaring over an aerial shot of a sheriff's helicopter flying low over the stark desert terrain outside the city and landing at a remote, rocky site. On the ground, several medical personnel were loading a body into an ambulance as the news anchor said, "The body of Bruce Singleton was found tonight at this remote desert location northeast of Las Vegas. Mr. Singleton apparently died of drowning some eight hours before his body was discovered."

"Died of drowning in the desert? Now that's a trick," I said as the camera moved in on the dead man, his arms folded across his chest. I reached with one arm out of the shower to turn off the TV, not wanting more dead men interfering in my love life.

"Wait! That's the man who was in our bathtub!" Callie squealed. I jerked the shower curtain back as if getting a better view of the screen would make the video frames slow down, but the photographer was already rolling on something else.

"How can it be the same guy?" I tried to calm Callie, telling her we were both just tired and nervous. It couldn't be the dead guy.

"I mean that it's his clothes, his hands, his body…I don't know. Singleton was murdered, that's what I'm getting," she said and hopped out of the shower, grabbing a towel.

"Getting from whom?" I asked, knowing full well from whom. Callie was inexplicably plugged into the cosmos, and apparently her lines were up and running.

We dried off and climbed into bed, Callie disturbed and preoccupied. I was disturbed and preoccupied too. I couldn't believe we were about to go to sleep without making love.

"I'm sorry," she said, hugging me close. "I'm just exhausted and a little freaked by this."

"No problem," I lied, thinking Barrett and Mary Beth and probably two or three other women would love to be lying here in front of me, but I wanted the woman with her back to me.

Callie rolled over, wrapped her arms around me, and held me tightly, in one tender touch erasing my doubts and increasing my desire.

CHAPTER SIX

At dawn, Callie burst into the room having gotten up, dressed, and hit the lobby without my ever stirring. She plopped down on the edge of the bed, jarring all of my synapses into firing at once while I tried to remember where I was. Callie had the morning paper so close to my face I could smell the type. I rose up on one elbow.

"Check the photo!" she said excitedly. I tried to focus. There was Bruce Singleton's tanned body on a stretcher being loaded into an ambulance.

"Look, he's wearing a tuxedo!" Callie said.

"Like half the dealers in Las Vegas," I replied. I wasn't sure why Callie was so excited over Bruce Singleton, since we didn't know the man. The photo of him didn't really show his face but merely gave us a side view of his belt, right shoulder, and arm.

"His finger. Look at his little finger. It's white, not tan. That's where he wore a ring, but the ring's not there!" When I was slow on the uptake Callie finished her thought. "He's the guy from the tub. He was wearing the bird ring. Now he's dead in the desert without the ring."

"It was probably nibbled off him by prairie dogs," I said. She punched me playfully for not giving his mysterious death my full attention. "Is there coffee?" I asked.

She produced some black liquid in a ceramic mug that she'd brought upstairs especially for me since she never touched the stuff. "You drink it too strong—" she began, but I cut her off by pulling her down on top of me and kissing her. She sighed and seemed to relax for a moment.

"You have the most luxurious lips!" I sighed in return. Elmo sighed too, making us giggle. "He thinks they're luxurious and he's ten feet away. So what am I supposed to do with this startling information you've brought me?" I asked, gratefully sucking down the coffee and pulling Callie in closer.

"Bruce Singleton was dating Karla Black, wife of Mo Black, the now defunct owner of this hotel." She smiled smugly. "The waitresses in the restaurant downstairs were buzzing about it. I guess Karla and Bruce Singleton were quite an item, because he was fifteen years younger than she is." Callie could see I wasn't enthused. She bounced the bed as if kinetic energy would jar my enthusiasm level. "You love great stories. You write great stories. You sell great stories. This is a great story…and it will help my client. Come on, get excited! Word is that Bruce Singleton was set to come over here and run the *Boy Review*, become its executive producer, but he died before he got to do it."

"Significance being…?"

"I don't know, but Karla's at home this morning. I rang," she said. Callie pulled a slip of paper bearing an address out of the pocket of her tiny jeans, and just the way she moved her hip to get her hand into her pocket looked sexy.

"You got the phone number and address from the waitress?"

"Nope. My client knows her. And I called her and she's invited us over."

I complained about having to leave the room. In other circumstances I, too, would have been curious about Karla Black, a woman who had managed to trap a big-time gangster into marrying her, and then outlived him to enjoy a hot young guy like Bruce Singleton. "If I'd been Mo, I would have at least inserted a prenup that specified, in case of my death, she couldn't screw her new lover in my hotel," I said.

"You would do that," she said flatly.

"Damn straight. Let the next Bozo take her to Motel 6. How did you get Karla to agree to see us?"

"Told her we're thinking about writing an article on astrological architecture and we want to feature the hotel lobby."

"Her lover just died and she's up for an interview on astrological architecture? I'd say the woman isn't too heartbroken."

"People cope in different ways," Callie said nonjudgmentally.

❖

An hour later, we crossed the starstruck lobby, where a domed ceiling, painted in nighttime blue, held hosts of twinkling stars raked by hidden strobes that seemed to make the heavens come alive. Callie stood in the middle of the celestial display and stared up in wonder, leaning against me for support. It was a compression of stars and planets and asteroids, each carefully placed and correctly named. As if God hovered above the entire array, light filtered down through the stars, somehow managing to cast their images onto the floor below. Other images embedded in the floor were backlit, casting their shadowed shapes up into the sky. So looking up at the ceiling, we were, in fact, partially looking down, God-like, and looking down at the floor, we were, in fact, looking up. It was a wonderful, mind-boggling experience. I hadn't really taken time to admire the ceiling, having spent most of my time admiring Callie.

"I was so proud to be part of this at the time." Callie's voice was barely audible as she pondered the astrological implications.

"You worked on this ceiling?" I asked in awe.

"Mapping out the design. Mo directed it. He was obsessed with eights, can you tell? Look at all the eight clusters. He said he always won on eights and that the number eight had the best odds."

I stared at her wondering how many things I would learn about her over time that would surprise me. I couldn't expect at our age that life would only begin from the moment we met, but there was a piece of me that wistfully wished it could. How sad that there had been so many wonderful and interesting experiences she had already had without me—memories I wouldn't share with her, places she would talk about that I wouldn't have seen. I longed for us to have a history together, to be able to say, remember when we went to Sedona? Or, remember that time in New York? I suddenly felt cheated of her presence, as if God had left me to wander the desert alone for forty years before giving me a mate. *Why couldn't we have met in our twenties?*

As if reading my mind, Callie took my hand. "Had we known each other twenty years ago, we wouldn't have hit it off." We exited through the large front doors on the way to retrieve our car.

"Because you were busy designing the astrological equivalent of the Sistine Chapel?" I asked.

"No, because you were too cocky and arrogant." She jabbed me with her forefinger for emphasis.

"That *could* be construed as a negative remark," I mused.

We got into our car, and I tipped valet parker Sheik Skippy and headed north off the Strip.

❖

"Right, right, right!" Callie suddenly shouted as we drove up into the hills above Las Vegas.

"Sorry," I said, making the turn at the last possible moment. "Thought you were just agreeing with me."

"You have no sense of direction, do you?" she asked kindly, as if inquiring about a loss of hearing.

I insisted I did have a sense of direction but merely became preoccupied. Her silence made me want to argue the point, but she quickly added, "The address is 888. You passed it!"

I threw the car into reverse and backed up in front of a two-story Spanish mission–style home with an arching entryway that led into a huge courtyard. *Not a bad cottage,* I thought, but the pink and turquoise walls, with inlaid tiles of half-naked girls, and the garish fountain, featuring three peeing lads, made me think that Mo Black had more money than taste.

❖

"Hiya, kids." Karla threw open the door in a grand gesture, as if we'd known her for years. "Come on in." From what I could tell, she didn't appear to be in the emotional vicinity of any of the five stages of mourning.

Karla Black was what gangsters in the twenties called a floozy, a woman of disreputable character. When she was sober, her walk was a stagger, her massive head of bleached-blond hair looked as if she'd tried to comb it with an egg beater, and her makeup was Ringling Brothers. She was forty pounds too heavy, and her clothes needed another trip through the wash cycle; nonetheless, she had sadness behind her soft green eyes and a ready smile that made me mentally slap myself for being judgmental. So she liked sleeping with mobsters. Maybe they told her she was pretty and bought her nice jewelry. Who was I to judge?

Callie introduced us and explained we were on a literary mission. Karla didn't seem to care why we were there, as long as we would sit and chat. She obviously didn't get much female company.

A half hour into the conversation, Karla let out a big sigh. "Always wondered about all that crap on the ceiling. Some little chickie came in and sold him a bill of goods about the hotel bein' a livin' person and some jibberish about the planets. He just wanted to get in her pants, was my take on it." Karla laughed. I furrowed my brow at Callie, who avoided my stare as Karla rambled on.

"Aaaanywho, that was pre-me, so I didn't give a shit. Exceptin' he spent a zillion dollars of what woulda been my dough on the damn thing. People like it, I guess. So whadaya wanna know about it?"

Callie explained that the kind of color commentary Karla had just provided was exactly what she was looking for, and she artfully moved Karla away from the astrological design of the ceiling and onto her love affair with the builder. It was a subject near and dear to Karla's heart.

"So, Mo and me was just, ya know, like in our second childhood and in love, humpin' all the time, not worryin' about nothin', then a couple of his buddies come along and they decide to build these kinda gigantic houses out here in the middle of nowhere! Ya know, for me, the desert was just like, well…deserted! But Mo, he was like a sand-schlepper, so we pulled some money together and times was tough, but then, I don't know, he hooked up with the right guys, and well, here I am in this desert palace, as Mo called it." Saying his name made her chin tremble, and tears came to her eyes. "I miss Mo. He was my baby."

"I'm sorry," I offered.

"Yeaaah, he was hot stuff, Mo was. That's him," she said and picked up a photo off the mantel of a chunky, Italian-looking stud. She gave the picture a big lipsticky kiss. "I got life-size cutouts of him stored down in the hotel basement. Used to have 'em in the lobby, but people said it made 'em sad. God forbid they should be as sad as me, huh?"

Next to that photo were other pictures of her and Mo at the beach, both looking well-fed, but less decadent and decidedly happier. There were photos of Mo kissing a large golden retriever, and Mo with an attractive woman. *Must have been a relative*, I thought. *Or Karla would have chewed that portion of the picture off with her teeth.*

Karla put her chipped red nail on the image of the woman. "That was Mo's first wife."

"So you must have liked her," I ventured, definitely surprised.

"Sure, 'cuz she was dead right after I met her. They had a couple a kids together, and she blessed Mo and me on her deathbed, so I figure, why not let her sit up on the mantel and look good, ya know, 'cuz she don't look so good now."

I was beginning to wonder how our conversation could transition from wonderful Mo, the love of her life, to Bruce Singleton, a shorter-lived love. I decided diving right in was the best solution.

"So I guess you met Bruce after Mo died…"

"Bruce died too! You hear about that? I just don't have any luck with men. Bruce was comin' over from another club to run the *Boy Review* for me. It was originally called *Boys in Review Daily*. BIRD. In honor of the big-winged finale. Mo named it that. *The Bird Review*. But we was gettin' so many calls from people wantin' to know how to get rid of starlings or clean out a martin house, for God's sake! Can you believe it? So we changed the name to *Boy Review*. Bruce was gonna run it, but not now. He drowned! You gotta go to a helluva lot of trouble to drown in the goddamned desert, ya know what I mean?" Karla's shoulders shook and she began to sob. "Cops comin' to talk to me…funeral plans…his mother bawlin'. It's a mess!"

"How did he drown?" I asked.

"Under water." She looked at me as if I were an idiot. "He couldn't breathe underwater."

I suppressed a grin as Callie dove in to save me. "What were the circumstances of his being out in the desert alone and then being found in that small lake?" Callie asked.

"How would I know that?" Karla was suddenly suspicious, "You're not like cops trying to be somethin' else, are ya? Because if you was, I would call some people you would not like to know. Because I had nothin' to do with my husband Mo's death or with Bruce's death. Bruce was a drinker, ya know, and for all I know he coulda passed out and fallen in the goddamned lake…"

Whatever Karla was on, it was starting to kick in. She was slurring her words, and her eyes rolled ever so slightly, as if she were about to faint. "I think you two better get the hell out," she said without malice, and rose unsteadily to her feet. Then, just as suddenly, her mood shifted again. "Don't be mad at me. I'm just not feelin' too well, ya know. Got a lot of things on my mind. Come see me another time."

"What do you know about the ghoul pool, Karla?" Callie asked as we walked to the door.

"Howcha hear about that?" Karla revived, shocked back into consciousness.

"I have a friend on the list," Callie said.

Karla gave us a large, tired shrug, her soft fleshy upper body jiggling with the effort. "Bruce said he was on the list, but I don't know. I was on the list one time. Mo was. It's like a naughty night that everybody in town wants to be invited to 'cuz they want to brag about bein' on the list."

"When the show was called the *Bird Review*, did you give anyone a gold signet ring with a bird on it?" I asked.

Karla let out a sharp laugh. "The day I pass out fourteen karat gold anything, you call 911, okay? You're soundin' as crazy as those women who call about the starlings! I'm not feelin' well. Good-bye." She closed the heavy carved door in our face.

"Well, she closes doors as abruptly as you end phone calls," I remarked.

"When there's nothing more to say, move on." Callie shrugged, seeming to understand Karla.

"Why are you fixated on this ghoul pool deal?" I quizzed Callie.

"Let's go have lunch and we'll talk," she replied, getting into the car.

"Okay, but start talking now."

"You sound like a cop." She grinned at me.

"Well, I *was* a cop, just not a very good one. I feel too sorry for people, like poor Karla. What a wasted life."

"Not in her eyes," Callie said in her typically cosmic way.

"So you're the little chickie who talked Mo into spending all that money, and he did it because he was trying to get into your pants?" I said, only half kidding.

"He was not trying to get into my pants," she said firmly, to put an end to further questions.

"Then he really was a dumb gangster." I slid my hand under her and squeezed her cheeks, and she yelped.

❖

We stopped at a little sandwich dive with a couple of tables out front. Not much ambience but at least some fresh air after the stifling atmosphere of Karla's drug and booze den. We stood in the takeout line and Callie ordered a ham and cheese sandwich. I ordered a tuna melt. The words had no sooner left my mouth than Callie spoke up, "I wouldn't do the tuna."

"You're right. I'll smell like a fish, and cats will follow me down the street. Make it a ham and cheese," I said agreeably.

"I'm just cautious about food," she said. "I was poisoned in another lifetime, and it's a carryover."

The sandwiches came flying across the counter before I had time to respond to that startling confession. Callie took them both with her and unwrapped them, lifting the bread as if it were a manhole cover, staring down intently at the ham. I waited expectantly, amused by this blond woman of great insight who held all nourishment in suspicion.

"Are we safe?" I kidded her.

"Are you making fun?"

"Absolutely not." I smirked. "Just waiting for the green light on this sandwich so I can eat and then find out about the ghoul pool."

"Eat." She smiled and pushed my sandwich toward me.

"You were poisoned in another lifetime?"

"Around 1500 A.D. Conditions were hideous, of course."

I stopped midbite to stare at her.

She continued, "I think it was accidental. I don't recall the specifics, but I…" She stopped, realizing this was far beyond my ability to comprehend, believe, or perhaps even endure. "Let's talk about something else. We have years to discuss things like this."

"That last sentence was comforting," I said and reached over and gently wrapped my hand around the nape of her neck. She let out a great sigh, not unlike Elmo's.

"I've missed you," she said, looking up at me, and her translucent blue eyes sparkled. There was a long pause, neither of us quite knowing where to take the conversation. I let my hand drop from her neck, and Callie changed the subject.

"My client in Tulsa, Randall Ross, is a wealthy man. I've known him for years. He's been contacted by a man"—she seemed to be selecting her words carefully—"who told him his daughter is in trouble. This happened two months ago when I was in L.A. with you. He called, begging me to come back to Tulsa immediately. He thought his daughter's death was imminent. I've been trying to help him. Then a few days ago, he phoned me in a panic. His daughter had called from Las Vegas to say that she'd attended a party where she'd been put on a ghoul pool list."

"Who's the man who contacted him?" I asked.

"He...wasn't sure," Callie said.

"And your client's daughter is Rose Ross?"

"Yes. The problem is that people on the list actually do die with some regularity. Whether they are on the list because they are about to die, or they die because they're on the list, is the issue. Hard to prove. No one has the list. As Joanie Burr said, each name is 'read out loud and dropped into the flames, and only the ghost remembers the names.'"

"Pretty convenient. A bunch of drunks hear thirteen names and get drunker. No list. No evidence. So this trip is business, and I'm a nice adjunct to that?"

"I knew if I told you I was here on business, you'd feel slighted," she said.

"You think? Because the corollary of that is, had there been no business, you would not have bothered to meet me."

She leaned over and, in front of the couple dining at a nearby table, kissed me warmly on the lips in a lingering promise of even warmer things to come.

"I will always find you," she said softly.

"Not as good as I will always be with you," I replied.

She kissed me again and her lips were intoxicating.

"Callie, you've got to level with me," I said, unable to prolong the pleasure for fear of the pain. "You could have arranged to see me if you'd wanted to...you didn't want to."

"I wanted to," she managed to say.

"We've been apart for over two months. I know you want me, I can feel it. And God knows, I want you, and yet...we've been here for twenty-four hours and we haven't made love?"

"There was a dead man—"

"Why aren't we making love?" I gently interrupted and looked into her eyes. She shifted in her seat and looked away, then tried to formulate her thoughts. Apparently the truth was difficult—even for a psychic.

"It's…in L.A.…it got to feeling so…permanent…so quickly."

I was hurt by the fact that Callie Rivers had just admitted she wasn't rushing headlong into my life, but I was glad to have the source of her anxiety out in the open. Obviously I wanted more out of this relationship than Callie did. I let that sink in and then the survivor in me kicked in, that piece of me that always made sure I was okay. *After all, this is the woman who confided in me that she'd made love for years and never let herself climax, so why am I surprised that she can keep her emotional distance? Just take a different approach,* the voice in my head commanded.

"So 'permanent' is our problem?" I asked casually.

"It's just bad timing, that's all. Astrologically, I'm emotionally reserved right now. My Saturn has been opposition my Venus for weeks…"

"But that aspect," I said, noting she was pleased I'd learned the word aspect, "is short lived, right? You did say when you met me that I was destined for you. So I'm hanging my hat on that. However, my immediate problem is that I've been put on planetary pause, or asteroid avoidance, or whatever, and it's wearing on my nervous system. So how about we just have some amazingly…impermanent…sex? Would that be all right?" I kissed her gently.

The middle-aged woman in tennis togs sitting directly across from us cocked her eyebrow at me and gave me an appreciative smile. She was apparently picking up on our conversation. I grinned shyly at her in return, lowered my voice to a whisper, and tried to pull myself together.

"Okay." Callie reached over and slid her hand playfully between my legs.

I rocked back reflexively. "You're an exhibitionist."

"You told me when we first met that you hated routine. Don't want you to get bored," Callie said.

The woman wearing tennis clothes walked past our table on her way out and hesitated a moment to say, "You two continue to have a nice day," and she gave us a radiant smile.

"Thank you." Callie smiled up at her.

The woman's husband let out a large belch and hoisted his belt buckle to adjust his pants. "Men." She shook her head and laughed, obviously hooked on them and unable to understand her own attraction for them. "We marry them wanting all their masculine strength and testosterone, and then we want them to be as playful and close as women can be, like asking an elephant to perform a ballet. Even if we could train them to do it, it would look unnatural." The woman grinned again as her husband shouted for her to come on.

We left the café and headed for our car. I stepped off the curb to open the driver's side door, still laughing over the straight woman's catching Callie in the act of groping me. I didn't see the car that came out of nowhere heading for me. Callie screamed at the top of her lungs. My mind slammed a thousand thoughts across my brain in a nanosecond. Leaving my physical body unattended, it moved fearlessly to a four-beat musical choreography, an orchestrated dance of danger, my head keeping count like a metronome: Arms overhead, *three-four*, dissolve to pirouette, *three-four,* away from oncoming car, *four-one,* spin, spin, turn, face to the car, *three-four,* back to the car, *three-four,* side mirror grabs my jacket and I'm up, spin and down, *three-four*. Land on my feet, dip back, bounce off my hip, *two-three-four,* Callie's incredible strength hauls me out of the street, *three and four and cut!* Take two. Cue the effects: screech of tires, grinding of gears, car backs up at high speed, snap zoom to wide shot, car comes back for the kill! Callie's viselike grip on my shirt collar, and I'm off my feet, up and backward through the air and I land on the café patio. Standing ovation from the gathering crowd. Callie dials 911. Cut. Wrap! My mind snaps back from outer space, slamming into my body, the pain of reentry making my head feel like it took a bullet. Callie was kneeling on the ground beside me, cupping my head in her hands and whispering, "You're all right, Teague. Everything's okay."

How does she know that? I wondered.

The police arrived. No one had gotten the license plate number, so there wasn't much else to do but ask the usual questions. "Any reason someone would want to kill you? How do you know it wasn't an accident? How long will you be in Las Vegas?"

"He was a mid-thirties, muscular guy, like a wrestler with no hair," I offered.

"Got it down." The cop took notes. "We'll be on the lookout for the car, and we'll contact you at your hotel if we need anything else."

One, two, three, wrap! I thought.

Chapter Seven

That guy who tried to hit me was pretty damned determined. Well, he failed and may his dick be torn off by wild dogs," I said, limping slightly.

"Teague, I know you're angry but please don't say those kinds of things into the cosmos. It's like a curse and—"

"I like curses, particularly those that torture the perpetrator for centuries." I smiled.

"That's not funny." I could have sworn Callie glanced up at the heavens. "Here, give me those. I'm driving." Callie took the car keys from me and helped me into the car. "I need to get you back to the room." Callie's voice was filled with concern over my near demise.

"No, I'm okay. I'm fine. Just a little shook up, that's all."

❖

We pulled into the valet park at our hotel, and Callie told the man opening my car door to help me out.

"I'm fine," I reiterated, embarrassed at the attention. "Come on. Let's go over to the theater and tell your friend Rose what happened and see if the description of the driver clicks for her."

Moments later Callie, still protesting my not going directly to our room, followed me to the theater where a skeleton cast was doing a somewhat sloppy run-through of a new *Boy Review* routine. The theater company's production assistant tried to head us off, leaping from his seat and dashing down the aisle as if to greet us, rather than throw us out. Rose spotted us and hurried down off the stage, letting the boy know that it was okay, she knew us. I remarked that it appeared she never slept and spent her entire life in rehearsal. She smiled and said they actually got two days off a week but those days varied.

"We're here because someone tried to kill Teague by ramming her with his car." Callie was direct and her voice held no emotion.

Rose gasped. "Are you sure? Maybe it was an accident. People around here drive like—"

"When he missed, he screeched to a halt, backed up, and tried to hit her again. It was no accident," Callie said.

I watched Rose's face for a reaction. She looked a bit like a deer in the proverbial headlights.

"He was mid-thirties, bald, and beefy. Do you know anyone like that? Do you have any reason to suspect someone?" Callie asked.

"No," Rose said breathlessly as a drag queen even more gorgeous than Joanie Burr strode toward us. She was a proud jungle cat cruising rapidly and effortlessly down the aisle, muscles taut, head high, her large, angular frame gliding to a stop in front of us. She graced us with a sensual smile. *European good looks,* I thought.

"Someone tried to run over my friend with a car…a man," Rose said.

"That's horrible!" she said. "I'm Marlena Mercado."

We introduced ourselves. Marlena said a quick hello and added, "Rose, you're up next. Better get back onstage."

Rose looked flustered and torn. She glanced up to see the director, a tall, thin, gay man, signaling her that she was about to miss her cue, and she hurried back up the aisle.

"Sorry, I have to go," Rose's voice trailed behind.

Marlena cocked her head slightly in a studied theatrical way that made sure her best features were always on display. "Are you in town on vacation?"

"That, and I'm very interested in what's frightening some of the performers," Callie said pointedly, hoping for an entree, but Marlena was too schooled for that.

"I would say they're frightened that their looks, or their legs, or their bank accounts will give out before they find Mr. Right. Isn't that what all girls are afraid of?" Marlena shot us a dazzling smile. "Gotta run. Maybe we'll all get together before you leave town—if you're going to see Rose again."

"We'd like that," Callie replied, and we watched Marlena bound up onto the stage.

"Damn, I wish I could look that good." I sighed.

"Darling, you look much better," Callie said sincerely as we headed up the aisle for the heavy double doors that separated the theater from the hotel lobby.

"Notice how every time we see Rose Ross she gets dragged off by a drag queen? Maybe that's why they call them drag queens." I gave her a silly grin.

"Maybe it was just her cue to go onstage. You and I are always a bit suspicious."

A tall, handsome Italian woman approached from the balcony staircase and introduced herself as Sophia Pappagallo, another cast member. She was older than Rose, a beautifully put together dark-haired woman in her mid-thirties with riveting dark eyes, ample breasts, and great self-confidence. She said that Rose had explained why we were here and that she was grateful we'd cared enough to come and check on her friend's well-being. She offered to get us something to drink and indicated the best seats for us to watch the rehearsal. I quickly declined on all counts, wanting only to be with Callie. Sophia sized us up with a slow smile.

"Of course, you probably have many things to do," she said mercurially, and then remarked that she sincerely hoped she would see us again as she disappeared into the dimly lit theater.

"Attractive girl," Callie said.

"Gay girl," I replied.

"How do you know for sure?"

"Let's go back to our hotel room and I'll show you how to recognize one." I turned toward the door and a piercing pain shot through my leg. In fact, both legs were throbbing and my shoulders were now aching from the whiplash of my auto ballet. "I need a muscle relaxant for my shoulders."

"You shouldn't take those," Callie said. "I'll work on your body."

"Best offer I've had in the last hour," I said.

❖

I greeted Elmo with a hug and a Milk-Bone, bribing him to cut me some slack and lay low. In the quiet of our hotel room, Callie crawled into bed and pulled me up between her legs with my back against her chest and wrapped her arms around me, saying nothing, just breathing. She felt much larger than her actual size—strong and solid. She placed one hand on my forehead and one on my heart, took three deep breaths, and threw something away into the air.

"Now you'll feel better," she assured me, still holding me.

"So you're removing evil spirits?" I asked, letting myself sag back into her arms, happy I hadn't been taken from her.

She began kissing me along my neck and down my shoulders, pausing occasionally to ask me if I was hurting anywhere.

"One or two places unrelated to the accident," I said.

"I can take care of that," she whispered, and I thought perhaps it was worth being nearly hit by a car if this was the reward, or perhaps Callie could only focus fully on me if she thought she'd lost me.

The wonderful thing about passion is that it releases endorphins, and they mask pain. Very quickly, I wasn't hurting and I could turn my body a hundred and eighty degrees to embrace her and unbutton her blouse.

"I'm worried about this," I teased as I unsnapped the single hook holding her bra together. "Why does a girl have a bra that snaps in the front?"

"For those who aren't very adept at undressing women." She kissed me fervently.

"You are a lot to handle, Callie Rivers." I smiled.

"Let's see how well you do." She smiled back.

I tried to begin at the beginning, kissing her lips, letting my mouth wander slowly down her gorgeous neck, then letting my lips make teasing side trips to her breasts and across her belly as she ran her hands through my hair, but I wasn't doing too well on the lingering part. Foreplay had been taking place in my head for months so now, just like the guys, I wanted to skip the preliminaries and be in the wet, wonderful orgasmic center of her, and with that single thought in mind, I buried my face in the soft golden hair between her legs, letting out a moan that said, much like Elmo, I'd reached nirvana. She was instantly wet and thrusting into me as I reached under her to hold her small soft hips in my hands. Suddenly she pulled away and rolled me over on my back so that she could lie on top of me, and she buried her face in me, while I was in her, so that we could enjoy the tastes and smells and feelings of one another simultaneously. And that was the exact moment in my life when sixty-nine became my favorite number. I decided I would have it put on a football jersey with today's date or perhaps even have it tattooed on my arm! The woman was masterful. There was an art to sliding effortlessly into that position, but there was a chemistry to climaxing at the same instant. We were overwhelmed by our chemistry when our bodies had barely had time to know one another. I reversed my position to hold her in my arms and kiss her golden hair.

"I hope you know what you're going to do with me, because now you completely own me," I whispered.

"I do." She pushed me onto my back and straddled me, managing to position all the wet, warm areas I'd most recently kissed directly onto my own still-throbbing parts. "You're not getting off that easy." She grinned at her double entendre, sitting upright astride me and rocking back and forth, smiling down at me, revealing how gorgeous she was from golden head to voluptuous breasts and her tiny lower torso.

In only seconds, I was unbearably hot again, pushing against her with my hips, pulling her down on me to kiss her and caress her breasts. I lay back almost unconscious from the sheer pleasure and excitement of her touch. She lay on top of me, gently, rhythmically thrusting into me, and in minutes, I was rolling her over again and sliding my fingers inside her and kissing her so deeply that we were both on fire and climaxing. When we finally came up for air, I whispered, "I can only say I've been in more positions than the Dallas Cowboys."

"Complaining?" she asked.

Weak and happy, we stared into one another's eyes with utter amazement at how completely we had come together to become one. We fell asleep wrapped around each other and didn't move until light shifted on the shutters and the clanking sounds of room service trays clattered up and down the halls.

We stayed in bed for hours exploring one another's bodies as if they were unique to the planet. Holding fingers up to the light to notice how long and slender they were, examining the shape of feet, putting them sole to sole and sighing over the touch, marveling at the two inches of the inner leg just next to the pubic hair where it was so soft that it was mesmerizing to touch, and then we would make love again. We could not tell night from day. The order of things was lost. Eating or sleeping or making love had no appropriate time. It was all randomly driven by hormones. And so, Las Vegas was truly the town for us, because love plays havoc with time and Las Vegas knows no time. Lights are always on in Vegas. Breakfast and dinner are always ready simultaneously. Crowds always fill the streets. People are always wide awake. We could make love for six hours and not miss anything.

In the silence, we heard something brush the carpet. A piece of paper was slowly sliding under our door. I crawled out of bed, my body beginning to stiffen now, and picked up the letter and opened it. The typed note said, *Congratulations! We have captured your homo-fucking on tape. Be careful what you try to expose, or be exposed.* I stared at it. "What in hell?"

I yanked the door open and poked my head outside, but the hallway was empty. I was still naked, so there was no chance that I would go sprinting down the hall after anyone. I went back to bed with the note, and Callie leaned over my shoulder to read it and then said, "Call the police! We're not going to be blackmailed by anyone for any reason."

I ignored her demand in favor of making a thorough search of the room: yanking back the drapes, checking the TV set for suspicious wiring, looking up and into every crevice, corner, and cobweb I could find. *Maybe there is no video. Maybe it's all a threat*, I thought as I crawled up on the dressing table to examine a picture. Callie warned me to watch my step as I clambered down and Elmo freaked. He apparently could take a lot of things in his basset life, but my being butt naked and mounting the furniture wasn't one of them. He wanted out.

I pulled on my jeans and told Callie I'd call the manager after I walked Elmo. I wanted time alone to pull my thoughts together. Until I knew for sure there was a tape, I didn't want to expose our sex lives to the hotel employees, particularly security, whom we'd already met during the non-dead-body caper.

Elmo and I went downstairs to his favorite spot on the grass where he went about leaving his calling card as I pondered how to begin the conversation with the front desk. I rehearsed under my breath. "Hi there. So does in-room movies mean that people are in the room making movies—or not? Or how about, I got a letter saying you'd captured my homo-fucking on tape and I wondered if I could get a copy for my agent?" I sucked in air so loudly that Elmo stopped to see if I was all right. *There is no way this can go well.*

I took Elmo back upstairs and gave him two cookies and a rawhide bone to chew on as I prepared to leave to go talk to the front desk. He looked at me as if to say my recent attempts to entertain him were lame and insulting. "Look, I know. But at least you're not going downstairs to talk to the front desk about who you've been humping!"

"You're not really worried about telling the front desk what happened, are you?" Callie asked.

"Looking forward to it. Something I've always wanted to do—share my sex life with total strangers who come from countries where they still stone people to death for wearing lipstick or, if I get lucky, share my sex life with a prepubescent theater person, disguised as a front desk person, whose age is most likely higher than her I.Q."

"Don't underestimate people, Teague. They're more in tune than you think."

❖

Moments later I was at the front desk where a very pretty multi-ethnic woman in her early twenties, swathed in gold cloth, smiled at me and asked if she could help. I hesitated, envisioning her perhaps cultural reaction to the word "homo-fucking," but decided to go for it. She was either front-desk material at a big hotel in a sophisticated city or she wasn't.

"I received this threatening letter in my room." I handed her the letter.

She bent her head and dutifully read the letter, after which she looked up with a confused expression. "Where is your homo-fucking that was captured?" she inquired, her brow slightly furrowed.

"What?"

"I don't know what the homo-fucking is that was captured," she said sweetly but loud enough that the businessman next to me stopped checking in and stared at me.

"Could you get Ms. Loomis, please?" I asked.

"She is very busy. I can handle this with you, if you will tell me about your"—she glanced down at the unfamiliar word—"homo-fucking so that I can help you find it."

"Get Ms. Loomis, the hotel manager, now!" I said, my tone beyond urgent as I took the note back from her.

In seconds, the very tired and very thin, but nattily dressed Ms. Loomis stepped out of the door behind the long marble main desk. Her black hair was just this side of lacquered and lay tightly against her head. She had the look of someone who worked for powerful and demanding bosses. I told her that, like many people vacationing in Las Vegas, I had made love in my room, and I then received a letter under the door telling me that my lovemaking was captured for posterity, and if I chose to expose them, they would expose me.

"And who are *they*?" she asked.

"I have no idea," I said, realizing for the first time how hard it is to report an act of near-criminal behavior.

"So you have no idea what they might be afraid you would expose?"

"None," I replied.

"To the precise point, there were pictures taken of you in our hotel, making love, is that what you're saying, Ms. Richfield?"

"That's what the note says." I laid it on the counter in front of her, looking for a reaction to "homo-fucking," but to Ms. Loomis's credit, she never altered her expression.

"I want to know who wrote the note, and who took the pictures, and where those pictures are," I said calmly.

Ms. Loomis looked me squarely in the eyes. "Ms. Richfield, there is no conceivable way that the hotel could take photos or videos of you in your room doing anything." She picked up the phone and rang security. Roy arrived. The same flattopped, flabby Roy who had shown up to find nobody in our bathtub. I sighed when I saw him, imagining what he would think upon hearing that our lovemaking had been taped, but that there was no tape. Ms. Loomis assumed her most crisp, executive tone in addressing Roy. "Ms. Richfield believes that her privacy was violated with in-room cameras, the images from which are being held by someone in the hotel."

Roy stared at me. "Pictures were taken of you in your room? Not possible, ma'am. No cameras in any rooms anywhere."

I stood quietly for a moment trying to decide if I should demand they summon the police. However, I was fearful that the LVPD might find the camera topic less interesting than the same-gender-sex topic. I had no evidence, no perpetrator, not even a suspect. I decided to drop it, drawing the dialogue to a halt by summing up my current needs. "I want security to keep an eye on our room."

They both assured me they would have someone available at all hours if we rang, and someone would make it a point to patrol the halls. As Roy spun on his heels to execute that order, Ms. Loomis looked deep into my eyes. "I will personally file a report and follow up on this matter, and I will be in touch with you on what we find. It appears to me that despite this terrible thing having happened to you, you have the makings of a lovely vacation, and we at the hotel wish you one." Ms. Loomis gave me a pleasant smile.

The young golden woman standing at her side replicated her smile and craned her neck slightly to one side to be able to make eye contact with the person behind me, thereby dismissing me with practiced body language. I strolled back over to Callie, who was just getting off the elevator.

"What did she say?" Callie asked.

"Well, the 'more-in-tune-than-you-think' young woman at the front desk shouted 'homo-fucking' loudly several times because she couldn't figure out what it meant. After that, Ms. Loomis implied that I looked like I was in love," I said, running my hand up her back and resting it on the nape of her neck, sighing over how good it felt to be there. "Nobody in this hotel knows the answer to anything! The only good thing about the front desk is that I can immediately locate the person who knows nothing rather than having to flag down someone and *discover* they know nothing. Maybe there's no video of us," I said, tired of the stress it was causing. "Maybe Gloria the Harem Girl slid the note under our door to pay us back for our check-in altercation like a waiter who spits in your soup," I remarked. "But then how would she or anyone know that we had just made love unless they were watching or listening, which gives me the creeps." *It could just be someone's attempt to make us nervous—and it's working, I'm nervous*, I thought. *Someone wants us to get the hell out of this hotel.*

"Let's not give it any more energy," Callie said, which I'd learned was the astrological equivalent of forget it, and we headed back to our room.

❖

Callie stretched out on the bed, thinking no doubt about what had happened. I wrapped around her, contemplating the evil done to us. It would have been quite a different matter if I were a man. A man could go downstairs, talk to another man at the front desk, and let him know that he was going to punch the lights out of any human being who had disgraced his wife by taping her in the act of making love with her husband. The hotel would bow down and no doubt apologize profusely to the injured couple. Investigations would take place. There would be a great deal of reporting back to the offended duo. Apologetic notes tucked into fruit baskets would be delivered to the room from the manager. Sex would not be the topic. Violation of privacy would be the topic. *When I reported the same situation on behalf of Callie and me, I was missing the two key ingredients that could trigger that kind of solicitous response: a marriage license and a chromosomal random act. Papers and penises. Absent those two things, the world is a far more difficult place, and our blackmailer obviously knows that,* I thought.

"I can't sleep with your brain churning." Callie patted me.

"I'm not moving or making a sound."

"Your brain is." She propped up on her elbow. "Let me tell you something, darling. Things are what we make them. If you believe things will be difficult and embarrassing, they will be. If you believe they will go smoothly, then they will. We create our own world, Teague. Repeat out loud 'My world will go smoothly,' and then let it rest for a few hours."

She kissed me and rolled over and went to sleep. I stared at her small, exquisite form, thinking what a positive light force she was. I whispered out loud the phrase she'd given me, wrapped around her, and went to sleep.

CHAPTER EIGHT

We tried to take our minds off the note we'd received, pretend it was all just a hoax, and think about each other and our vacation. Callie occasionally brought up the topic of Rose Ross, but I called a halt to the discussion. As far as I was concerned, we'd checked—the girl didn't want help. I had no desire to make us a target for someone who didn't want our assistance.

"Someone's trying to silence her," Callie said.

"We're done," I politely warned. "Come on, let's just focus on each other."

I knew Callie loved to gamble, so I took her to the casino to take her mind off everything else. She took off like a happy hound, her nose to the gambling trail, and I followed her. We moved through the casino lobby, which was dotted with slot machines, into the deafening roar of the main casino, where gambling took on the intensity of an illicit sexual encounter. We continued past the walls of mechanized monsters, their crowbar-like arms stretched out imploringly, eating silver dollars, dollar bills, and hotel debit cards as fast as the players could feed them. Men yanked the metal arms down, a whirring sound ensued, the tiny window in the machine erupted with symbols of hurricanes, volcanoes, and double diamonds as players screamed out encouragement.

"Sevens, sevens, seeevens! Sonofabitch!" a young woman yelled.

"Come on, baby, come on, come oooooon, baby!" A man's voice was orgasmic as he coaxed his machine, grabbing her metal edges as if he could tilt her into coming up with the right pictures.

Suddenly across the room a loud synthesized melody twanged

out, a red light akin to the one atop a police car flashed above one of the machines, a siren wailed, a woman shrieked, and people stood up and threw their arms over their heads as if they were caught in a police raid.

"That woman just won a hundred thousand dollars!" Callie said.

"You're psychic, go do that!" I ordered playfully.

"I wish it worked that way." She grinned back at me.

We meandered into the arena of blackjack and craps tables, where the winning was decidedly more subdued. The players were more knowledgeable and, therefore, fretful, understanding the odds were not in their favor.

The line at the blackjack tables was three deep and the craps table was loaded with high rollers, so I suggested we do a couple of spins at the roulette wheel.

"Give me your lucky number," I told Callie as I pulled out a five dollar bill.

"Seventy-two."

"That's your lucky number? Nobody's lucky number is seventy-two. Personally, mine is still sixty-nine." I grinned at her. "Give me a number between one and thirty-six or zero or double zero."

Callie laid five dollars on the table. "Twenty-eight," she said coolly as the dealer put a single five dollar chip down in front of her. The overhead lights reflected off his ring, a flat gold signet ring bearing a ferocious-looking bird with one leg poised in the air, its claws extended. I drew back. It was the ring worn by the dead man or, if not *the* ring, one exactly like it.

"Place your bets," he warned, putting the wheel into motion.

"The ring!" Callie whispered.

"Last chance. Place your bets. Game closed." The dealer put his hand up, warding off any further placement of chips on the numbered felt.

"Thirty-two!" he announced, deftly sliding chips off the table into a trough and paying the winners in a stack of tens.

"Where did you get your ring?" I asked.

"I used to perform in the *Boy Review,*" he said without looking up.

I glanced at his name tag, which bore the name Dealer Brownlee. Callie put money on double zero as the wheel spun around again. Twenty-nine came up, and he raked her chip away. I pulled another twenty dollar bill out of my wallet as an older, well-dressed man came up to the table.

"Mr. Smith, welcome back." Brownlee became downright civil. "What will it be?"

"Ten on sixteen," Mr. Smith said, pulling a stack of bills out of his pocket, not amounting to ten dollars, but to ten thousand dollars. Brownlee quickly raked in the cash and replaced it with a stack of thousand dollar chips, sliding them onto number sixteen and rolling the wheel again.

"Staying in the hotel?" Brownlee asked.

"Yes. Never see my room until about one in the morning, if you call that staying."

"Well, good luck on sixteen," Brownlee said as the wheel slowed and the round metal ball bounced in and out of numbered slots heading for a berth somewhere in the twenties. By the time it had landed, Mr. Smith had walked away and Brownlee had taken his money for the house.

Callie and I left the table amazed at the cavalier expenditure of ten grand.

"Did you see how the guy turned and walked away before he knew for sure whether he'd won or lost? It was like he didn't care either way. It was like he'd just come to give his money away," I said in amazement.

"The game he's playing isn't happening at that table," Callie said quietly, as if reading the man's mind.

"What do you mean?" I asked, but Callie had momentarily disconnected from this world to connect to something else—a place that undoubtedly provided her with more answers than I could.

"You play the slots for a minute. I've got to go check something out," I said, handing her Elmo's leash and putting her in charge of my hound. I walked to the front desk and told Ms. Loomis that I was curious about the bird ring I'd seen the dealers wearing.

She looked up slowly and smiled at me. "It's a medieval totem, popular in Italy during the Roman period," she said, in the tone of a docent wanting me to feel as if my question had been answered when, in fact, it had not. "The bird motif is very popular in the hotel. You can see it in the gargoyles above some of the pillars, and of course, the *Boy Review* is famous for its winged finale. It's the longest running show in Las Vegas."

"So how many years do you have to work here to get a ring?"

"I have no idea. I don't manage the casino," she said.

I returned to Callie, who was holding her own at the slots with Elmo standing guard. "Ms. Loomis tells me that the bird ring is a Roman totem. Of course, this is the same woman who didn't know a ninety-pound basset hound was being hidden in her office, so take it with a grain of salt," I said.

The dealers had changed shifts and the new man behind the betting line had no ring on.

My cell phone rang. It was Barrett Silvers. After a few moments I hung up and gave Callie a quizzical look.

"Barrett Silvers is coming to the hotel later in the week and wants to meet with me. She says she has a director with her who wants to talk about my theatrical. I'll believe it when I see it," I said, dismissing the call.

"She's coming all the way to Las Vegas to bring you a director like a cat dragging a mouse to its master?" Callie stared at me, apparently suspicious of Barrett's motive.

"A very big mouse! And it's only a forty-five-minute flight." I shrugged, trying to be nonchalant about the call. "I'm sure she does it for writers all the time," I said, thinking that was likely only if she were trying to sleep with them.

❖

We made a tour of the shops that lined the concourse under the Addizione VIII arch, with Elmo complaining the entire way.

Callie admired each designer's offering and tried on several fall outfits, modeling them for me. I told her she looked fabulous in every one of them, and she did. She settled on white slacks with cuffs held up by little gold buckles and a matching white V-neck shirt with a gold crest on it.

"You look so good in it I want to take it off you," I said softly.

She danced over and kissed me on the lips in front of the clerk, who asked if I was buying. I smiled and said, "I think the person who gets kissed buys."

❖

We went upstairs to our room. I had Elmo on his lead, and I carried the shopping bags full of pants, shirts, and shoes. Callie put the keycard in the lock and popped the door open, entering ahead of me. Elmo followed right beside her.

"Come on, let's go to the sauna," I said, dumping everything onto the overstuffed armchair. "You could use a little relaxation after a hard day of Barbie-dolling it."

"That is a rude, dismissive chauvinistic remark," she said, giving me a sensual kiss. "Besides, gyms can give you horrible diseases from other people's sweat," she added, unaware of the irony that we were both wearing sweats. Well, I was wearing sweats—she was wearing designer après ski pants that were sweats for people who don't sweat.

"Rose uses the hotel gym and sauna about this time every day and we might see her there."

"How did you find that out?" Callie stared at me.

"I'm psychic," I said and then added when she gave me a raised eyebrow that while she was trying on clothes this afternoon, I was talking to the young clerk who did stagecraft work for the *Boy Review.* She knew Rose's schedule because they used to go to the sauna together sometimes after rehearsal.

Minutes later, we exited the elevator at the penthouse level and entered the gym and sauna. Callie wasn't a workout person. It wasn't that her muscles weren't strong and that she wasn't well built, she just didn't believe in the process. "Tell your mind what you want your body to look like and it will do it for you. You don't need a lot of clanking metal with seats that other people have sat on," she said.

"You wipe the seats off," I said.

"*You* wipe them off. I'm not sitting on them at all."

I glanced up to see Rose Ross wrapped in a towel and headed for the steam room. I alerted Callie. She jumped into action, apparently forgetting what vermin might thrive in moist heat, and demanded that we strip and follow her. We were wrapped in large white towels and inside the cedar-lined hot box before you could say Legionnaires'.

Rose seemed nervous but relieved to see us, and I hoped she was anxious to talk. Callie set the stage, explaining that she was psychic and that she could sense things about people and that she knew Rose was afraid. I assured Rose that whatever she told us would be in confidence.

"People on the ghoul pool list do die. I don't know if they were chosen to be on the list because they were sick like people say or if they were put on the list and then that caused them to die," she said.

"But they draw the names randomly, don't they?" I asked.

"They say they do, but someone always holds up the bowl containing the names to be drawn. I mean, a lot of people touch the bowl, and this whole town is one big magic trick. Something is happening underground but no one talks about it, and you can't figure out who knows and who it's safe to talk to. I know, it sounds ridiculous but…"

"You've got to stay in contact with us," Callie said.

"That could be hard," she said as the door opened and two older women emerged through the fog. Rose exited without even telling us good-bye, obviously frightened and suspicious of everyone.

We toweled off quickly and pulled on our sweats, heading back to our room.

As we passed the casino, I tugged at Callie's sleeve, indicating we should just go by the roulette wheel one more time. The mystery of the ring had me baffled. There never seemed to be more than one dealer wearing a bird ring at any given time.

We had no sooner stepped up to the table than a man approached and put down ten thousand dollars in cash. Dealer Brownlee brightened. "Mr. Emerson, how are you this fine day? Staying at the hotel?"

"Your front desk is pretty busy. I'll be lucky if they check me in by midnight. Put it all on fourteen," he said and the dealer froze for just an instant, as if Mr. Emerson had chosen the wrong number, but he dutifully placed the bet nonetheless. The wheel spun, and we all waited to see if the ball landed in the fourteen slot. The wheel slowed, the ball landed, and jumped, and jumped again. It just missed fourteen. We looked to the man for a reaction, but he had left the table, disappearing into the crowd.

"Lotta money," I remarked.

"They're not betting, they're buying," Callie murmured. I stared at her, not understanding what she was saying. "I dreamed that sentence last night. I just remembered. I woke up in the middle of the night and thought, I have to remember this."

"Okay, so what are they buying?"

"Sex," Callie said and her voice was far away.

Callie was jarred back into reality by her cell phone ringing. She answered, spoke for a few seconds, and then hung up. "Mom and Dad will be in early in the morning. Their plane was delayed."

"Great," I said and Callie looked at me, I presumed, for signs of sarcasm. "Great that they're still coming," I said and monitored my tone for believability.

CHAPTER NINE

Callie was in high spirits because her parents were finally here in the hotel and in the room right next to ours. The moment she heard their key in the lock, she dashed next door to greet them, returning fifteen minutes later to suggest I wait to say hello until they'd had time to get some rest. Their flight had indeed been delayed, their room wasn't ready, then they were put on the third floor by mistake and finally moved up to the twelfth floor, so they were pretty worn out and ready for a rest. Callie was disappointed to learn they were only going to be here for twenty-four hours—her dad had a meeting back in Tulsa. That meant one full day with them and I got Callie back. I would meet them at breakfast and some afternoon socializing and then it would be pretty much over. So I was in good spirits myself.

Callie's upbeat mood made her playful and amorous, a state I breathlessly awaited but not exactly at this moment. I was sound-shy when it came to sex. It had to do with the insanity of my upbringing.

By the time I'd reached puberty, it was stamped into my DNA that my Midwestern parents would not approve of my having sex in the abstract, much less approve of my having sex in the specific, and they would definitely not approve of my having sex with a person of the same sex, because sex should be preceded by a wedding and followed by a honeymoon, the purpose of which was the procreation of people who looked and sounded like my parents. That last thought served as a mental prophylactic.

My parents, Ben and Lu, had evolved over the last twenty years, and I was over forty, for God's sake, so why was I nervous? Nonetheless, Ben and Lu's heads loomed as large as the Wizard of Oz, bobbing over my bed if ever I lay with my lover in any room adjacent to theirs. Therefore, the idea that Callie's parents had checked into the hotel and were now in the adjacent room, with only the thin-as-a-cardboard-box wall between us, was just one step removed from having my own parents present.

"What's with you?" Callie said, snuggling up to me. "Come here."

"Shh," I whispered.

"Why?" She giggled at me.

"We're right up against their wall."

"Whose wall?"

"Your parents'."

"So what? They know you and I are together." She rubbed her hand across the soft hair between my legs.

"Okay, fine. I just don't want them to *hear* that we're together."

"Are you ashamed of us?"

"No, not at all. Of course not! I mean, I don't want to hear them either. I just think lovemaking is private, that's all."

"So, are you going to have a very quiet orgasm?" she said, leaning over me and putting her tongue where her hand had been. I bolted upright in bed, banging my head against the headboard, which in turn banged against the wall, and I yelped like a teenager, drawing back from her touch. She laughed. "Well, I'm sure they'll wonder what *that* was about."

"Sorry," I said and took a deep breath.

Suddenly the TV came on as if possessed. On the screen was a still shot, like the opening frame of a video on pause. It was a shot of our hotel room, Callie and me in bed together, in such an intertwined position that it was hard to see whose legs belonged to whom. The text beneath the image said: Check out now or this tape will be broadcast throughout the hotel.

"That's us on TV!" Callie shrieked.

I picked up the phone and rang the front desk, getting Ms. Loomis upon request. I told her frantically what we were looking at on our TV screen. She offered to send someone up to investigate as, mercifully, the image disappeared and the closed circuit network of the hotel took over, describing where to dine and what to see. I told Ms. Loomis the image had just disappeared, and she assured me that she would immediately contact the hotel audio/video department and find out who was on duty and what had occurred. I hung up, knowing whoever had done it was long gone, and I squirmed over the existence of such a shot, our not knowing if it was an idle threat or if it would indeed be broadcast in every room including 1252, where Callie's parents were staying.

I stared up at the ceiling, analyzing the location of the camera from the angle of the video. The camera would have to be up high, shooting down in a wide angle onto the bed. I jumped up and pulled the chair over to stand on it so I could examine the walls, running my hands across the smooth paint looking for pinholes of light or slits in the crown molding, any place a camera lens might hide, as Elmo rolled his eyes over my repeated gymnastics. I found nothing, and whoever put the camera in our room could just as easily have removed it, for all I knew.

"Teague, call the police," Callie ordered. I hesitated. This would mean describing what was on the tape, perhaps locating and viewing the tape in public. It would involve her parents. It would be invasive and embarrassing.

"We have nothing to report," I stammered as I got down off the chair. "I couldn't even tell if it was us, and the image is gone and—"

Callie handed me the phone. "Call the police now, or I will!"

I shook my head in agony over being in this situation. *Good grief! How the hell did this happen?* I rang the police and got a desk sergeant. He listened to my statement and said he'd send someone over to the hotel within the hour.

"Thank you," Callie said, then picked up the phone and called her parents, asking if they would meet us downstairs at the coffee shop, an attempt to get them out of their room immediately and away from their TV.

I slung my shirt on and stepped into my tennis shoes.

"Wear this shirt. It makes your eyes pop," Callie said.

"My eyes are popping without a shirt! What difference does it make what I wear if they've just seen me butt naked making love to you! That was our Dallas Cowboys night, in case you've forgotten!" I said, my voice going up an octave.

"I'll never forget that night!" Callie squeezed my hand, reassuring me.

With that, we went downstairs to determine what, if anything, had appeared on her parents' in-room TV. I had to keep reminding myself to breathe. *What I do is my own damned business.* But I knew from years in the motion picture business that it took days with a talented director, lighting designer, cinematographer, and makeup artist just to get a nude kissing scene to look good, and that raw, poorly lit, unstaged sex scenes could look absolutely horrific.

"I hope you're not embarrassed over our lovemaking," Callie said, picking up on my thoughts as we got off the elevator and scanned the lobby for the police, who apparently hadn't arrived yet.

"I'm not embarrassed. I just don't want it to look bad on camera," I said.

"Good." Callie gave me a look that said she didn't believe me.

I stopped at the front desk. "The police are looking for us."

"Of course they are," Ms. Loomis said without looking up. I decided not to take offense.

"If they inquire at the front desk, we're in the coffee shop," I said and continued on with Callie. "Every time I walk up to the front desk, I'm demanding a security guard, threatening to call the police, or meeting the police! In fact, since I've known you, I've met more police than when I was on the force! Furthermore, and more importantly, this is not a good way to meet your parents for the first time, right after their having seen me naked on top of you!" I stopped ranting when her parents came into view like a nightmare on the horizon, there to avenge their daughter's deflowering, ready and waiting to suck the life from me and pick my bones clean.

"You okay?" Callie said in what would be our last private words together.

"Sure." I shrugged.

Paige and Palmer Rivers were seated at a corner table in the coffee shop, neither smiling at us nor frowning at us, just fulfilling our request to show up. Callie greeted them in a chipper tone, kissing each on the cheek, and then she introduced me with an amazing amount of pride in her voice, given the circumstances.

Paige said, "Hello, dear."

Palmer nodded. Palmer struck me as a man who had a lot to say but picked his time to say it. I imagined he was the last of the concrete cowboys pulling his big rig across the state to deliver oil field pipe that would crush anything that got in its way, delivered to men who would crush anything that got in theirs. Palmer was the kind of man who didn't trust you at first, but when he did, he'd get up in the middle of the night and drive five hundred miles to give you the shirt off his back, and never expect a thank-you. On the other hand, if Palmer didn't like you, I suspected that he might just beat you to death with a tire iron and call it a day.

Callie asked if they'd slept well, Paige rattled on about how nice the room was, quiet and with a good mattress. But the conversation was strained.

The waiter showed up and took our order. I felt Palmer watching me like a peregrine falcon through one intensely focused eyeball with the iris dilating in and out. I ordered pancakes, silently preferring a sedative. That out of the way and small talk diminished, Callie took charge.

"Did a video come on in your room just before I called you?" she asked flatly.

"Yes," Paige said, wincing. "I didn't know who to call about it!"

Callie assured her that we had called the police, and that they were going to appear within the hour. I felt my chest tightening and my ears turning red as Paige and Callie launched into a dissection of the injustice of what had occurred, the invasion of privacy, the perversion of the perpetrator, the deplorable idea that someone could invade a hotel room with a camera—all while Palmer and I sat silently avoiding eye contact. Paige went on about it as if it were a movie starring two strangers and not her daughter and me.

"I saw the whole thing!" Paige said loudly. "I was shocked, because I thought, 'I didn't order this movie. What in the world!' And then two women doing God knows what, and I got confused, thinking, well, how did this get into my TV? I was so shocked I didn't even know if he was awake. Did you see it, Palmer?"

"Just the climax," Palmer said without expression.

That startled even Callie, who said she'd better go to the lobby and wait for the police officer. Paige went with her, leaving me with Palmer.

He sipped his coffee and stared up at the constellations that ran across the top of the ceiling, a universe of stars shining down on sausage and hash browns. He didn't say a word. I tried not to let my mind imagine what he was thinking. It seemed like an hour before he finally said, "Callie's psychic." I let all the air out of my body in one relieved sigh, grateful that he wasn't going to stab me with his breakfast fork. Palmer lodged a toothpick somewhere back in his bicuspid and left it there. "Her mother's psychic too. So I've lived with psychic women all my life," Palmer said and my mind filled in the rest of his sentence: *And that's how I knew you were messin' with my daughter,* or *That's how I knew this whole thing was going to come to no good.* But Palmer seemed contained. I told myself to relax.

"The trouble with Callie and her momma is, even when they don't know what you're doin', they *think* they know what you're doin'. And to make matters worse, it's someone out in outer space tellin' 'em what you're doin', someone you can't even talk to. She told me that you stay up in your head all the time. Well, at least that's a *place.* She and her momma are out of their bodies most of the time. They're talkin' and communin' and hearin' from people. I learned a long time ago that information from the cosmos can override plain common sense, but you won't convince them of that. It's a challenge." He shook his head in wonderment. "Now when I met Paige, this psychic stuff didn't even come up because, of course back then, they'd just throttle you, and take you to the priest, and try to scare the demons out of you. It's only been recently that people are into that, if you know what I mean. TV and all that. Television can get you in a lot of trouble." He looked me square in the eye, longer than anyone had ever looked at me in my lifetime, and rolled the toothpick across the front of his mouth and into a crevice of the other bicuspid.

He's like a cat who's decided to play with his breakfast first and eat it later. He's toying with me, trying to wear me out. Well, I'm a grown woman! I don't need to put up with this shit!

"Look, Palmer, I'm a very direct person." I added quickly, "I'm in love with Callie. I am. And I'm sorry you saw us making love in our hotel room, but I'm not sorry we were doing it...only sorry that you saw it."

There was a long pause and he breathed in real deep. I thought that if he spoke next it could only go downhill, so I decided to get my say in first. "She's a phenomenal person, and a phenomenal lover, and if I could just make love to her all day long, well, hell, that's what I'd do, and that's the truth...not eat, not sleep, just love your daughter. You're a man. Surely you can understand those feelings. We're over forty, for God's sake, and we deserve some happiness. So if you don't want to invite us to Christmas dinner or whatever, fine. But I'm not sorry about the videotape of our lovemaking. I mean I'm sorry someone else made the tape, but I'm not sorry we're in it."

There was another long pause during which the only thing

that moved was Palmer's jaw muscle as it twitched and tensed and tightened. Palmer adjusted his silver Spandex watchband. He twirled the cowboy hat that rested on his knee. He picked up a fork by its tines and set it down and pressed the tines down onto the tablecloth with his fingers—again and again and again—as if he thought the fork might actually stay like that.

Mercifully, Paige stuck her fairy godmother head into the coffee shop and signaled for us to join them, saying the police officer was here. Palmer reached for the check, and I launched myself out of the chair like a bottle rocket, unaware of how badly I wanted to get away from this table until the opportunity to do so appeared.

The police officer was a gray-haired, pot-bellied detective who'd obviously seen and heard everything one could conceivably see or hear in a town with twenty-four-hour vice. He pushed his hat back on his head, pulled out a pad and pencil, and suggested we go sit on a large settee in the lobby.

"What's in room 1252?" the cop asked.

"That's my room," Paige interjected.

"And you're…?"

"The mother," Paige said seriously, as if she were in an ancient episode of *Cagney & Lacey.*

"Where's the tape now?" he asked.

"We don't know. That's why you're here," Callie replied.

"Girl sex," her mother whispered, "that's why you're here."

"Invasion of privacy and blackmail, that's why you're here," Callie corrected.

"Well, that too," Paige said.

"And it played in every room?" the cop asked.

"How would I know that?" Paige said.

"The super on the screen said, 'Check out now or this will play throughout the hotel,'" I interjected.

"Maybe it was a commercial. 'Check it out now! Playing throughout the hotel,'" Paige said like an announcer.

"Mother, stop it, please. You're just confusing things." Callie tried to calm her down.

"What am I confusing? I don't want this man to get the idea that I order dirty movies."

"I would never think that, ma'am." The officer smiled.

"*Girls Galore!* That was the name of the movie that came on this morning. I remember now! And these two girls were doing sex acts!" Paige said.

"With each other?" the cop asked.

"With everyone! There was even a man there too!" Paige giggled and the cop laughed.

"So were Callie and I on your TV?" I asked.

"No! How would that happen?" Paige asked, utterly surprised.

"Good question. You should be a cop." The officer stuck his pen back in his shirt pocket. This was a noncrime in his books, and he was looking for a wrap-up and a quick exit. "I'll file the report, talk to the manager, and if anything else happens, call this number." The officer handed me a card that said Sergeant Lane.

I stood there in utter shock and embarrassment. "The video never came on in room 1252? Your mother saw part of an X-rated movie?"

"Yes!" Callie beamed. "You see, I told you everything would work out."

"Except that I just told your dad I'd rather make love to you than eat."

"What did he say?" Callie's eyes flew open wide.

"Nothing. He just sat there and stared at me, and his hat, and his watchband, and his fork…"

Callie burst out laughing.

"I can never look the man in the face again," I said.

"You were so afraid he'd hear us making love through the wall and now you've described it for him! What you fear you bring to you." She grinned mischievously.

CHAPTER TEN

A nice-looking couple did a double take to look at Callie and me as we walked by, giving us an odd look. Moments later a man walked past and then turned to look again.

"What are they looking at?" I asked.

My question was answered by two short, stocky, pro-bowler-looking ladies in their late fifties. One pinched my arm as they went by and said, "You girls are hot!"

"I have a feeling she's not talking about our wardrobe," I said as the women flew past, destination unknown.

"I think the tape played in *someone's* room," Callie said.

"But how?" I asked.

A man in his late forties approached us, pulled his business card out of his pocket, wrote his room number on the back, and asked if we did three-ways. "Saw your ad this morning on my in-house channel!"

I blew up at him and the man hurried away looking confused. We glanced across the room where half a dozen people were going about their vacation routine uninterested in us, so not everyone had seen us. I suggested we abandon Paige momentarily and take a walk so we could talk.

Down the long corridor, under the Addizione VIII archway, I found a spot out of the stream of tourist traffic where I could get cell phone reception and rang George, my attorney in L.A.

"We're going to sue the hotel!" I said.

George's upbeat, Hollywood voice took on a nervous tone when he got the gist of my request.

"Teague, I'm an entertainment attorney. I don't do invasion of privacy. I do entertainment. Now if you want me to book you for a lap dance…"

"Not funny, George. We were entertainment for a lot of people in this hotel. George, are you there?" I asked loudly in response to the silence. Then I heard muffled laughter. "Are you laughing, George? So help me God, if you're laughing…"

"Jesus, Teague, cut me some slack, will ya? Most people can't even get toast brought to their room and you manage to get an entire video shot of your sex life!" George's laughter was choking him up.

"I want you to contact the hotel's attorney and tell them we're suing."

George got his laughter under control, but now his voice was agitated. "How are you going to prove that people saw you?"

"I'll get proof, George! What if I had broadcast you having sex with your wife—"

"I'd be proud! Hasn't happened in years!" he interrupted.

"George, scare them. Send an e-mail, a letter, an assassin. I don't care."

"Okay, okay, okay," and George hung up.

"I need to get a woman attorney. George has no balls. No balls!"

"So what rooms got the video?" Callie asked.

"Let's ask," I said with an anger that stemmed from a lack of support in serious matters. I stopped several people and asked them point-blank if they'd seen me, or anyone else like me, naked on their TV several hours earlier. They gave me an odd look and moved away from me.

Callie yanked me aside. "Stop it! You're acting crazy."

"Now that's an odd thing for a psychic to say, and negative too, I think."

Back down the corridor and into the lobby, we saw the two pro bowlers. I approached and began quizzing them.

"Well, we did see two people who looked like the two of you…" the smaller and younger of the two said, fidgeting now that she was being pinned down and couldn't fly by and just tell me we were hot. I asked for her room number and she hesitated as if she thought we were contemplating bringing our act to her bedroom. I told her we needed the room number to find out who was broadcasting this video, and she finally gave in. I thanked them and went back to Callie, leaving them with their jaws ajar.

"They saw us and they're in room 332."

"What are we going to do?"

"Demand top billing out on their marquee?" I said, trying to lighten the mood, but Callie only frowned.

❖

Back in our room, I sat down on the bed and stared at the business card the middle-aged man who wanted the threesome had given me. His room number was 413. I looked at my other scribbled notes from the people I'd spoken to. The ladies were in room 332.

"Callie, look at this. All the room numbers add up to eight. The guy's, the two women's, our rooms. We were in 1142 originally, and 611, and 1250 where we were videotaped. They all add up to eight! But your mom and dad were in 1252, which adds up to ten…"

"Actually to one in numerology," she said as I stared at her. "Ten is one plus zero which equals one. You have to reduce it to the smallest increment."

"Ten, one, whatever. Not eight. And they didn't see the video. But they were put on the third floor, remember? And I'll bet you that room number did add up to eight, but we moved them into the room next to us!"

Suddenly I flashed back to the Roman numeral VIII carved in marble on the archway of the hotel. I grabbed Callie's laptop and went online for an Italian dictionary and then typed in "Addizione VIII." Callie stood beside me watching silently as *addizionare* came up on the screen—the verb meaning "to add up."

"So it could have been put there to say it adds up to eight. That really freaks me. How would Mo Black know, from the grave, what's going on right now?" I called the concierge to ask if the hotel had ever had a wing added. I looked at Callie as I hung up the phone. "Under the Addizione VIII archway, where the shops are, that entire area was added just before the builder died. So maybe Mo…"

"…knew what was going on and maybe he knew they would kill him. I'm getting chills," Callie said in a whisper.

"Maybe the rooms whose numbers add up to eight have cameras

in them or pointed at them. Wait a minute," I said, reaching a moment of clarity. "Remember when Ted said 'I got 1142 moving to 611'? He told the desk that. They didn't tell him. The desk normally tells the bellman or security where to move the guest, right? But Ted told the front desk where he was taking us and then put us in a room that added up to eight. Maybe Ted is more than a security guy. Suppose that was all an act with the head of security and Roy." I was on a roll now, pacing and talking. "Remember what Rob from the theater said—everyone plays many roles. They could come up here pretending to investigate a dead body or a threatening letter or a video when all they're really doing is concealing it. Maybe the hotel employees are all acting. Think about it. They could be working as a group. They could choose to put people into those rooms for surveillance, blackmail, or murder."

"Everyone in the entire hotel? That means there's no one we can trust," Callie said.

"That's exactly what Rose said. What is she afraid of that is so serious she won't even talk to us about it privately?" I plopped down on the bed and glanced at the phone, and that's when I saw it—a newspaper article partially hidden under the lamp. Callie and I stared at it, wondering how it had gotten into our room, tucked under the lamp as if a friendly force had visited us. I slid it out and opened it carefully, its edges frayed and yellowed. It was an old copy of a decades-old newspaper article—a murder story about a young boy killed at the new Desert Star Casino in what the article said were "mysterious circumstances." The article stated that it was unclear from police reports whether anyone had accompanied the boy to the hotel. "Who do you suppose put this in our room?" I wondered.

"I don't know. When I was here years ago for the opening, I never heard anything about a boy's death in relation to the hotel." Callie stared at the newspaper article. "Look what's written across the bottom of the page: 'This story was pulled from the press and never made the papers.' So it must have been typeset but got pulled before the run. This could be a proof someone kept."

"Who would have been able to get their hands on a proof?" I asked.

"Someone who worked at the newspaper or someone who pulled it," Callie replied.

"And today, that someone would have to be over forty. I guess they covered it up so it wouldn't ruin the glitz and glamour of the new hotel," I said.

"Or perhaps for other reasons." Callie was deep in thought. "I touch it and it feels like an old story, but it has new energy. Why would that be?" she asked herself and then just as quickly began piecing things together. "The person who left us the Stellium in Scorpio chart is the one trying to uncover the darkness. That person knows the answer to all those questions," Callie said.

❖

The following day, we prepared to drive Paige and Palmer to the airport. My goal was small and short term: to get them through the hotel lobby before someone else tried to book us for a ménage à trois. I had them loaded into the car before Sheik Skippy could even find their door handles, and I pulled out of the drive so fast it blew his four-foot feather back. This was the first time I'd been in close proximity to Paige and Palmer since my spontaneous sexual confession at the coffee shop and I was feeling the strain—in fact, every part of me was puckered. Paige talked about the scenery, Callie listened, Palmer stared out the window, and I pretended to be intensely focused on maneuvering through traffic. At the airport, they insisted on leaving us at the curb, saying they were going to board right away and were taking their carry-on bags. Callie gave her parents a big good-bye hug and told her mother to put the white light around them. I hugged Paige and told her I was so glad I got to meet her. Palmer stood back and then at the last minute stepped up like he was going to quickly shake my hand but then, instead, he turned and headed inside. He was almost out of sight when he stopped and reversed directions—heading right for me. I braced myself, not knowing what he was going to do. He came to a halt just inches from my face.

"Don't let things get ya down, kid," he said in his first attempt at conversation since I'd told him the intimate details of our sex lives. "And if you need somethin', call me. I can be here in an hour." And with that, Palmer swept Paige through the double glass doors and they were gone.

I took a deep breath. That was the familial Good Housekeeping Seal of Approval as far as I was concerned. It was also the first comforting thing anyone, except Callie, had said since this whole mess began. I expected that if I ever called on Palmer to "be here" it would mean that he'd come to knock somebody's lights out, since he struck me as a man who believed in rapid retribution. I also took it to mean that if it came down to it, Palmer Rivers would be on my end of the tire iron. That thought warmed my heart. *Funny how just a little show of support can change the energy*, I thought.

❖

On the drive back, Callie placed her small hand in mine and sat close to me. "My parents like you," she said.

"And I like them. You're mom's kind of out there," I said and Callie smiled, rubbing her hand gently down my arm and then back up again. I asked what she was doing.

"Just feeling the strength in your shoulders and arms. You're such a strong woman."

"You must be in love. I have absolutely no muscle definition." I laughed.

"I didn't say you were buffed. I said you were strong. You have great strength."

"Buffed would be better. Maybe I'll start lifting weights or taking steroids…" I teased.

"You will not!" Callie said.

Once inside our room, I let no time lapse before I began slowly undressing Callie, gently removing her shirt from her shoulders and unsnapping the little hook in the front of her bra.

"What are you up to?" She smiled at me. "I thought you couldn't make love next to thin walls. There are people checked in next door."

"Not our people," I said, unbuttoning her jeans and slipping them down her soft, pale thighs. She bounced backward onto the bed as I pulled her jeans off completely.

"In many countries several generations of people all share the same big sleeping area. With your obsession about privacy and silent lovemaking, you'd be in real trouble," Callie said as I helped her tiny white panties take the same trip down her slender legs while she tried to maintain her concentration. "Or what if you lived in a cave…" she asked as I knelt by the edge of the bed and pulled her toward me and rested her legs on my shoulders.

"I would make love down by the stream," I said, burying my face in her and listening to her moan.

Chapter Eleven

Later that evening, having freshened up and walked Elmo, we strode across the plush mauve carpet and through the arches of the Star Bar. I could already make out Barrett's tall, suave form from just the way her pants creased and her shoes shone. She was butch-elegant. Either she shopped at very posh men's stores for genderless European fashion or she had her clothes custom-made. Either way, she looked great.

"Does it bother you that I'm tagging along?" Callie asked.

"Not at all," I lied, fearful that Barrett might say something inappropriate and alter the good vibes I had going with Callie.

"Teeeague," Barrett said, extending my name and her hand at the same time. "It's so good to see you. You look smart. This is Jeremy Jocowitz. Jeremy, Teague Richfield." I shook his hand and then took Callie by the arm and pulled her into our tight circle to introduce her. It was an awkward introduction, but only in my head. *Is she Callie Rivers my lover? Callie Rivers my partner? Callie Rivers a friend from Tulsa? Callie Rivers a well-known psychic?* I settled for just Callie Rivers.

Jeremy, however, fell into the time-honored Hollywood greeting, "And you are...?" leaving room on the end for her to fill in the blank. This was the moment when Callie Rivers—lover, partner, friend, psychic—could respond Hollywood-style with, "I'm a writer. I have a studio deal at Marathon." Or something that would let Jeremy get comfortable. Directors could be very uncomfortable if they felt they were in the company of people who couldn't name their latest movie, admire their body of work, or fund their next picture.

"Working on a story with Teague," she said.

"Ah, good, another story," he replied.

"I told Jeremy about your screenplay," Barrett said. I had no clue which screenplay she was talking about. Callie obviously tuned into that, asking outright which screenplay Jeremy loved, making me instantly grateful she had "tagged along."

Barrett replied, "*Shades of White,* and we flew in on Jeremy's plane to hear you pitch it, Teague. Pitch him the story."

Jeremy was an overweight man in his late fifties wearing a rumpled white shirt and scuffed loafers. He wore large black glasses, had a bulbous nose and a gray, scruffy beard which, I think, was more about image than the fact that he hadn't been able to locate a razor. I was surprised to hear that he liked *Shades of White* because it was a woman's flick: romance, heartache, love lost, love found. It just didn't seem like a picture the man across from me would want to spend six months filming, even if it were on location in England.

"Pitch it now?" I asked, trying to remember the plot points.

"Unless you'd like to do it up in the suite," Barrett said with a smile intended only for me.

"Here is fine." I took a deep breath. "This is the story of a beautiful English woman who falls in love with a young duke while she's taking a tour of Windsor Castle."

"Ahh, period piece, nice costumes…" He smiled, not overly attentive. "Maybe shoot it in Scotland."

"Possibly," I said brightly. "The duke's stodgy, aristocratic family finally blesses the engagement after exhaustive background checks, particularly into her ability to produce an heir—"

"Waiter, another drink over here." He glanced at me. "Sorry, go ahead."

"She and the duke are mad about each other and meet clandestinely to make love—"

"Good, we're getting to the part that sells tickets," he said.

"She becomes pregnant by him. Then she learns that the man she believed to be her grandfather is not, and that her real grandfather was a Nigerian man who had an affair with her grandmother."

"Now there's trouble. A friend of mine had sort of the same situation—" Jeremy interrupted, behaving as if we were just sharing anecdotal information.

"She keeps that secret," I continued forcefully, "not wanting it to prevent her from marrying the man she loves, and of course, when they have their first child, it's—"

"Let me guess...purple!" He laughed, then tried to sober up. "Of course today who cares?"

I glared at Barrett who gave me a blank stare, as if to say she hadn't noticed that he was rude throughout the pitch and that the only movie this man would be interested in making would be one in which there were lots of tits, ass, and explosions.

"Teague just pitched a terrific film about three hookers who go on a cruise and are shipwrecked on a remote island with a man who is completely impotent since the age of ten," Callie said, nearly shocking me out of my shorts.

"Now that's a film I can get made!" Jeremy salivated.

"That's what three other directors said. She sold it just like that." Callie snapped her fingers and a waiter appeared, thinking she was summoning him. "I'll have a Coke, please," she said.

Jeremy's cell phone rang and he stood up and turned his body in two or three different directions, trying to improve reception, then finally wandered out into the lobby to face the etched glass panels where he could hear.

"What are you doing bringing that guy over here for me to pitch that story? It's not his genre, and furthermore, I don't even like the damned story! I only developed it because I was asked to do it for Marathon years ago," I hissed at Barrett.

"Calm down. It didn't hurt anything. He's a good guy to know. Smart and connected. Besides, I got to see you"—then she remembered Callie—"and your friend." Barrett slouched back in her chair, resting her head on her French-cuffed hand, letting the other arm dangle over the side of the chair and staring at me as if I were a watering hole in the desert. In the dim light, it was impossible to tell on which side of the testosterone scale this exquisitely dressed studio executive would land. I knew, of course, having slept with her.

"So, Callie," Barrett's voice was even, and her eyes never moved from mine, "what exactly are your intentions with this woman writer across from me?"

"I'm taking her to bed," Callie said just as evenly, and then added, "It's late, and we've had a busy day." She rose and took me by the hand, pulling me up from the chair. "Enjoy your evening, Barrett, and give our regrets to Jeremy," she said, obviously not meaning it, and Barrett grinned and gave Callie a look that said she appreciated her style.

❖

Callie's smooth tone dissipated into near-choking sounds as we left the bar.

"I don't like that woman! She was fucking with you before she fucked you, and now she's hitting on you!"

"Odd sequence of events, I agree," I said. "Three hookers who go to a desert island with a guy who's impotent? You sound like that director who pitched with me at CBS."

"He liked it." Callie led me into the casino past the craps tables and over to the million-dollar slots. When I mentioned that I thought we were headed for bed, she snapped at me, saying she needed to play the slots to unwind. Barrett had apparently gotten to her. She plopped down on a padded seat in front of a machine with American flags and put in ten dollars, jabbing a finger into the slot machine buttons as if they were Barrett's eyeballs. On the third roll, the screen locked up momentarily, turned red, and began to spin. The amount went from $7.00 to $107, it paused, remained red, then spun again. This time the number read $257. It did that three more times until finally the bell rang on top of the machine, and it made a sound like a fire truck. The screen lit up and flashed us.

"You just won twenty-five hundred dollars!" I exclaimed.

"I did!" she squealed. "I always win when I get that mad!"

"Glad I could help." And I leaned over and kissed her.

A young woman approached us and got Callie's ID and other information and said she'd be back shortly with the money. We were both suddenly relaxed and happy again. For a few minutes, we were alone and having a vacation just like regular people. In fact, I was beginning to rethink my fear of boredom in a relationship. I longed to be just a regular person with Callie Rivers, going shopping at the grocery store, sitting around in the evening watching TV, taking walks in our neighborhood.

A man wearing a hotel uniform appeared and addressed Callie. "Congratulations, you're a winner." He returned her ID, paid her out in cash, and handed her a small slip of paper. She glanced at the paper, folded it up, and put it in her pocket. "Quit while you're ahead and go home," he said pointedly. Then he added, "The real winners leave," and he turned and did exactly that.

"That guy looked like a drag queen in a suit, like one of the performers pictured in the *Boy Review* posters."

"It's a drawing..." Callie pulled the paper he'd given her out of her pocket. "It's a sketch showing a pathway leading to a cemetery with an *X* on the building next to it." I scanned the room in search of the man, but he was gone. "I think he's telling us that whatever is going on here at the hotel is somehow connected to a cemetery," Callie said.

I spotted the drunk guy I'd elbowed on the first night I'd joined Callie in the bar. He was wearing the same silk pants and had drawn a bead on us, missile locked on Callie, obviously drawn by the flashing lights. He looked drunker than the first time I saw him. He staggered up to her, his words slurring as he reached into his pocket.

This is just all we need tonight, I thought. "Okay, fella, we're done with the Paco number, let's—"

He slid his hand out of his pocket and lunged at Callie. For a moment, I thought he was attacking her with his silly puppet, but then I realized in his pocket was a small knife, and we had been lulled into complacency because we expected it to be a puppet. Callie jumped back, but she was trapped up against the slot machine. His knife slashed her jacket. My mind got stuck on that image: a knife slicing through Callie's jacket, next to her perfectly formed body, a knife—so close—a knife—her jacket—a knife. My terror at losing her causing my neurons to lock up—short-circuit—the chemical communication to go suddenly speechless—frozen—frightened—my mind replayed knife—jacket—knife—as my reflexes, unhampered by my brain's issues, kicked in, and I grabbed his wrist, twisted, and swung his arm out at a ninety-degree angle from his elbow and cracked it back against my knee. I pried the knife out of his fist and was preparing to drive it into his stomach when Callie screamed for me to stop.

By now, we were surrounded with name tags of every description: security, gaming management, hotel bar, clerks, front desk, everyone pressing the crowds back and separating us from the attacker.

❖

It took about an hour to fill out the paperwork for security, who told me their procedure was to do an internal investigation and the police had already been notified. I smirked as the young kid filling out the paperwork for the hotel moved his arm just long enough to reveal Palace Guard Greg on his uniform. *Great guarding, Greg,* I thought. The LVPD officer arrived looking serious and formal this time—the near knifing of a tourist definitely higher priority than a sex video. The officer conducted the appropriate questioning and then took Paco-man down to the precinct. I was certain the hotel would have him out on bail in a matter of hours since they all seemed to know him.

When the crowd cleared, Ms. Loomis took us aside to say how grateful she was that we were all right, but that, as we had undoubtedly noticed, trouble seemed to be following us at this hotel, and the management felt that for our safety, and the safety of the other guests, we should check out. I became incendiary. This was a neat trick: someone who wanted us out of the hotel had threatened us with dognapping, illicit videotaping, and attempted knifing, and now was trying to make *us* the threat!

"Ms. Loomis," I said, my voice like steel, "this hotel has a secret. Perhaps more than one. I am beginning to think you are aiding and abetting that secret. Your telling me to leave further supports my belief that you're an accomplice and you're covering up something. I know your owner, Karla Black, and perhaps Karla will be happy to tell the FBI what's going on here."

Ms. Loomis backpedaled, explaining that she was merely fearful for us, and the insurance problem that all of this might cause the hotel, but certainly she never meant to imply that we should leave if we didn't want to go.

❖

I stepped over to the only section of the lobby where I could get reception on my cell phone and called my old police buddy in Tulsa, Wade Garner, who'd helped Callie and me on the Marathon Studio murders a few months earlier. Wade was the big square-jawed cop I'd worked alongside at the TPD, and our time together had an odd bonding effect. We were known on the force as the Odd Couple because there wasn't one thing we agreed on except that we'd lay down our lives for each other.

"I think you've encountered more crooks as a writer than you ever did as a cop," he said. I gave him the rundown on what was happening and the names of a few of the players, just to see what he could dig up on them: the drag queens in the review, Karla, Mo. "It would also help if you could match any current hotel employees with employment at the local newspaper here, say fifteen, twenty years ago."

"Oh sure," Wade snorted. "You think TPD stands for Teague's Police Department? You know what kind of work all this shit involves? I'm not the desk flunky on your crazy-ass cases," he said. I told him to forget my request and implied that he was probably incapable of finding anything out about them anyway. The response was instantaneous harassment and snorts on his end of the line.

"By the way," he added, "I ran into your mom and dad, and they mentioned that you hadn't called in a week. Do I have to wipe your butt too?" he asked and hung up.

❖

I rejoined Callie, who was in a snit. "I'm trying to find someone in the hotel who can sew up my jacket. That man sliced a hole in it, and it's my good jacket!"

I shook my head in wonderment. "You're nearly knifed, and you're worried about your jacket."

"You kept me from being stabbed," she said and sagged into my chest, holding me close, and I realized that sometimes she focused on small tasks to keep from feeling the enormity of larger issues.

"You want to go up to our room?" I whispered into her ear, not being able to bear seeing her upset.

"Just long enough to see Elmo, then I want to go out. I'm too upset to stay in a small space. I don't think that was just the act of a drunken man. I think he's been stalking us from the day we arrived, and now, we're starting to get close to somebody or something the hotel doesn't want us to see," Callie said.

"Or maybe he's merely a drunken lounge performer who, in his own mind, is paying me back for decking him in the bar the night he called us dykes. But none of that matters right now. What matters is, are you okay?"

Callie nodded that she was. I asked if I could have another look at the drawing the stranger had handed her before he walked out the door.

Callie pulled it out of her pocket. It clearly showed a pathway from the casino to a cemetery, but from *where* in the casino and to *which* cemetery?

We moved over to a bank of phones and checked the phone directory, but there were no cemeteries that were a "pathway" away from the hotel.

"I wish if people are going to give us clues, they'd think it through a little more, you know?" I said in exasperation.

"Maybe the people trying to help us aren't used to being in this situation and don't know how to provide clues. Maybe they're doing the best they can," Callie said.

"Well, they're going to have to do better if we're going to stay alive," I said darkly.

CHAPTER TWELVE

Having showered and changed clothes, I sat down on the bed and speed-dialed Mom and Dad. Mom swooned when she heard my voice, saying she'd been so worried when she couldn't reach me in L.A.

"Mom, if you were worried, why didn't you just pick up the phone and call me on my cell?"

"If you don't have time to call your mother, why would you have time to take a call *from* your mother?" she said.

Years of experience had taught me to let those remarks go unanswered. Instead I put Elmo on the line so she could baby talk to him. He pressed his ear into the phone and moaned with joy upon hearing her voice.

"What did you say to him?" I asked her, taking the receiver back.

"That's between him and me," Mom replied. "He said you're with Callie, is that true?"

I shot Callie a look, having caught her in the act of talking to my mother without telling me. "Your father said Callie would have you living with her before long, and I said would that be so bad? At least you wouldn't be alone and maybe you'd move back to Tulsa with her."

"Just wanted to tell you that we're safe. Gotta go, Mom." I sent her my love and hung up.

"Your dear friend, my mother, says she fully expects that we'll live together." I looked at Callie with renewed interest.

"That's because she thinks you sleep around too much," Callie said.

"What?" My voice elevated.

"She says women are at your house a lot when she calls. She worries about disease."

"What?" My voice was going even higher now. "Let's talk disease. I am not the one who married a guy. I believe that was you. Do you know the disease you can get from guys? They will put it anywhere! A blow-up doll, a knothole, a sheep—have dick, will stick! *I* am a woman."

"And a very sexy one. Take me to dinner." Callie laughed and patted me in an indulgent way, and I was glad to see that she was coming out of the darkness brought on by her attacker.

❖

The hotel's top floor contained a big Italian restaurant with arched ceilings and painted frescoes taller than the restaurant was wide. It was a quiet, relaxed atmosphere away from the noise of the gamblers, and I was happy to have a few hours alone with Callie. I made a mental note that Elmo would love an order of meatballs.

Callie was dressed in a pair of navy slacks with a navy blazer, a designer crest on the pocket, and a white starched shirt. The overhead lights bounced off her polished gold jewelry and her gorgeous swept-back blond hair with an intensity that could have lit up an airfield at midnight. When she walked through the door, every head turned to see where she'd land.

"You look great in that jacket," she said, referring to the green suit jacket I wore to highlight my green eyes.

"I think everyone's looking at you, not me." I smiled.

"I think they're looking at both of us, thinking we make a nice couple."

The waiter tried to seat us in the middle of the room at a small table because we were two women without men. I stopped him, letting him know we'd take the corner booth. He hesitated, wondering no doubt if he should say that the larger booth was reserved, or that it was being held for a larger party, or that he had no wait staff for that area, but one look into my eyes and he undoubtedly knew, in order to preserve peace, he should fold on this one. He nodded his acquiescence, and we were seated in a large corner booth where I could slide close to her and we had a view of the entire room.

"So, Ms. Rivers, when this assignment is over, are you going back to L.A. with me and spend some time so we can get to know each other in a normal setting?"

"We agreed we weren't going to do anything permanent."

"I didn't say it was permanent. We can re-up the deal every ninety days—for the rest of our lives."

"I don't think I…"

"Do you want me dating other people?" I asked in my blunt way. She looked at me for a moment and blinked.

"I never thought you wanted that," she replied, seemingly hurt.

"I *don't* want that, but…"

"Then why would you do it, or even suggest it?"

"Because…because you're making me crazy." We both laughed. "I think, I'm not sure, but I think I'm a nester. Now, before I met you, I never was, and frankly, I abhorred the idea, but all I want right now is to be together with you in the same cave, apartment, house…hell, even town would be nice! To find out if maybe you like that too."

"You're proposing…" Callie teased out the words.

"Yes, in an impermanent fashion!"

"…that we live together." She completed the sentence.

"To please my elderly mother," I said.

The waiter arrived with a napkin over one arm and a pad and pencil in hand. "Are we ready, ladies?"

"That is the very question we were just discussing." I gave Callie a meaningful smile, and we ordered our meal.

Callie sat close to me, reached over, laced her fingers through mine, and pressed her shoulder into me. A musician moved from table to table playing love songs. He was wearing black tights, a blousy white shirt, and had a big colorful sash wrapped around his substantial middle. I wondered when he was growing up, if he ever conceived of the day when he would have to dress like Geppetto to find work. After the last strains of "Arrivederci, Roma," the violinist removed his violin from his shoulder as if taking a break in a musical interlude and then reached into his pocket and suddenly produced an explosion of red. I lunged across the table and intercepted it before it could reach Callie. It fell to the table…a small red paper rose. I felt foolish and sank back into the red tufted leather booth as the musicians moved on to the next table.

Callie rested her head on my shoulder. "Relax," she said. "It's okay."

"It's a rose! Do you think that means anything?" I asked.

"Just that Italians are romantics," she said and kissed me. "Maybe I'm Italian."

Her kiss felt so natural that I wasn't even shy about being out in public with this gorgeous blonde hanging on me. In fact, I was grinning, betting that the men at the other tables were wondering what in hell I'd done to deserve this or what I had to offer that they didn't. I was happily wondering myself when a dark, swarthy Italian man in his sixties, with the masculine softness of an opera singer, came to our table and introduced himself as Giovanni, a friend of Karla Black's. She had told him that we were very interesting writers, and he wanted to invite us to his home later that evening for a party.

"Many beautiful people from Las Vegas will surely be there." He smiled and squeezed my hand warmly.

Callie asked for directions, and he said once we were at Karla Black's home, we merely had to proceed up the hill another two miles and the road would dead-end at his estate. I could tell Callie was interested in going.

"I heard that you are the ghost of the famous ghoul pool," Callie said, smiling.

"The ghosts are everywhere in Las Vegas, even this hotel," Giovanni said, and then at her probing he tried to explain. "It's an old tale, really, that a ghost watches over the hotel and guards it. In exchange, the ghost demands a cut of the earnings. So every night, after the money is counted, a dollar bill is taken to the ghost to make him happy. A dollar's not much, but over time, I would say the ghost is doing better than the 401Ks, no?"

"So who really gets the money?" I asked.

"Like throwing pennies in a fountain Las Vegas style. It brings good luck and everyone in Las Vegas is superstitious about luck. Perhaps when the hotel is destroyed a hundred years from now, the money will be discovered." Giovanni reiterated that he hoped to see us at his party later in the evening, and he took our hands again before leaving us in a flurry of spirits.

"He said after the money's counted," I whispered, watching Giovanni's retreating backside. "So the money is probably counted in the cashiers' main cage on the north side of the hotel. maybe that's where the pathway begins."

"I think it's more than a pathway. I think it's an underground tunnel," Callie said.

"Why do you think so?"

"I don't know. Just a feeling," Callie defended herself.

Callie and I finished our leisurely dinner just as a tray of cream-filled Italian pastries arrived compliments of Giovanni. It was a nice gesture, and we took a few, along with the meatballs, back to the room for Elmo.

❖

Elmo was lying patiently inside his wire show cage and jumped to his feet as the meatballs and pastries were unwrapped. I placed them in his doggie bowls and set the bowls on the morning newspaper, anticipating a lot of action. Elmo dove on the meatballs and in his enthusiasm scattered them all over the floor.

Callie grinned. "Give me a washcloth. He's got it all over the ends of his ears and on his paws."

"Hey, at our house, Elmo and I have a rule: If it's good enough to eat, it's good enough to wear."

I glanced down at my hand and nearly jumped out of my body. Clearly printed on the inside heel of my right hand was a jumble of letters: ƎSOЯИAOſƎƆUЯB. I screamed for Callie to take a look, and then we both stared in disbelief.

"Where did you put your hand?" she asked.

"Nowhere!" I exclaimed, my mind racing.

"It was written somewhere and you pressed your palm down on it. What does it say?"

"Nothing, just letters!" I nearly shouted.

"Hold your hand up to the mirror," Callie demanded.

I held my hand up and both of us stared into the mirror…clearly written was BRUCEJOANROSE.

"Bruce Singleton is dead," I breathed, not wanting to think that maybe the other two were scheduled to die. I held my palm away from me as if it belonged to Sigourney Weaver. "I am totally freaked out. How did this get on my hand?" I rushed into the bathroom and scrubbed the ink off, watching it dissolve almost immediately.

"You took a shower before we left, so it had to have gotten there between the hotel and the restaurant. Think about everywhere you've put your hands," Callie said.

"All over your body, for one thing!" I replied. "I think whoever did it wanted to frighten us."

"Everyone here is frightened of someone, and it's not all the same someone," Callie said.

❖

We harnessed Elmo up and took him down to the lobby, where his arrival always caused a stir. I walked him out the front doors and over to a grassy landscaped area, carrying a plastic bag with me. Having walked Elmo in other people's yards in L.A., I'd mastered the inside-out baggie for poop pickup. I quickly sealed and tossed the airtight baggie and its odiferous contents into a Dumpster outside the hotel. Elmo scratched the ground with his hind legs, pleased with his efforts, as we looked up to see Rose Ross heading our way. Callie called out her name, and she looked relieved and quickly joined us.

"Hi," she began nervously. "Is this a bad time?"

"Not at all," Callie said. "Have you met Elmo?" Rose knelt down and put her pretty manicured hands around Elmo's head, swooning over how beautiful he was. I noticed a man watching us from the hotel. He was a security type with headset and radio.

"There are some other things I wanted to tell you that I didn't get to say in the sauna. I don't know what they mean," Rose said, and started to get up.

I touched her shoulder, signaling her to stay on the ground with the dog. "Pretend you're just admiring Elmo, because there's a guy watching us, and I'd just as soon have him think this whole meeting is about your love of basset hounds."

"Okay." She stroked the Milk-Bone shape on the top of his caramel-colored head. "Every night, money from the tables is put in a vault, and the vault has a slot for the money to go in, but no way to get the money out: no opening, no key, no combination, and no door. They call it the ghost's money."

It was odd that we'd just heard this tale from Giovanni, and now we were hearing it in more detail from Rose, who seemed overly distressed about it. *Rose said "money from the tables." That's certainly more than the innocent nightly dollar Gio described.* When I asked her why anyone's putting money into a slot for a ghost who protects the hotel was a concern, she said because it was somehow tied in with what was going on with the male performers, something sexual that they talked about among themselves in a dark, joking way.

"I think some of them double as prostitutes. Joanie told me she was seriously thinking of going to the police to try to put a stop to it. I guess it's gotten worse over the years. First boys, then really young boys. Sometimes they get hurt, depending on who the guy is they're meeting. They talk about that."

"So you think the money from the prostitution ring goes into this vault?" I whispered.

"I don't know…there's talk, you know, about how much could be in the vault. Guys saying things like, 'Hey, I humped for 400K of it!' Jokes like that."

"Would Joanie talk to us about it?" Callie asked.

"I'll ask her," Rose said and then paused. "A very good friend of mine could be put in danger by my talking to you. I might not be able to be in touch anymore."

"What's your friend's name?" I asked, but Rose ducked her head and wouldn't answer.

"Be careful. Everyone here plays many different parts. It's fun but it's dangerous. No one is who he appears to be…just like the *Boy Review* says. I have to go now," she said.

"Well, Elmo likes you as much as you like him. He's a sucker for pretty women," I said loudly. "Stop by anytime and say hi, and we'll try to get over and see your show."

"Great." She waved good-bye and proceeded into the hotel. We waited a moment and then took Elmo back up to the room. He'd had meatballs, a walk, and an evening with a pretty girl. What more could a guy ask?

"Well, I guess now we know part of the dark secret—child prostitution," Callie said.

I told Callie that while the discussion with Rose was interesting, Rose could be overreacting. After all, she was a young girl in a grown-up world. Prostitution was a timeless game, and young showgirls or boys being exploited was a crime, but most likely not a crime anyone would investigate until the story was bigger.

"Like someone dying?" Callie said, unhappy with my jaded opinion.

"You could knock out a million prostitution rings, and in a week, like weeds, they'll be back, because there are always creeps who want to run them and naïve kids who need a quick buck."

Callie said nothing in reply and I knew she was thinking about Rose and how deeply involved she might be. I was wondering about the truth behind Rose's statement that everyone played many roles. The performers seemed to roll off the stage and out into the hotel like a thick human fog, morphing into staff and vendors and guests…no one knowing who anyone really was.

"You're the only one I really know is *you*!" I said to Callie. "On second thought, you could be an alien!" Callie just smiled at me.

CHAPTER THIRTEEN

Giovanni Gratini's estate was a massive stone and marble structure protruding off a promontory that looked like a large sand dune. The wide circular drive was dotted with valet parkers poised to assume the burden of parking cars fifty feet away from the mansion. The rough-finish stone walkway lit by centurion torches and the night air filled with celebratory chanting that echoed outside the home made me feel as if I were about to join crowds at the Colosseum for a large sporting event. The doorman, looking stiff and starched, held the door for us, and a woman stood by to inquire if we'd like our coats checked. Ten feet farther on, a servant offered us a drink; another ten feet and we were served hors d'oeuvres. Finally, at the end of the food gauntlet, Giovanni, in a purple velvet dinner jacket and black silk slacks, smiled at us as if we were the most important arrivals of the evening.

"You made it, my lovely friends!" He kissed Callie's hand as I held her drink for her. He had positioned himself against a large sculpted fireplace with a mantel shaped like birds' wings and an oil painting of an Italian opera singer above it. He was obviously a man of drama. The room was sprinkled with young men from various theatrical venues, several we recognized from their pictures in the *Boy Review.* They stood in gay groups of twos and threes, interspersed with the occasional heterosexual couple, and made smart jokes and drank heavily.

Off to Giovanni's right, around the massive marble pillars separating the drawing room from the dining hall, came a recognizable figure dressed in a tight-fitting, long-sleeved, low-backed black gown: Karla Black, her massive head of curls looking coiffed in an intentionally disheveled sort of way. She swept into the room, in far greater control of her faculties than when I'd last seen her, and she gave Giovanni a big kiss on the cheek. He ran his hand idly down her back and over her rump but I noticed his focus was divided, half of it going to Marlena, who was giving him the eye from across the room.

Karla smiled appreciatively at Giovanni and then caught sight of Callie and me. "Hello, I was hoping you'd come," she said.

"We were glad to be invited." I shook her hand.

"You asked about the ghost of the ghoul pool, well, you can now say that you've met the ghost firsthand. We hold the party every year at the hotel. It's the most fun. People love it! Hard to get an invitation!" Karla said, in contrast to her earlier statement of knowing virtually nothing about the event. I chalked it up to her having been in a near-drugged state at our last meeting.

"In fact, you just missed the last one…too bad," Karla lamented.

"We have a friend, though, who made the list. Rose Ross," Callie said brightly as if Rose Ross had won a scholarship.

"Oh, Rose." Karla elongated the name lovingly. "What a cutie. To be that young again."

"I like my women just your age, and your height with your looks," Giovanni said gallantly, and squeezed her buttocks right in front of us.

"Ghostly promises." Karla giggled. "Now you two go enjoy!" Karla moved on to other guests.

One look around and it was easy to see that this was a hookers and mafia kind of party. The men looked tough and suspicious, the women were dolled up and used up, and the young boys were there for decoration and entertainment. Several of them had a Ouija board set up on a table in the corner, and they were asking questions, watching the planchette move across the board, then squealing over the answers and accusing one another of moving the planchette themselves.

Callie joined them and asked if Joanie Burr was at the party.

"Ask that queer over there." One of the young men pointed, and Callie and I strolled over to the handsome, metrosexual man they'd indicated, who was seated at a horseshoe-shaped bar in the middle of the room. He wore a dark pair of pants and a dark shirt and sunglasses despite the dark room. Unlike the very feminine drag queens in all their finery, he seemed to be gay publisher chic, or record industry executive chic. I could imagine him holding down a job in the entertainment industry, marching about with a clipboard, and snapping a pencil down on it in aggravation over something late or wrong. I wondered what role he played in the *Boy Review* since he didn't seem to be as exotic as the other performers. He extended his hand as if we were there for a job interview. "I'm Elliot Traugh, rhymes with how, or as my roommate at Princeton once said, 'How now, Elliot Traugh, will you fuck the bull or kiss the cow?' I was having some gender confusion at the time," he said, his tone acerbic. "So you know Karla." Elliot Traugh laughed. "She changes boyfriends more often than I do underwear, but then this whole town's about who's doing who. So are you two with someone?"

"Each other," I said.

"That's refreshing." He flipped a cigarette ash onto the floor with disdain. "Most everyone comes here to hook up; you arrived already hooked."

A female hand slid onto Callie's shoulder, and we all turned in unison to find Rose Ross in our midst. She was smiling radiantly. "I had no idea I'd see you here," she breathed and then swirled around our tight circle to kiss Elliot, who presented his cheek to her as one would a hand to the manicurist.

"And they're an item," Elliot Traugh said. "Isn't that nice?"

This was apparently new and startling news to Rose, who perhaps hadn't contemplated that a woman who was a friend of her father's could have a sex life, much less one with me. She stared at us with renewed interest. "Really? You're together-together? Wow." Rose introduced her friend Sophia. I recognized her immediately as the woman we'd spoken to when we went to the theater for the first time. She'd thanked us for being interested in helping her friend Rose.

Rose could barely take her eyes off Sophia, who was easily ten years her senior. Sophia was taking in the room, aware of her surroundings, seemingly sensitive to what was safe and what could explode. Rose was only taking in Sophia.

Suddenly, a large, rough man on the far side of the room yanked a woman to the ground by her hair and twisted her arm. She screamed, and he slapped her. As things were about to get decidedly rougher, a gay man stepped up and playfully cupped him in the balls, distracting him from the woman. There was muted conversation between the two, the attacker left for the bar, and the gay man shot the hooker a look that warned her to be more discreet.

"Rough party," I remarked.

"They're all on good behavior tonight because it's a mixed bag." Elliot Traugh spoke in a bored way, and his eyes scanned the room, seemingly in search of people more interesting than us. Callie asked Elliot if he'd seen Joanie Burr. Elliot, his focus waning, replied that it was too early. Joanie liked to arrive late and make a dramatic entrance.

Callie and I had hoped to get Joanie alone and ask her about the very thing she wanted to report to the police, but the odds of that now appeared slim.

Sophia slipped her small black lacquered makeup mirror out of a thin slit that was her side pocket and began running the lip liner around the edges of her full Italian lips as Rose watched, visibly aroused, if one could judge by the condition of her nipples inside her tight silk blouse.

"Sophia must be the one who left us the newspaper article," Callie barely whispered.

"Why do you say that?" I asked.

"The way she looks at me, as if she's trying to ask if I got her message."

"She could just be cruising you, in which case I'll be sending *her* a message," I said.

"She's not cruising me," Callie said.

Sophia glanced up at me, then trailed her fingers across Rose Ross's shoulder as she departed to talk to someone else, smiling as Rose involuntarily shuddered at her touch. *You're right. She's cruising Rose*, I thought as I steered Callie out into the large ballroom past the massive dining hall. Rose trailed along behind us out of earshot, most likely trying to see where Sophia had landed.

The ballroom was a sea of mottled terrazzo with gold inlay separating the five-foot squares. The windows on the south and east part of the room were tall and arched at the top, overlooking a beautifully landscaped garden that must have required enormous tending in the midst of the desert. A few other people had made their way into the room, admiring the architecture as much as anything. I asked Callie if I could freshen her drink. She nodded, and I moved back across the floor that made me feel as if I were gliding across ice in my search for a bartender. Rose went with me, saying if there was food I'd need more hands.

As we walked, Rose leaned in to my ear, ducking her head just slightly to talk to me since she was taller than I.

"So, how long have you been gay?"

"Longer than you've been alive," I said, not being particularly interested in young people.

"So how long have you and Callie been together?"

"I just met Callie a couple of months ago."

"Omigosh! So, you're just now…getting together?" She squealed like a teenage girl.

"Getting together?" I asked, to torture her into having to say what she meant.

"You know…you're just now…" she said, and I gave her a direct and blank stare. "Well…*dating*," she said with quick word replacement. "What's it like exactly?"

I didn't reply but ordered Callie a Coke and got Rose's bourbon and Seven, an old oilman's drink, and I wondered if she'd picked up the habit from her father.

"What's dating like?" I finally repeated, teasing her with my tone. She lowered her gaze in slight embarrassment, not at all the confident, arrogant young woman who'd easily accepted Callie's compliment in the greenroom.

"*Dating* Callie is the sexiest thing on the planet."

Rose let her breath out, collected herself, and then followed me back in the direction of the ballroom like a puppy.

"So who are you *dating*?" I asked, giving the word her emphasis.

"I don't know," she answered obliquely.

"You don't *know,* which means you're dating *someone,* but you're confused about who he—or she—is? Does that mean you're dating a drag queen?"

"No!" The look on Rose's face said she was truly shocked, and I laughed at her uneasiness, remembering what it was like to be in my early twenties and totally inept at answering the questions of women nearly twice my age. However, in fairness to me, Rose would have to learn not to start things she couldn't finish.

"So, is it Sophia?" I turned and looked directly at her. She reddened.

"No! Of course not," she nearly shouted at me.

You've had each other so many times mentally that the rest is just detail, I thought but instead replied, "Too bad."

❖

It was while we were away that Callie saw the tall female dancer from the *Boy Review* whom she and I would discuss after the party. The dancer was wearing tight black leggings, black fur balls dangling from her Russian-style boots, her colorful shirt bloused at the sleeve and cut low on her chest. Her waxen hair, black as coal, was combed flat to her head, giving the impression that the head was all of one molded piece like a porcelain doll. She turned gracefully on one foot to leave the room, lost her balance, and fell—her head cracking against the terrazzo, blood spilling from her skull. Callie let out a small yelp and ran to her side. The other people in the room were seemingly oblivious to the poor woman's plight. Callie looked up at the older man standing nearby to ask for his help, then caught his placid expression and stopped herself. Instead she ran through the dining hall and found me. In an urgent whisper she said, "Teague, a woman has fallen on the terrazzo and her head is split open. She may be dead. Come and help me quickly!"

"I'll get Giovanni," I said, but she held me by the arm.

"No, I want you to come help her." Callie pulled me with her. We scurried through the dining room and back to the ballroom, where people were milling about laughing and drinking.

"Where is she?" I asked.

Callie's body sagged up against me as if to say it was exactly as she'd suspected. "She was right there." Callie pointed at a pristine area of the terrazzo floor. "Right there."

"So she was moved?"

"I don't know. I don't know," she said, shaking her head, and yet, I sensed that Callie Rivers did know. The pieces of whatever was happening were beginning to take shape in her mind—pieces that might frighten me if she spoke them out loud.

Chapter Fourteen

Callie said very little on the drive home. No amount of coaxing on my part was going to get it out of her. Whatever she thought she saw at the party either didn't happen or it happened in the same way it happened in the bathtub in our room. I decided just to give her some space. I opened the moonroof so we could see the bright stars against the dark desert sky, and I turned on the radio. It was a country song about somebody who thought they were picking up a hitchhiker, and he turned out to be the ghost of a famous country singer.

"Everything's a sign," Callie said, and receded back into her own private world.

What would living with Callie Rivers be like? I thought. *Sometimes she'd be present, and sometimes she'd be out in the ether and I'd be with her, but alone.* I reached over and took her hand, content to have something to hold on to until she came back.

She was silent as I pulled up to the valet parking stand, and the plumed boy asked how our evening was. I refrained from saying, "It was just swell: hookers, hoods, and homicide." Instead I settled for the Midwestern version and muttered, "Fine, thanks."

We rode up in the elevators in silence. After unlocking our bedroom door, I quietly hooked up Elmo and left the hotel room to walk him, leaving Callie to her thoughts. When we returned fifteen minutes later, she'd fallen into bed and was asleep before I'd even had a chance to brush my teeth. Apparently flying around outside her body took its toll. As I leaned over to kiss her good night, she murmured in a half sleep, "Don't leave the bed in the morning, I do want you."

"I'm not the one who leaves," I reminded her, and she smiled.

"Can you tell me more about what you saw?"

"Just a woman in an exotic Russian costume. She slipped, she fell, she died, she disappeared."

It was evident that she knew nothing more and didn't want to dwell on it.

❖

With the first rays of morning sunshine, I awoke to Callie's kissing my neck and unbuttoning my nightshirt. I moaned into awareness, loving that the first thing I was feeling as I awoke was her nude body pressed against mine.

"You are so sensual. I'm so glad the planets have aligned to bring you to my bed. Although, since they're aligned exactly as they were twenty years ago, I would still like to have had you then," I said. My remark made Callie pause and then look up at the ceiling for a long moment. "What's wrong?" I asked.

"What you said about the planets aligning just as they did twenty years ago. It's made me think about something related to the chart." She jumped out of bed and headed for her computer, locating the scrap of astrological paper bearing the Stellium in Scorpio. "The ghoul pool always takes place on Halloween. This chart was created on Halloween. That's one thing he's trying to tell me. Mo must have had this chart on his mind when he died, because it just has his presence. Whatever happened on this most recent Halloween at the ghoul pool gathering is what brought the energy of this hotel's natal chart back. You see, it's a retrieval of energy from the Halloween Eve in which the groundbreaking occurred. Sun, Moon, Uranus, Venus, Mercury, and Mars, all lined up like little soldiers."

"Come back to bed. I am so sorry I mentioned the damned planets. Get over here, please!"

"Don't curse the planets." Callie stood up at her computer, too excited to sit. "A Stellium is the conjunction of three or more planets in the same sign of the zodiac. In this instance, if we want to be liberal about our orbs and allow ten degrees, one could say there's a double Stellium: Sun, Moon, and Uranus within eight degrees of each other, all in Scorpio in the Eighth House, and Venus, Mercury, and Mars all within ten degrees Scorpio in the Eighth as well. The Eighth House is just packed! Every aspect, every sign, every planet, every asteroid has a positive and negative energy attached to it. We use it for either good or evil, depending upon our own will. Scorpio in the Eighth House is inherently intense, secretive, sexual, power seeking. The Eighth House relates to many issues, including reincarnation, death and dying, and other people's money."

"Sounds terrible."

"It's all in how you use it. Someone with that aspect in their natal chart could use the energy positively to become a powerful surgeon specializing in reconstructive surgery, or on the negative side, he or she could be a murderer. You see, two ways to use a knife. Positively, one could be a brilliant forensic detective; negatively, the same person could be a sexual predator. Again, two ways to use the power of tracking an individual. Positively, a power seeker in the sense that he marries or becomes the head of state; negatively, that same person could be a power seeker in the sense that he corrupts the head of state. You see how that works?"

"So who makes the choice—that person or the cosmos?"

"Another question becomes, when are the choices made: before you ever arrive on Earth or as you live each day?" Callie smiled, enjoying our being able to share a conversation like this.

"So someone who knew Mo Black and the story about this chart is passing us the word that something dark and Plutonian is going on in his hotel right now, or that the old darkness is about to be brought to light—or both?" I asked.

"Exactly. We know Rose is on the ghoul pool list, but we don't know why. We know Mo Black was on the list at one time. Karla mentioned that. It's possible that he was on the list right around the time the young boy was killed. Then Mo died as well. Maybe Mo was on the list as a warning to be silent regarding the boy prostitution ring, and he ignored the warning and he and the boy were both murdered—the boy first to make Mo suffer, and then Mo. And if I'm right about the retrieval of energy, Rose is on the list as a warning to be silent, and if she's not, maybe someone else dies along with her. Retrieval of energy, a present-day event mirroring the past. But usually you go back to retrieve energy in order to change it and correct it." Callie took a deep breath.

"Let's hope so," I said.

Callie threw her head back, and I could see the elegant lines that made up her neck and the exquisite structure of her cheekbones and her nose, Greco-Roman carved and perfectly sculpted.

"In the Eighth House Stellium, Venus is involved. It sits right in the middle. So there is a woman in the middle of this, and Venus is Retrograde so the woman is going back. Back where? Back to do what? Look at this." She picked up a book from her suitcase that contained something called Sabian Symbols. She explained that every single degree through which a planet can pass has a particular meaning.

"Venus is at 19 degrees and 6 minutes in this chart. If you consult that symbol, it says something like an exotic bird hearing and then talking. Now I know that's strange and makes no sense, but I've come to realize that there is sense there. I simply can't decipher it right now."

I was totally worn out from the conversation, the kind of fatigue that comes from concentrating intensely on trying to understand someone talking to me in a foreign language.

I turned on the TV to catch the morning news, accepting that our time in bed together had been waylaid by the cosmos. As the picture came into view, the reporter announced, "Investigators were at the home of a well-known Las Vegas showman, Johnathon Burr, known in Las Vegas show circles as Joanie Burr, who died late last night. Mr. Burr came home from his late-night second performance and apparently slipped on his back patio, falling to his death." The news broadcast cut to performance photos of Joanie Burr in costume wearing black tights, Russian boots, and the blousy shirt Callie described.

"That's the woman who died on the terrazzo floor at Giovanni's home. She's the drag queen, Joanie Burr!" Callie shouted.

"So she died twice? Once at Gio's party and once at her own home?" I asked, totally confused.

"No, her face was different at the party, but it was Joanie," Callie said.

"I'm lost." I shook my head in frustration.

"The woman who died on the terrazzo floor at the party was the drag queen Joanie Burr, who died last night at her home, and they showed her on TV just now, but at Giovanni's house, her body and her clothing matched the clothing Joanie was wearing on TV. Her face was a woman's face because she was dressed in costume, but it was almost like the face of the man in the bathtub."

"Well, that clears things up," I said, trying to be funny, but Callie was obviously too upset to laugh. "It's weird that twenty-four hours ago, we asked if Joanie Burr would talk to us, and now she's dead. Is she dead because of that very thing?" I asked.

"Rose is the only one who knew we wanted to talk to Joanie, but I don't think she would ever have anything to do with her death. In fact, if your palm imprint is correct, she could be next," Callie said.

"Let's go talk to her," I replied.

I gave Elmo a quick hug good-bye and Callie and I headed downstairs, past the ringing slot machines, under the celestially lit domed ceiling, beyond the ever-hot buffet and the ticket information booth, and down the long corridor and into the darkened theater, backstage, and up the staircase to the greenroom where we found Rose Ross sitting alone sobbing. She said she never even got to ask Joanie if she'd talk to us. She died too suddenly. Still, something didn't feel right. With everyone in this hotel seeming to know our every thought and deed, maybe someone did know we wanted to question Joanie Burr.

"Rose, you're obviously not telling us something," I said.

"Too many people. Even I don't know who's on whose side," she said almost inaudibly.

"We think you landed on the ghoul pool list to ensure someone's silence or your own. True?" I asked.

The door opened and Marlena filled the doorway. "You shouldn't be alone, Rosie. Come on, you're too upset." She gave us a look that indicated how sorry she felt for poor Rose, and she helped the girl up. "We have to go," Marlena said to us, and we watched her shepherd Rose away.

"They always seem to know where Rose is," Callie said.

"Let's hope they're protecting her. Ever since those names appeared on my palm I've been worried it's a gallows list."

❖

As we headed back down the stairs and through the maze of ropes and pulleys backstage, the phone rang and Wade Garner's voice sounded solemn as he asked me if I'd told anyone else about my request that he do some investigating for me. When I assured him I hadn't, he said he'd gotten an anonymous call warning him off the case.

I apologized profusely and told him to back off. This wasn't his affair.

"No way," he replied. "I'm just impressed that you're dickin' around with crooks who have the balls to call me a thousand miles away to threaten me. Must mean you're getting close. Stay in touch," he said. And I knew he was saying stay safe.

While my body was moving through the theater, my mind flashed back to the Star Bar, where I'd been the night Wade called and I'd stepped outside to get better reception. Everyone always met at the Desert Star Bar. Everyone had to step out of the bar to make a call because no one could get reception inside, and everyone had to face in the only direction one could face and get a cell phone to work. The spot outside the bar where the phone would work faced a series of overhead glass panels just off the lobby.

They're scanning everyone's cell phone conversations through the glass. It happens in the lobby, I thought. I picked up my pace, wanting to get out of the theater and back to the glass panels to check out my theory.

I don't know what made Callie look up as we proceeded across the theater's back stage. I only heard her gasp and my eyes followed the tilt of her head. Up above us, a man stood on his tiptoes, on scaffolding that jutted out away from the tall theater walls. His anguished expression seemed to communicate that he was committing suicide. He let out a piercing scream and my heart nearly leapt out of my chest as he tumbled down, diving to his death. Our hands instinctively covered our mouths to stifle our own screams as we watched in horror, not wanting to hear the dull splat, but then at the last moment, he pulled out of the dive like an aircraft, his arms outspread, soaring above our head under his own power, shrieking and laughing in the most maniacally chilling flight. Callie and I ducked as he dive-bombed us. I searched for wires or filaments or any support system but saw none. Suddenly he seemed to lose control of his aerobatics and crashed to the floor, just missing our heads by inches, and now it was our turn to scream. We bent over the body and it was nothing but a dummy, a mannequin. Elliot Traugh stepped out onto the grid work up above our heads. "Oh, good heavens, I'm so sorry. Hector could have killed you! Are you all right? Hector is our flyboy test dummy!"

"Sound effects are pretty hair-raising," I responded.

"No one's supposed to be in here without permission," he said, fretting insincerely over the near tragedy.

"And if they are, you're forced to kill them?" I joked.

"Should I call the hotel nurse?" Elliot asked without the least bit of concern in his voice now that he presumed we were uninjured.

"No, we're leaving," Callie said and pulled me back toward the place where we had entered.

"Put the Do Not Enter sign up please on your way out," Elliot called to us.

"What do you know about Joanie's death, Elliot?" I couldn't leave without asking.

"I know it was tragic, a great loss to the theater community and to this show," he replied solemnly.

"Was it an accident…really?" I probed.

"That's what the paper said, and all the newscasts," Elliot responded.

"Who found her?" Callie chimed in.

"I sent Sophia to her house with a key when she didn't show for rehearsal. Sophia's still very upset. I don't understand your fascination with this…are you police or reporters…or just bored?" He went back to being the acerbic gay man.

"Sorry we bothered you," Callie said.

Out of Elliot's earshot, I leaned into Callie. "Why would he send Sophia? If he suspected Joanie was injured or maybe even dead, why wouldn't he send another drag queen who would know what things to remove or hide or who to call?"

"Perhaps he wanted to send Sophia a message. Perhaps he *knew* Joanie was dead and her corpse was an up-close reminder of what could happen to people who talk," Callie said. "But why would Sophia talk?"

"Maybe because of her relationship with Rose. If they're close friends, and one of them is in danger, I would imagine the other one should watch her back," I said.

❖

We retraced our steps up the steep incline, through the double doors, and back out into the brightly lit lobby.

"The dummy—was it an accident?" I looked into Callie's eyes as we found ourselves outside the darkened theater and once again in the hubbub of people having normal lives.

"No," she whispered softly. "The dummy flying down at us, the death of Joanie Burr…nothing here is by accident."

"I'm getting skittish, Callie. Too many places an attack can come from, and it always looks innocent."

"Wrap ourselves in white light," Callie said firmly.

I said nothing, thinking we'd most likely used up our personal ration of white light at this point.

❖

Callie and I took Elmo outside, taking solace in mundane activities. As the Queen of England purportedly said, the secret to success is never to pass up an opportunity to go to the loo. That was Elmo's secret to success as well. He hunched his body up at the base of an ornamental shrub, making it only slightly more ornamental when he was through. I was busy looking over my shoulder for would-be attackers and didn't have my plastic bag with me, so I left Elmo's token for the gardeners. I was thinking we needed to find Sophia and ask her about her discovery of Joanie's body.

When we reentered the lobby, I was struck by the number of businesspeople happily holding their conferences and meetings amidst what could only be termed total chaos: noise, lights, and throngs of humanity—like trying to hold a church service at a carnival. A man strode across the lobby and gripped the hand of a friend in a strong handshake that lingered just a beat too long, making me wonder if they were gay.

"Did you know that at one time there was a tribal group in New Guinea that shook penises," I said, causing Callie to stop walking and pay full attention. "They believed if you could trust a stranger with your most vulnerable body part, you could trust him with your life. I wonder how that got started. I mean, there had to be that first guy who said, 'May I shake your penis?' and then it caught on."

"Teague, your mind is a very strange place." Callie giggled.

"No, I'm dead serious. Can you imagine a New Guinea woman ever in her wildest dreams deciding that women should shake each other's tits? You see what I mean? I don't care where they are in the world, men's thought processes are just damned strange," I concluded.

As I thought about the men in the lobby, shaking hands instead of penises, my mind reached back into its databank and pulled up the image of Giovanni shaking our hands so warmly at dinner, first me, then Callie. "Callie, Gio put the letters on my palm when he shook my hand just before we left the restaurant. I remember thinking his hand was so warm, a bit sweaty, but he was so sweet holding my palm to his. He was transferring the ink. But did he mean it as a threat or a warning?"

"A warning—one that's too late for Joanie but not for Rose. Check the ring," she whispered, her lips barely moving.

I looked up and, sure enough, the dealer was wearing the signet ring on his pinkie finger. I looked past the dealer and spotted one of Hollywood's most famous leading men, Sterling Hackett, walking toward us. I punched Callie and nodded in his direction, and then we both pretended not to have noticed him.

I slid onto the end chair at the blackjack table, and Elmo and Callie stood beside me. Mid-deal, Sterling Hackett sat down to my left. "Is the dog winning?" he asked dryly.

"He just started playing," I said, not cracking a smile, but the dealer did.

The cards were dealt, and I checked mine—ace and eight—I waved my hand palm down three inches above the cards, giving the sign that I didn't want another. Sterling looked at his cards, two eights, and told the dealer to double down. The dealer laid a six over one of the eights and a king on the other: fourteen and eighteen. The dealer then turned his own card over, revealing a ten to go with his king and beating us both.

"Elmo, you lost," I said over the edge of the table as the dealer dealt us cards again.

"I'm busted," Sterling said, this time holding twenty-two, and the dealer took it all with twenty-one. "I've had fourteen be a winning hand," he mused. "Well, I'm hitting the hay and tackling this tomorrow."

"Good night, Mr. Hackett. I enjoy your movies, by the way," the dealer offered.

"Thanks," Sterling said without looking back, and he wandered off toward the elevators. Callie yanked on my jacket, and I cashed in my chips. Elmo, Callie, and I caught the elevator and got off on eighteen. Sterling entered room 1823. Callie said she felt strongly that we should hang around for a few minutes. I stood by the elevator with Elmo for fifteen minutes until he and I were both tired of shifting our weight from one leg to the other. Suddenly, *whoosh!* and the elevator doors opened and a young man who looked to be prepubescent walked down the hallway, escorted by an older, shorter man wearing lifts. He knocked on the door of room 1823, and I pulled Elmo back out of sight. Sterling opened the door and let the boy in, and the older man left. I could see Callie's countenance cloud over, and I knew what she was thinking. I didn't want to think about it. After all, maybe that was the boy's father who brought him there for an audition. *You know that's bullshit,* a voice in my head said. *Well, so what!* the warring voice in my head replied. *So what if Sterling had boys come to his room late at night? There could be a million reasons, none of them our business.*

Elmo was so tired he was beginning to stumble. When basset hounds wear out, they wilt like a flower in a matter of minutes, and Elmo had gone from being a tulip to a pansy. The voice in my head would not be silenced. *You know that Sterling Hackett has a reputation for sexual encounters with underaged boys. It's been reported in all the trades in L.A. You know that he's probably boffing that kid right now.*

"Do something!" Callie said as if residing in my head. There was scuffling and a muffled protest coming from the room.

"Like what?" I replied.

"Are you going to let him harm that boy?"

I knew from police work that the boy had probably been harmed before by many men. In fact, he was what older gay and bisexual men called chicken—fresh meat. But I chose not to tell Callie that.

"Teague…" Callie's voice was strained. I handed her Elmo's leash, telling her to hold him and get back out of sight. I charged the door, more out of frustration of being drawn into this drama than any idealistic view that I could save this kid. I banged on the door loudly with my fist and lowered my voice.

"Vice Squad! You've got five seconds to open this door! One! Two! Three…"

There was silence, and I jumped back out of sight. The door blew open suddenly and the young boy flew out of the room, his shirt hanging off him and his pants in his arms. He looked terrified, perhaps by Sterling Hackett or perhaps by the specter of the vice squad. I ran after him and caught him by the arm.

"You okay?" I asked him, panting slightly from my short sprint.

"Yeah." He ducked his head.

"What are you doing here?" I pulled him out of sight of Sterling's hotel room door.

"Nothing. Visiting," he said.

I pushed him ahead of me down the hallway and into a small linen closet. Callie and Elmo followed. "You're going to talk to us about what's going on around here. Who do you work for?"

"Whoever pays me," he said.

"To do what exactly?" I pressed.

He started to bolt, but I had him in a grip he couldn't escape. "I will turn you in to the police unless you talk to me for five minutes. What's your name?"

"Joey," he muttered. And suddenly I remembered him. He was the young kid who had served as our guide, leading us to Rose Ross the first night we'd arrived and had gone to the theater to meet her. He was Desert Greeter Joey! And it appeared he'd been giving folks a hell of a hello in his new role as boy prostitute. He was a small-boned boy, blond, rumpled hair, a little too boney. Feminine hands. Nice eyes. Just a boy.

"Okay, Joey, you went to that guy's room for what reason?" I said.

"To entertain. I'm an entertainer," he said.

Callie put her arm on mine to signal that she didn't want me to be too rough on him, but I ignored her.

"You do a lot of entertaining with your pants off?" I asked, and he blushed, letting me know that whatever sexual activity he was participating in, he hadn't been at it that long.

"No," he said. "I work backstage at a couple of shows. This one here too. When I get to be eighteen I can go into the review."

That's good," Callie said. "You'll be very good at it."

"So blow jobs for old guys…is that just to pay the rent?" I asked. Callie winced and Joey looked at the floor.

"Lot of guys do it," he said.

"What guys are those?" I asked.

"The guys in the shows," he replied.

I asked the kid how he'd found out this form of extracurricular activity was even an option. He said the older guys put him onto it. When I tried to find out more, all he knew was that he came to the hotel and hung around in the lobby and sometimes one of the staff would come up and tell him if he wanted to make some money he should go to a particular room. I realized I wasn't going to get much more out of him, and Callie was squirming. She asked what year, time, and day he was born. She said she wanted to do his astrological chart. He replied that he didn't know. He grew up with a relative and had no idea where he was born. She looked at him for a moment and then asked if she could place her hand on his hand. She closed her eyes and breathed deeply.

Suddenly she smiled. "Before you are eighteen, you are going to meet someone who is going to help you change the direction of your life. He will give you the things you have lacked. You will find love." She opened her eyes and smiled at him. He smiled slightly, briefly. I opened the door for him and he left.

"That kid's not old enough to be working anywhere. At least not the kind of work he can tell his mother about," I said. "He may be wearing a name tag, but he's lying about having a job here."

Chapter Fifteen

I lifted Elmo's front paws up on the edge of the bed, then grabbed his hind legs and gave him an alley-oop into the middle of the bed. He was tired of the hard floor and was very appreciative of a day in bed. He gave a deep shuddering sigh and collapsed in a heap. I kissed the top of his head and told him we'd be back in a little while. I rang the theater asking for Sophia Pappagallo, but the man who answered said she was out and they weren't allowed to give me her cell phone number. I rang Rose Ross, got her answering machine, and left a message for her to call but didn't say why—suspicious now of someone's overhearing and diverting her messages.

The theater lobby looked like a morgue. The theater entrance was draped in black, and a large display of personal and show-biz items honored the life of one of its longtime performers. There were Joanie pictures resting on easels draped with flowers, tributes posted on the walls, and young gay men passing by to read what others had written. It was mourning LasVegas–style for Joanie Burr.

"As long as we're depressed, I think we should go down to the morgue and have a look at Joanie," I said, and Callie wrinkled her nose in protest.

"Why? We know she's dead." Callie was trying to squirm out of going.

"Yes, but she slipped and fell. That's the part that's bothering me. Performers as trained and athletic as Joanie Burr don't fall on their own patios and die."

My cell phone rang. It was Barrett asking if I could make a meeting late in the day in L.A. with Jeremy Jocowitz.

"We've done this, Barrett," I said, irritated.

Barrett spoke so loudly that Callie could almost hear her, so I tilted the receiver to let Callie lean in and listen.

"Look, I was wrong. I was reaching for anything to pitch him and keep him interested in your work, and frankly, without you here, I couldn't remember what all you were working on. Excuse me for that, but I only work with about fifty writers. The fact that I'm pitching my balls off for you should say something, I would think. Do you know how many women would give their right tit for me to be pitching them to Jeremy Jocowitz?" I glanced over at Callie, who shrugged and rolled her eyes as if to say, "big deal."

"Whatever," I said.

"Whatever? What-the-fuck-ever? Is that what you're saying to me? Well, dear," her tone was suddenly acrimonious, "I have Jeremy lined up at four this afternoon in my office to hear you pitch whatever in hell turns you on. How about that? Whatever in hell turns you on! Why? Because he likes you, and he likes your talent, and he's just begging for some story that he can relate to. Do you think you can handle that? Do you want me to cancel?"

"I'm still in Vegas. I would have to leave now—"

"Yeah, and quit balling the blonde for a brief moment to get back to your career…"

I pulled the phone away so that Callie couldn't hear any more. "One more remark like that and you can stick your meetings up—"

"Okay, okay, okay, sorry!" There was a long pause while both of us breathed.

I looked at Callie, covered the phone, and mouthed, "I'm not going unless you go with me. We can drive back right after the meeting… round trip eight hours, plus a two-hour meeting."

Callie paused, then nodded.

"Okay, Barrett, but move the meeting to two, because I'm turning around and driving back. I have work here."

"See you at two," she said, and hung up.

"He must really like your work," Callie said.

"If Barrett's just fucking with me, I'm going to kill her," I said.

"I don't think she is. We'll have to pack everything and take it. I don't trust leaving anything here. Especially you, Elmo," she teased as if we'd even consider it.

"I'll buy him an In-N-Out Burger on the road," I said, marveling at a franchise that could get a name like In-N-Out approved at a board meeting. "What about Rose?" I asked Callie.

"We'll only be gone for the day. Maybe we'll come up with something while we're driving. We certainly haven't thought of much while we've been here."

❖

I loved road trips with Callie. She was the all-time best navigator and copilot. I could ask for things, extend my hand, and they were there miraculously: tissues, gum, water, more hot coffee, a doggie bone for Elmo.

"We love traveling with you," I said, after she'd handed me my third cup of coffee.

"You are the most needy driver I've ever met." She smiled sweetly.

"What? Am I annoying you? I'm sorry. I thought the fact that I am steering us safely through the desert at eighty miles an hour, shoulders tense, eyes glued to the road, senses alert to protect you, would be worth your having to hand me a few things," I said.

She slid her hand between my legs, and I jumped and took my foot off the gas. "Don't be doing that if you don't want to spend the night upside down in a sand dune," I warned, and she leaned over and began nuzzling me in a sensual crawl of kisses that spread from the base of my shoulder up my neck and behind my ear. I whined about her timing. "You are intentionally doing this when I can't do anything about it."

"No, I'm getting you ready for your pitch. Do you even know what you're going to pitch?"

"I'm going to pitch him a lesbian love story. One of the women is preparing to enter monastic life, and the other is married to an abusive husband, and they fall in love. It's a true story. In fact, I've always wanted to do it, but I just thought it was a bit ahead of its time for the general viewing audience."

"Oh boy!" Callie laughed. "If you thought he was ordering gin and tonics during your royal love story, he'll be sending out for a case of vodka by the time this is over."

We both got the giggles and couldn't stop. The idea of pitching the lesbian love story to Jeremy was almost a lark and not a pitch, maybe just a way of letting off steam, doing one's career duty, but not. Getting back at him for his short attention span. It didn't matter. We didn't really care. We just wanted to be together on a cool fall day, laughing and driving and singing along with a song about there being gold in a bank in Beverly Hills in someone else's name. And why that was something to sing about was beyond me.

As we came to a small desert town, I could smell burgers in the air. Elmo woofed loudly, signaling me to pull off and head for the drive-through. I ordered four hamburgers: two with everything but onions and two with meat and bread only. When we pulled through and the cute gay girl handed me the first plain burger, I unwrapped it, tore it in half, and put it on the sack for Elmo to eat in the backseat. He ate it while the lady at the drive-through window watched.

"He loves your burgers," I said, "and he's eaten every burger ever made. These are his favorites." Elmo woofed loudly, and I gave him the second one. He gulped it, looked up at the window, and belched for the girl. She laughed and we drove on.

"What does In-N-Out Burger really mean?" I asked Callie. "Is it the burgers that go in and out, or the people who eat the burgers who go in and out, or is it the cars that go in and out, or is it some more esoteric message..."

"Do you want me to drive? I think you could use a nap."

Watching Elmo devour his drive-through lunch must have reminded Callie of the hotel's food. "I don't think we should eat any of the food that comes through room service," she said. "Buffet's okay because they can't poison everyone, but no more room service in light of what's going on."

I couldn't disagree and wondered why I hadn't thought of it. I told her as long as we were on the topic, I wanted to go over what we knew about the case and focus on what we needed to know. I recapped for Callie that she'd gotten a call from Rose Ross's dad saying a man had warned him his daughter was going to die. Rose then called her dad and told him she was on a ghoul pool list and that was the last frightening straw. He called Callie for help. We came riding to the rescue, located the damsel in distress, and she seemed to think everybody overreacted. Silly her for upsetting people! She said all this in front of Joanie Burr. Later she tracked us down outside the hotel and admitted she thought the money left for the ghost wasn't just a superstition but had something to do with a boy porn ring. In fact, she thought Joanie was going to talk to the police about it, but before Joanie got the chance, she conveniently slipped and fell and died. We learned Bruce Singleton was about to come over to the hotel to run the *Boy Review* and then he accidentally drowned in the desert. Coincidentally, he was on the ghoul pool list.

As I paused to collect my thoughts, Callie interjected that we shouldn't forget about the ring. The ring on the dead man in the tub—the dead man who turned out to be Bruce Singleton with a white mark on his pinkie finger where the ring used to be…or where some ring used to be. Then there was the newspaper article left in our room about a boy who twenty years ago was killed in the hotel. Not to mention someone tried to kill me with his car, knife her, print a hit list on my palm, and then Elliot tried to smash us with a flying dummy.

"It's obvious that someone or several people are trying to protect the boy ring at any cost," Callie said. "But why would you warn people they were in danger of being murdered by putting them on a ghoul pool death and dying list?"

"Maybe not all of them are in danger. They don't all die. Maybe it's a warning to a select few, to keep them in line."

We both drove in silence for several minutes, trying to piece things together.

❖

We pulled into my Valley house, turned the alarm off, and made Elmo comfortable. He drank some water and plopped into his giant wicker basket with the padded mattress as if to say hotels were hell. I picked the mail up off the entryway floor where it lay scattered, having been deposited through the slot in the door while I was gone. I also retrieved the phone messages from my answering machine. Mary Beth's voice seemed exceedingly loud as she said, "Teague, I hope you're back and that you didn't get married! I've missed you. This is Mary Beth—" I hit Erase so fast that my finger hurt from jamming it into the button.

"Who is Mary Beth?"

"Salesperson," I lied.

"What did she say about getting married?"

"I think she's getting married or wanting to get married or something," I lied again.

"I hope you're not buying anything she's selling," Callie said knowingly.

"Nothing," I said, guilty with no reason to be other than Callie's piercing eyes staring at me. I broke free from her to go into the bedroom and get dressed for the pitch. We'd made record time and didn't have to leave for our appointment for an hour. It only took me twenty minutes to clean up and change into a nice double-breasted suit.

"You look very sexy," Callie said as I came down the narrow hallway from the bedroom.

"Well, thank you." I tried to move past her, but she trapped me up against the wall and kissed me. Her kisses were so hot that I could barely stand up.

"Are you trying to wrinkle my suit?" I whispered. Her mouth never let go of mine, her tongue searching and stroking as her hands deftly unbuckled my belt and unzipped my slacks. She skipped all the foreplay and slid her hand inside me, suddenly pinning me back against the wall and making me gasp. She was leaning fully against me, kissing me hard and long and making me weaker and wetter—her hands stronger than I had imagined they could be—moving inside me urgently as I moaned. I could no longer stand, but she held me like steel against the wall as I sank into her and let go, no longer trying to figure out how a person makes love against a wall, but just doing it—until there was no wall.

"I am ruined," I said afterward, breathless.

Still kissing me, she pulled my slacks up, buckled my belt, straightened my shirt, and said, "That should take the edge off," and grinned mischievously.

"I'll never think of this wall in the same way again. Perhaps a wall is nothing more than a vertical bed," I said.

"Hmm." She grinned and kissed me again. I began unbuttoning her blouse, but she stopped me. "Come on, we'll finish this later. You'll be late."

"But I..."

"It will give us both something to look forward to." She gave me that businesslike kiss that meant we were moving on, and I tried to pull myself together for my meeting.

I went into the bathroom to repair my makeup and caught sight of myself in the mirror. "I look so had," I said out loud into the dreamy green eyes that stared back at me. I practiced furrowing my brow and focusing my vision to a more businesslike look and finally gave it up. "Now I simply look like a business person who's been had."

❖

As we drove, hand in hand, to the Marathon Studio gates, I contemplated Callie's beautiful profile. "You know, for a woman who only a short time ago couldn't let herself go in bed, you're definitely making up for lost ground."

"And your complaint would be…?" She grinned at me.

We hadn't been to Marathon Studios since our infamous entanglement with Robert Isaacs, months ago, which had ended in his being arrested, along with half a dozen studio personnel. Barrett had survived to continue in her position as Executive VP of Worldwide Talent, which I assumed meant if your talent was only continental, Barrett wasn't your gal. The guard at the gate had been alerted to our arrival. He took our names, barely bothered to locate us on the list, and waved us through.

"Feels oddly familiar, doesn't it?" I asked Callie.

"More pleasant this time," she replied.

"That's due entirely to the sexual prelude," I said. "By the way, did you make love to me because we're seeing Barrett and you wanted me to keep you top of mind?" I teased.

"It's not a competition." Callie smiled serenely, then paused and added impishly, "But if it were, I would win hands down."

❖

Barrett's gay male secretary swooned when we came in, rising from his seat in awe and respect. "Long time no seeeeee. Let me tell her you're here," he said, veritably dancing into her office and returning to tell us we were welcome to go inside. I had personally noticed that Hollywood Studio greetings could range from rude, when I wanted something from the studio, to orgasmic, when I had something the studio wanted. Today was an orgasmic day, as if everyone on the lot had gotten the memo: Be nice, they have something we want. As we entered ahead of him, the secretary jogged in place in the doorway, demonstrating his desire to swiftly dash over to the commissary and get us any special drink we might require. We declined, and he jogged on.

Barrett's office was impeccably decorated. She'd had it completely remodeled since we'd visited last, maybe to entertain her guests, or perhaps just to entertain herself. Lots of leather and polished wood and museum quality objet d'art adorned the sweeping lines of her cherry-topped desk, held in suspension by nearly unseen silver legs in the shape of nude women whose arms stretched overhead, in a 1940s Esther Williams dive style, to hold the desk top aloft. A leather minimalist chaise stretched out near the window, beckoning someone to read a manuscript while enjoying the studio grounds. Her shelves were lined with elitist trophies, including some for rowing. She rose to greet us, wearing her signature pressed and pleated, cuffed dress pants, with expensive patent loafers peeking out from under them. Her shirt was the most expensive item, light blue textured cotton with navy accents around the buttonholes and a tiny navy crest. She was tall, flat chested, and smoothly gender-agnostic from her tiny gold earrings to her pinkie ring and gold coin cufflinks.

"I'm so glad you came," she said, in a double entendre every female writer in Hollywood could attribute to her. "And you too, Callie, of course." She extended a long, graceful arm, indicating we should take a seat together on the leather couch across the polished coffee table from two chairs where she and Jeremy would no doubt be seated. "Are you going to tell me what you're pitching to Jeremy?"

"No." I smiled.

"Then I can't jump in and help you if things go south." She gave me an I-warned-you shrug.

"South is fine." I shrugged back, truly not caring.

Moments later Jeremy came huffing in the door with a thick, black, battered satchel briefcase that I couldn't imagine was still being manufactured in modern times. His shirt had a lunch stain on it, his glasses needed a good cleaning, and his shoes had never seen polish.

This guy has to be rich and for real, or no one would give him the time of day. He's a nebbish, as my Jewish friends would say.

Barrett took his briefcase and stowed it away, remarking on what he might be hiding in it, including his mother, based on its weight. Nothing seemed to faze Jeremy. He was oblivious to insult and seemed only to be made nervous by his own personal time schedule. Barrett began with the usual "You remember Teague Richfield and Callie Rivers," and then we all shook hands, and said our hellos, and created small talk for a few minutes, after which Barrett set the stage with, "Jeremy has funds to deliver six pictures this year, and he's come to me for suggestions about the type of films that would be groundbreaking, but relatively low budget. So, that's why I asked Teague to leave her work in Las Vegas for a day and come over and pitch her absolute favorite theatrical to you." Barrett tossed the line off with the confidence of someone who embraced exaggeration as a staple of good business.

For a split second, I wished I had given this more thought. He was a big-time Hollywood director. He might be a schmuck, but he was a schmuck with bucks, and this was possibly my moment. I glanced at Callie, who gave me a riveting look that clearly said, "This is a great story, go for it."

"Okay." I looked at him thinking, *If you interrupt me one fucking time, I'm out of here.* "This is a love story between two women, one of whom is about to complete her religious training to become a nun, and the other who is married to an abusive husband. In the course of getting counseling from the younger woman, the married woman falls in love with her." I paused, giving Jeremy time to order a scotch, or scratch his crotch, or do something that would irritate me, but he never took his eyes off me. I went on for another fifteen minutes, describing the way the relationship developed, and what motivated them, psychologically and physically, and the moment of crisis in the middle of the film, and the climactic ending, and then I paused.

No one spoke for a few seconds. Then Jeremy slapped his leg with his hand like some old-timer hearing a funny joke, and yelled, "I love this film! I'm going to make this film. It's risky, it's romantic, it's a little raunchy even for Middle America. It will be talked about. We'll film it in New York. Do you have a treatment? I need a two-, five-, ten-page treatment, whatever tells the story. Get that to Barrett, and she'll get it to me, and we'll take the next step. I love it!" He stood up. "Sorry,

I have another pitch meeting across town. We'll be seeing each other. Good. Very good." And he left.

I was stunned and said nothing. Callie gave me a big smile. Barrett rose and paced proudly like a lion across her den. "So, you think I just fuck with you! Ha! He just bought your story, Teague. Great story. Who's representing you now?"

"I don't have an agent. I use my attorney."

"You're so stubborn. Why not an agent?"

"Agents don't get my work; they like very commercial stuff. Besides, let's enjoy this moment in which we just sold something without an agent."

"Have your attorney call me. We need to cut the deal," she said.

"I write the script," I said firmly.

"Sure." She dismissed my remark, but I knew the battle to come. "Okay, you two go back to Las Vegas. I'll be in touch. This is exciting. Callie thinks so." Barrett beamed at Callie.

"Very exciting," Callie said with genuine enthusiasm.

"Try to get your serious friend here to be enthusiastic," Barrett teased.

"I'll work on it," Callie said, and we left.

In the car, Callie hugged me, and kissed me, and congratulated me, until it began to sink in that one of my favorite films was finally going to be made.

"Let's go pick up Elmo and celebrate!" I said.

The road trip back to Las Vegas would have been long and tiresome had it not been for our ongoing speculation about shooting the picture in New York and how much fun we'd have there. We were already talking about how we'd have to teach Elmo what "quiet on the set" meant. I began practicing with him.

"Elmo! Quiet on the set!" I shouted, and he let out a piercing bark several octaves above his normal bark. We jumped involuntarily and then giggled.

"Elmo, come on," I continued, "quiet on the set!" The excited tone in my voice told Elmo something big was coming, and he barked louder. "Elmo!" I reached behind me and took his jowls in my hand to get his attention. "Quiet—" I whispered, and he interrupted with a bark. Callie was convulsed in laughter.

"He's going to need more work, but not in the car, I'm almost deaf," Callie said, and Elmo barked again. She hugged his big thick neck. "Elmo, you're going to be a star!"

Elmo licked Callie on the cheek in a very ungentlemanly manner.

"I can't blame you, Elmo. I've wanted to do that all night." I grinned at Callie.

Callie used an antiseptic wipe to clean her face while I patted Elmo's large head. Success on the horizon made everything okay.

My cell phone rang. A female voice said, "You return at great peril." The line went dead as Callie stared at me.

"Blocked call," I said and repeated the warning the woman had just given me. "I swear that voice sounded like Loomis, the front-desk manager. Why would she be warning us not to come back?"

"How would she have your cell number?" Callie asked. "Wait, she does have your cell! You gave it to her and said don't remove anything or put anything in our room without calling me. She's in a position to know a lot about what goes on there. Maybe she's not trying to scare us, but just trying to save us. Rose is next, Teague. I have to go back there."

"Well, you're not going alone," I said and took her hand, all conversation about the movie put on hold.

Across the Nevada state line, just outside the Las Vegas city limits, a police car pulled up behind us. I was doing eighty-five and reflexively slowed to seventy-five. He flipped on his red lights, signaling for us to pull over.

"Damn!" I said.

"How fast were you going?" Callie asked.

"Ten over," I replied.

I fumed over how much this was going to cost me as he opened his car door and got out. He wasn't overly tall, chunky, with an antiquated crew cut and dark wraparound sunglasses. He wore his gun holster high on his hip like all the cops I'd ever known and clenched his metal ticket book, snapping it against the side of his leg in a statement of aggravation, indicating he might have been tailing me longer than he liked before I realized he was behind me and pulled over.

"Just be careful, Teague. You have a combative square in your chart today."

I was missile locked on his image in my rearview mirror, something about the way his green pants hung. "He's not a cop," I said and dialed 911, handing Callie my cell phone as the man in uniform swaggered toward us.

Callie asked for dispatch. "They're taking forever!" Her voice contained a frantic note. The officer was halfway to the car. Someone came on the line and Callie gave them the squad car number. The officer dropped his pen on the ground ten feet from our car and leaned over to pick it up. Callie listened to the operator. The officer's belt buckle and chest blotted out the landscape and filled our car window. She hung up and repeated almost inaudibly, "Not a Nevada police car. They're sending backup."

He bent down and leaned his head in to see us. "Hello, ladies."

My mind was racing; he could kill us right now. Callie went silent, clenching the armrest with fingers that went white at the knuckles. He asked for my driver's license. I reached into my pocket, making a mental note that my gun was in the console and not accessible, but I had the short-handled fire ax I always carried next to me between my seat and the door. I could swing the door open as if getting out, and then smash it against him, giving me time to grab the ax.

"What did I do, Officer?" I asked flatly.

"Tell you in a minute," he said and went back to his car and picked up the radio, seemingly checking my license. I took my gun out of the console, snapping shut the barrel.

"There's no safety on these, so don't touch it," I warned, sliding it between my seat and the console and putting the edge of Callie's purse over it.

He was back at the window and said, "Ten miles over the speed limit. I'm going to write you a warning." He looked into my eyes. "You ever had a warning before?" And before I could answer, he opened his silver book, wrote something, and ripped the page out, giving me a copy. He sauntered back to his vehicle, and I let a whoosh of air escape from my lungs as I watched him depart. I absently handed the warning to Callie.

"Look at this," Callie whispered.

The police car pulled out and slowly cruised past us.

"It's not a ticket. It says, 'Ring the vault,'" Callie said.

My skin was covered in goose bumps. "I was right; he wasn't a cop. I swear to God he looked like security-asshole-Ted. That jutting chin looked just like Ted."

"He's setting a trap," Callie said.

"What do you mean, a trap?"

"That's all I know."

"Well you know, nobody knows enough! Everybody knows something they can't explain or share or figure out, and it's just not very damned helpful!" I said, losing my cool.

"Being psychic isn't like putting a penny in a gumball machine, Teague. At least not for me. I get what I get. I don't know why or how or when. So stop berating me because I don't have the whole story."

"You're right. I'm sorry. I'm just nervous. Hell, I don't know anything, so you're ahead of me."

"You knew he wasn't a real cop. How did you know that?" Callie asked.

"Green pants. Nevada HP wear blue."

❖

It seemed forever before the red flashing lights lit up the dark night sky and the police backup went by us in the opposite direction. We didn't bother to flag them down. The crisis was long over. We drove slowly back to town, shaken by what had happened and still trying to piece together the puzzle.

"There's a boy porn ring. That much we know, if we can judge from Joey," I said.

"But what does that have to do with Rose? And who's going to such trouble to keep us out of it?" Callie remarked. "We think Mo wanted the ring broken up; Karla doesn't seem to think it exists, and someone in the hotel is making sure the ring stays alive."

"Where does the money from this ring go? I'm sure it's not funneled into the hotel coffers. No one wants that audit nightmare. We need to find out where the money's flowing," I said. "Ring the vault. Just phone?"

"It must be the dealer's ring that gets us into the vault. We need to find a way down into the tunnel. I think the answer's in the tunnel. That's the image I get when I meditate," Callie said.

"Well, walking through the cash room of a big casino without being an employee with security clearance is about like getting into Fort Knox," I reminded her. "While Ted was jotting us a note, it would have been nice if he could have told us how to get to the vault."

"Someone will tell us. They want us there," Callie said quietly.

CHAPTER SIXTEEN

I spoke with Loomis at the front desk as we checked in to tell her we'd been warned not to return and looked into her eyes for a sign that she was the one who had called us on the road. Her expression was impassive, and she said she was delighted that we had chosen the Desert Star for our stay. I told her I wanted security to keep an eye on us and our room, and that I'd let my police contacts know we were back in the hotel. She didn't have to know that my police contact was Wade, and he was in Tulsa, not Las Vegas. Saying his name reminded me to call him. I stepped outside to get reception on my cell phone and to avoid the glass panels in the lobby, and I rang Wade's desk. After a few minutes of describing our situation, I could almost hear his big jaw stiffen.

"Teague, do you really need to check back into that place? Vegas has its share of bad guys."

"Something's happening here, and I think we have to be here to find out what it is."

"Want me to come out?"

"You've got no jurisdiction here," I said.

"Yeah, but I got a hell of a lot of testosterone!"

I grinned at his macho offering. He was a true friend. "Tell you what, keep searching the players for me, and I'll take a rain check on the hormones."

"Don't wait until it's too late; I don't own a black suit. By the way, nobody at the hotel, as far as I can tell, ever worked for the newspaper. Happy?"

"No. But thanks."

❖

I returned to the front desk, where Callie was still waiting for our room keys. She'd requested room 1250, the room we had before.

"You want the same room?" I whispered.

"So we can try to find the source of the videotaping." She turned her head so that no one could hear her as Harem Girl Harriet typed our information into the computer.

Suddenly Ms. Loomis looked over Harriet's shoulder, placed her hand lightly over Harriet's briskly typing fingers, and caused her to pause mid-strike. With a flick of her finger, Loomis pointed to something on the screen, then looking up she said, "I think you'll like the view in room 1248, and housekeeping hasn't cleaned room 1250 yet." Loomis's eyes held mine for just a second too long, making me wonder what she was up to.

She's moved us to a room that doesn't add up to eight, I thought.

"Six," Callie said, reading my mind.

"Thanks for taking a personal interest in our comfort," I said.

"I see Mr. Elmo is still with you." She smiled and began talking a moderate baby talk to him.

In another twenty minutes we were in 1248, had tipped Desert Bellman Bob, tossed off our trip-wrinkled clothes, and flopped back onto the bed.

"Shower," I said, dragging myself away from her. "Got to do it before I pass out. My adrenaline high is starting to ebb." I kissed her quickly and headed for the bathroom, turning on the water and letting it steam up the room, then climbing in and savoring the hot water pulsing across my back and buttocks. Callie's hand reached into the shower and turned the water down to tepid.

"Hot showers zap your strength," she said. "Cool is better."

"No!" I complained as she stepped into the shower with me.

"Hot baths killed off the Roman Empire, cooked their sperm so they couldn't reproduce," she said, placing her hand between my legs.

"Probably saved a lot of women from having to be pregnant in a very dirty and disgusting time," I said, rubbing the soap into my hands and then onto her stomach, shoulders, and back, then turning her away from me so I could gently scratch and rub her soapy back. She leaned into me.

"Now don't you love cool showers?" she said and reached back between my legs.

"I will take a bath in ice water if you will do exactly what you're doing now." She turned to face me and put her cool, sensual body against mine, the water flowing down around us like a waterfall. She kissed me until I was so hot I could have made the water steam from my own body heat, and then focused on one small area of my anatomy, massaging all the tension out of my entire body through that single spot.

"Would you like to finish this in bed?"

"Too late," I moaned, climaxing only minutes into our lovemaking. "I can be harder to get?" I tried to defend myself.

"Really?" she said and resumed where she left off, getting exactly the same results in only slightly more time. I was a limp rag.

"Okay," I breathed. "I am so damned easy it's embarrassing."

Callie grinned, patted my behind in a brisk upbeat way, and hopped out of the shower, her voice trailing. "But you're very sexy, darling."

I stood under the pulsing showerhead, shaking my head in wonder. This woman really had me, literally and psychologically.

I dried off and slid into bed next to Callie, anxious to return the favor. She was sitting up, her shirt off, her glasses propped down on her long, exquisitely shaped nose, reading a book on energy transformation. She fended off my advances by capturing my arms and wrapping them around her waist and continuing to read.

"This is just one more example of your being in control of the relationship instead of its being mutual. This is the second time you've fended me off after making love to me and—"

"I thought we were just having impermanent sex and not a relationship," she tortured me.

"Well, yes, that was the deal, but it has to be two-way impermanent sex," I insisted.

"You keep changing the rules," she said, absently massaging my neck with one hand as she continued to read. I fell asleep before I could complain any further.

❖

Elmo and I awoke several hours later. Outside our room other hotel guests in the hallway were preparing for their vacation sightseeing or their business meetings. The morning paper slid into the room under the door, and Callie bounced out of bed to get it and make me some coffee and find herself a Coke. The front page featured yet another story on Johnathon Burr. The paper said that he was drunk when he fell to his death. I told Callie that I hated to ruin her day, but we needed to pick up where we left off, and that meant a trip to the morgue.

On the drive over, I rang Rose's cell phone. Callie knew exactly what I was up to, and she took the phone away so that she could deliver the message in a more palatable fashion.

"Rose, it's Callie Rivers," she said when Rose answered. "Elliot said Sophia was the one who found Joanie's body. We're on the way to the morgue to see her." There was a long pause while Rose sobbed and attempted to collect herself. "Is it true that your friend Sophia found Joanie dead?" There was apparently an affirmation from the other end of the phone. Then Callie asked if Sophia would talk to her about what she saw when she went to Joanie's house. That must have sent Rose into a nervous state, because Callie begged her not to hang up and told her that we desperately needed to talk to Sophia. The phone went dead.

"Scared girl," I said. And we drove in silence.

The morgue was a strange conglomeration of dead misfits. People who'd arrived in town on a big vacation and had died of a heart attack from too much sex, too much food, or too much excitement; guys who'd overdosed in their hotel rooms; and old folks who'd come to gamble their social security checks, and ten thousand nickels later had keeled over. The guy in charge of the records said many of the bodies went unclaimed. Maybe they were out of touch with family before they showed up here. Maybe their families had decided that their gambling had used up whatever would have covered their burial. Whatever the reasons, the morgue drawers were crowded and the lobby was empty.

Callie talked the skinny, pimply-faced desk jockey into violating at least ten rules by letting us have a look at drawer 137, where Johnathon Burr, aka Joanie Burr, was laid out. The skinny guardian of the dead turned his back to let us slip past him into the morgue and said quietly, "Might as well. No one else has come to see him. Ten minutes."

The morgue room was depressing and freezing cold. The center of the room hosted steel tables on sturdy gurneys, the entire area illuminated by lights that could be lowered over the body during autopsy. Lining the walls were huge steel sinks which I imagined had unspeakable contents dumped down their drains, and beneath the sinks lay floors with permanent dark stains in them. Along two walls were the most recently dead. Drawer number 137 loomed large. I strode over, trying not to show how much this place creeped me out and wanting to get the whole thing over with. I slid the long filing-cabinet-type gray drawer toward me. A dead man's feet emerged with a toe tag and number on it. The tag read Johnathon Burr.

"Must be our friend," I said quietly, as if I thought I might disturb Joanie Burr.

"Can you slide the drawer all the way out, so I can see her face?" Callie asked.

I complied, hoping that I wouldn't get to the end of the drawer and have her tilt forward on me. I slid her out slowly. It was weird to think of being dead and being in a drawer like a pair of socks or kitchen utensils. Her once gorgeously made-up face was now flaccid, gray, and rubbery. It was a face someone once kissed. A face that laughed and ate and drank and now just sagged sadly back against the drawer floor.

"Bruises on her neck," I whispered. I wondered why people whispered around dead people. It was the one time you could shout if you wanted to, but mostly people whispered.

"Check that out." I pointed to a wide expanse of bruising. "Looks like someone with large hands had them around her throat before she 'slipped and fell,'" I said.

"They say she was alone," Callie said.

"Now that's a trick...choking yourself until you slip and fall over dead." I tried to humor her, the morgue being a particularly humorless place. I wondered if guys sat around working on bodies, having a doughnut or candy bar and shooting the shit. Actually, I didn't really want to know.

"She's important enough to be on the ghoul pool list, but not important enough for anyone to claim," Callie said.

"Nobody's talking about the bruising: not the medical examiner, not the police, not the news. Doesn't seem like anyone wants this to be anything more than an accident," I remarked.

I slid the drawer closed and silently said, *Rest in peace, Joanie Burr.* Callie and I walked back out into the lobby. Two gay men were there, obviously distraught.

"His name is Joanie—" the younger man whimpered, and his friend interrupted him.

"His name is Johnathon Burr. We're here from the hotel to have him sent to the mortuary for the funeral."

"Yeah," the skinny kid said, "we got him."

The front door opened and Sophia slipped into the morgue lobby. We glanced at her but made no outward sign of recognition. *So Rose got word to her that we wanted to talk.* Sophia made her way to the ladies' room. We gave it a few beats and then Callie said that she needed to use the ladies' room before we left. We entered the gray metal bathroom where Sophia had her back to the wall facing us as we came in the door.

"Joanie had bruises on her neck. The kind that come from strangulation." Callie cut to the chase.

"Maybe she liked rough sex," Sophia said. "You've got to leave Rose alone. That's what I'm here to tell you. You keep trying to talk to her, and you'll get her killed just like they killed Mo," Sophia said. "You get her killed and I'll have you killed, so help me God." She tried to appear tough, but I could tell from the way her whole body went rigid that she was scared to death.

"Tell us what you know." I ignored her threats. "The three of us are Rose's best chance, and I think you know that or you wouldn't be here."

She paused, perhaps trying to decide if she could trust us. Finally, her voice barely audible, she said, "The porn ring has its roots in the theater. And the theater is a huge moneymaker in its own right. So Karla doesn't want to lose the legit side of the business. One of the boys had sex with Traugh when he was drunk, and Traugh kept mumbling about the church and its money, so the church is in on it. I think that's how they launder the take, but I can't prove it. But you figure this out without Rose."

"Was Joanie alive when you got there?" I asked, surprising her and watching all the blood drain from her face. "Did she tell you who did it?"

"It's hard to be strangled by someone shorter than you are," Sophia said.

The door opened, and a female worker entered. I dove into one of the stalls, Callie washed her hands, and Sophia exited.

Minutes later, safely back in our car, we analyzed the conversation.

"Joanie was killed and Sophia knows who did it, so I'd say Sophia's in danger," Callie said.

"Joanie was a big gal. Who's taller than Joanie?"

"A man, most likely," Callie mused.

"Or another drag queen. Let's go see what our dear, close personal friend Karla has to say about all this," I said, and headed our car in that direction.

❖

Karla greeted Callie and me like an Irish setter who hadn't seen its owners in a month. She literally draped herself over us and gave us big kisses on the cheeks. She kept chucking us under the chin and grinning at us, and saying what a hot little couple we were, and how sexy Callie was. I knew something was up, but I couldn't decide what, until she opened a drawer in the hall table.

"Have a little gift for you," she said. It was a flat, slender clear case housing a DVD. On the cover someone had written in black marker Room 1250 Sex Scene. Callie's and my lovemaking had been reduced to Room 1250 Sex Scene. I asked Karla how she'd gotten the tape. She let out a long sigh and braced herself against the entry table, as if talking to people this stupid was sapping all of her strength.

"Kiddos, this is a town built on money and sex. You got sex going for you, you can get money. You got money, you can get sex. Tapes like this happen a lot, but not in my hotel," she said proudly. "I don't tolerate that stuff. My guests have to feel as safe as if they're stayin' at their mama's house. When Loomis called me and told me what happened, I called the chief of police. He listens to me. Schmuck better listen to me. I got him outta a lot of jams. I told him top priority, get this goddamned tape. So he did."

"Who had it?" I asked.

"Some punk kid who tips the maids to let him in. He rigs hotel rooms and shoots the tape and then blackmails the people, or just sells it on foreign markets. Gotta give him an A for smarts."

"I want to see him, and I want to pursue charges," I said.

"Not part of the deal. Deal is you got your tape back, the kid gets turned into his rich parents—nothin' more. Guys down at the precinct loved this tape." Karla smirked. "Two hot women gettin' it on. Every boy in blue musta had a hard-on."

I was getting red faced I was so mad. Perhaps because I'd been a cop, I figured she could be right—a whole bunch of cops had probably gathered 'round someone's computer screen and watched it again and again, slowing it down, rewinding and shouting. I cared for Callie. I was incensed for Callie. I wanted to kill someone or something for this indignity.

"Keep your shirt on, sugar," Karla said, sensing my anger. "It's sex. We all do it. We all act like we don't do it. We all point and whistle when we see someone else do it. Get over it."

Karla was a lot of things, but she wasn't a fool. *So why did she fork over the disc?* I wondered. *Maybe it's to show us how she controls the police and that it would be useless for us to ever go to them for help. Or maybe it's to make us worry that she's kept a copy and could use it against us if we ever crossed her. Or maybe she's trying to befriend us mob style: she does something for us and we go away and forget everything we've seen.*

"Elliot's here. You know Elliot. He always makes me laugh. You look like you could use a good laugh," Karla said, disrupting my thoughts.

"Elliot, the guy who tried to kill us with the flying dummy?" I said.

"Sweetheart, you think one of us is tryin' to kill ya?" Karla gave me an acidic grin. "If I was tryin' to kill ya, you woulda already been dead. Those kinda things ain't that hard. It's all who you know. Now you need to lighten up; somethin's got your knickers in a twist. The sex tape, huh?"

Callie took my clenched fist, unwrapped my fingers slowly, and laced them in hers. Karla led us into the living room where Elliot had his shoes off and his feet curled up under him like a swami, seated on the couch munching grapes, looking a bit more on the feminine side. He leaned as far forward as his body would allow and extended his hand. We took it in turn as if greeting an elderly Queen Mother. At least we were half right.

"This time you are safe," he said. "I can only drop grapes on your head. We were just dishing Gio." Elliot grinned.

"Gio prays all the time at San Hidalgo. If he's not partying, he's prayin'. Makes you think that whatever happened at the party requires forgiveness, don't it?" Karla burst out laughing at her own joke.

"Well, for my money, nothing happens. The man is lacking in the man department," Elliot said.

"He's got big chalangas!" Karla said slyly.

"Oh honey, he's got his gun, he just don't ever fire it!" Elliot roared.

"Well, not at us!" Karla said, offering her lips to Elliot for a condolence kiss. He complied as joyfully as a politician at a pig-kissing contest.

"Elliot and I love the same flavor ice cream—pissedatgio!" Karla roared over her play on words.

"We came here to talk about Joanie Burr," I said, and the two of them stopped laughing and stared at us. "We think she was murdered. Marks on her neck."

"Joanie was like every other performer in this town: wrong men, wrong meds," Karla said quickly. "One makes you want the other."

"I think she was strangled—by someone taller than she was. How tall was Joanie, Elliot?" Callie asked.

"There was no one taller than Joanie." Elliot teared up. "She was a mountain of a human being." Karla put her arm around Elliot to console him. After a few moments, he pulled himself together and ran his long, slender fingers through his thick brunette and somewhat oily hair, and tossed his head back, jutting out his jaw and striking a pose that seemed to be the trademark of *Boy Review* performers. "You seem far more interested in dead performers than live ones."

"On the contrary, I'm very excited about coming to see you perform," Callie said, and she told him she'd heard wonderful things about his work. Since Callie felt lying was bad Karma, I knew she was referring to all the publicity posted in the hotel lobby, and it made me smile that he was so flattered. She asked him how he'd ended up in the show, a question that seemed to give him the giggles again. He admitted that he'd "auditioned," and he strung out the word, giving it a mischievous little twist. Karla handed Elliot a new drink and then plopped down beside him, putting her hand in his crotch. He jumped, but left her hand there.

He kissed the fingers of her other hand and then stared up at us. "Why are you here?"

"We were invited in?" I suggested, and the two of them burst into laughter again.

"Well, then, out!" Elliot waggled his fingers at us jokingly, as if to say, if we could be so easily summoned, then we could be just as easily dismissed. Then, suddenly, Elliot Traugh noticed the time and jumped up saying he had to run because he had a show to do. Karla blew him a kiss, and he said, "Bless you, darling," as he headed for the door.

I realized that I had only seen Elliot seated on a bar stool or a couch or standing onstage. As he dashed past us and disappeared from sight, I realized that Elliot Traugh was tall.

CHAPTER SEVENTEEN

"Let's drive up to San Hidalgo Chapel. Isn't that where a praying Italian might hang out?" I said.

"If he's smart. Imagine having Elliot and Karla both wanting your chalangas!" Callie giggled. "Take a right," she said, correctly assessing the situation. "I was undoubtedly sent to you to keep you from driving in circles for the majority of your life."

"What makes you think you were sent to me?"

"Because all my parts fit exactly into yours." She pressed herself up against me and kissed my ear.

"You win. I am a disaster. I don't know where I am half the time, and I'll do whatever you want, as long as you just keep kissing me."

"Never say you're a disaster. You're not. And words have power."

❖

We stopped to grab a sandwich and gas up before wending our way through the sandy hillside, away from the bright lights and slightly above the city. On a plateau stood a Spanish mission with adobe arches and a small bell tower overlooking the city below. Early Mass was in progress and the singing could be heard through the huge wooden doors, one of which was ajar. The wind blew the bell rope and our shirts and our hair, and it was a glorious feeling, as if God had moved uptown to escape the cacophonous sounds of the casinos and to hear the birds sing again.

A man walked out of the church, then a woman and her son, and finally two dozen people exited. Mass was over. They stood in the courtyard and waited for the priest, a tall thin man in his black cassock and skullcap. Giovanni was the last to exit the chapel, still bent over, looking prayerfully at the ground. The priest put his hand on Giovanni's shoulder and thanked him for something. Giovanni looked oddly shy and boyish in response, but obviously pleased.

"Weird guy," I remarked. "I mean, contrast Giovanni the prayerful with Giovanni of the ghoul pool. It's like he's two different people."

"Something strange about the priest." Callie's brow furrowed.

"You mean aside from the fact that he wears a dress, never has sex with a woman, and has a cannibalistic desire to eat the body of Christ?" I said, making light of the belief system ingrained in me when I was a child. "Archeologists a hundred thousand years from now are going to have a field day with this set of beliefs."

"I don't know, just the aura around him. I feel like I know him," she said.

"Are we speaking this lifetime?" I asked, as the priest stepped back inside the chapel.

"Don't make fun, Teague, you're distracting me," she said.

"That's my goal, to distract you!" I kissed her neck while Giovanni, oblivious to us, got into his car and drove slowly down the hill.

"Okay, we were fooling around and we missed him!" she said.

It was true; Giovanni was out of sight now. I leaned back in the car seat and felt the wind blow in through the open window. "I was always bad on stakeouts. I couldn't focus."

The double doors swung open again and we spotted Sophia taking her time exiting the church, dipping her hand in the holy water and crossing herself. The priest talked with a parishioner, and Sophia lingered there in the courtyard, watching him complete his duties, and then approached him, smiling and attentive. The two of them laughed and chatted.

"She must have come straight over here," I said. "Like she's afraid if she talks to us, she needs the Last Rites or something?"

"I think she's trying to find out what's going on up here with the money, just like we are."

I was about to suggest we leave so that she wouldn't feel threatened if she spotted us, but then I saw the headstone a hundred yards away from the car. Callie saw it too.

"Maybe it's a cemetery," she whispered. We drove slowly across the dirt and rocks to the old headstone west of the church, and there surrounding it were other flat markers, some of them dating back to the 1800s. "A cemetery next to a building with an *X* on it," Callie said, referring to the map given to her at the casino.

I looked over her shoulder. "Leave it to a Spiritualist. That's not an *X*, it's a cross. This has to be the place." I turned my back to the markers and faced the direction of the hotel. *Two miles? Five miles? How long would a tunnel have to be? And does this mark the location?*

"It does," Callie answered the unspoken question in my head. "Now we have to find the entrance to the tunnel."

❖

I clocked the distance back. Slightly more than five miles and then just a short drive down the Strip to the Desert Star, and the bright lights, and the valet parker with the giant feather in his hat. We were back in the swing of Vegas nightlife, both still trying to decide what the cemetery meant.

"Where's the tunnel entrance? Under a tombstone like a big fake rock used to hide house keys?" I asked flippantly.

My cell phone rang and I stood outside by valet parking to take the call. I mimed to Callie to go on into the bar and order me a drink.

"Hello?" I said loudly into the phone, shouting over the roar of the traffic.

"Teague, it's me, George. I've been on the phone with Jocowitz's counsel, who's a dick. You there?" I assured him that I was. "So they don't want you to do the script. They want to hire someone who's written for Jocowitz before. They'll pay you for the first draft—"

"Then they won't get the story rights," I said sharply. "Tell them they just lost the movie."

"Well, I told them you might agree if you—"

"No!" I nearly shouted. "They don't rip off the idea, have a crony write it, and then fuck up the script. Tell them thanks, no deal, goodbye."

"You sure?"

"I'm sure," I said.

"Makes *my* life easy. Talk to you later." He hung up.

That's always the way it is! Love ya, love your work, love your writing, love to steal your stuff, love to fuck you over, love to pay someone else, who's not as bright but who I know from PS 180 in the Bronx. Fuck Jeremy Jocowitz, I thought. I tried to shake my angry, gloomy mood as I headed back toward the bar. It was more crowded now, and there were several men halfway blocking my view of Callie, who was seated on a bar stool in profile to me talking to an attractive older man with silver hair and a very expensive suit. He looked well groomed in a slick, expensive way, like a mafia type. I strained to see who he was, and what they were doing, when suddenly, I was jostled by a waiter carrying a tray of drinks. We both staggered slightly, and I apologized. When I looked up, the silver-haired man was gone, his bar stool empty, and Callie was talking to the bartender.

"Hi," I said, approaching her. "Who was that?"

"Who was who?"

"The man you were talking to."

"I wasn't talking to anyone," Callie said, and looked at the bartender.

"She's just been talking to me, that's all," the bartender said.

"So you lie, and he swears to it?" I asked sarcastically. Callie looked shocked, and the bartender lifted his eyebrows in reproach and moved on down the bar to less obstreperous patrons. Callie was incensed that I'd called her a liar, and she said, with great seriousness in her voice, that she wouldn't tolerate it.

"Well, Callie, you were talking to a man with gorgeous silver hair and a very expensive suit and jewelry, and I, on the other hand, am out of the room, so I'm just asking what I missed." Callie stared at me like I'd lost my mind. I sat down and she pushed a drink in front of me.

"Apologize," she demanded.

"For what?"

"For the tone of voice you used on me."

"I apologize," I said, somewhat confused.

"And don't do it again! You're angry over your phone call, and you're taking it out on me."

I chose not to respond. She was right, but she was rubbing it in. Callie Rivers would be a very difficult person to live with. Every word received analysis, every joke a sermon, and every remark was infused with a positive or negative implication. Henpecking, men used to call it.

"While we're asking questions, who was on your phone?" she asked, pecking a bit harder.

"My attorney. It's already started. They don't want me to write the script."

"What? It's your story!"

"Doesn't matter. They always want to take it away and give it to a friend, or to someone they owe a deal, or to someone who's won an Academy Award, or to someone who's a big box office hit, or to anyone who's not the person with the idea they like, want to buy, want to steal…whatever."

"I'm so sorry, but listen to me, you're going to get to write it."

"Oh sure, they'll let me do the first draft. Then they thank me, pay me Writer's Guild minimum, and put the script in the trash. Now you've gotten to write, now good-bye." My cell phone rang and I excused myself again to go out into the lobby and seek quiet and better reception.

It was George. "Okay, you scared 'em. My suggestion, however, is stick with no. They're going to be a big fucking pain in the ass if we do this deal. Just let me know."

He hung up and I felt slightly vindicated, but only slightly. These kinds of deals were always a battle, and they left me feeling less than. I took a deep breath, let out some air, and prepared to have a better night. As I reentered the bar, I could see Callie clearly across the room this time, in a corner with the same silver-haired man. He was standing so close to Callie that their bodies were nearly touching—could have been touching. He leaned in to kiss her.

My heart sank into my shoes and my mind flooded with images of L.A. and Robert Isaacs and the way Callie had omitted the fact that she'd been married. Now here was another man, and he'd returned minutes after Callie had denied his existence. He was sharing her airspace as if they were intimate. I was insanely jealous, and on top of that, lying was my hot button. I didn't want to be lied to and I certainly didn't want a relationship with someone who could summon lies so readily. I stood and stared for what seemed like minutes, then I made my way over to the two of them. By the time I got to her, the silver-haired man had left. Callie looked shaken. My heart was broken.

"What the hell was that about?" I asked coldly, flatly. *I knew this entire relationship was too good to be true. Callie is a fantasy. The idea that she would be monogamous is insane, of course!*

"It's okay, Teague, come on." She took me by the hand, and I pulled away. "Come with me. Let's go back to the room."

"I'm not going anywhere with you, Callie. I'm going back to L.A." I turned and walked to the bank of elevators.

I could hear Callie's heels clacking on the floor behind me as she struggled to catch up. "Teague, listen to me, please." She had me by the arm now and I could feel the tears on my cheeks. I pulled away as the elevator doors opened, but she got in with me.

"It's not what you think," Callie said, and the man in the elevator standing next to me looked at her quizzically.

"It's not what I think?" I whirled to face the man, and in true Callie fashion, I aired my pain in public. "If your wife were kissing another man, and then told you that it's not what you think, what would you think?" I asked the stranger riding on our elevator.

The man blinked. "I'd think about divorce."

"Bingo!" I said and the elevator doors opened. I dashed ahead of Callie and opened the hotel room door. Elmo looked fretful, as if he knew the kind of angry energy coming his way.

I grabbed my clothes and began flinging them into suitcases.

"I owe myself this much. I'm not dating straight women and I'm not dating bisexuals. It's called pick a flavor and stick to it! No one should be turned on by the entire planet. Fifty percent of the population should leave you cold. Which fifty percent is entirely up to you, and while you figure that out, I'm out of here!"

Callie grabbed my arms, then my hands, then finally grabbed the suitcase with Herculean might and flung it off the bed and against the wall. "Listen to me! I am not running around on you!"

I froze, staring at Callie. She looked intense, and serious, and in control, like a hero in a movie who has to convince a disbelieving comrade that a bomb is about to explode and they only have minutes to survive. Something about her look and her energy dissipated mine.

"Look, Callie, you don't have to go to this extreme to end our relationship. Really, a simple 'it's not working' will do. I know I've been pushing you, and that's why it's taken you ten weeks—"

"You don't know anything! Listen to me, please. I think he's the man who told Randall Ross that Rose was in danger."

"And what does that have to do with him slathering over you?"

"I knew you wouldn't get it…"

"Get it? You were married, you fool around with older guys, hell, you look straight, I don't know what I was thinking."

"No one understands what I do…"

"Glad you could make it global...cosmic...no one on the planet understands you!"

Callie stared at me for a long moment. "Don't say things you'll regret."

"Is that a threat of some kind?" I asked, and she didn't answer. I could feel silent tears rolling down my cheeks. "I don't know what to say, and I don't know what to think. I just need to get some sleep." I hooked Elmo up and took him downstairs for his walk, hurrying out to intentionally leave Callie behind. I needed some time alone. Elmo padded along in silence, letting me mull things over. Out by the bushes where we always made our nightly stop, I looked up at the stars and said a small prayer: *I don't get it, God. Whatever help you can give me, I would really appreciate. I just need to understand. I just need a little guidance here. Amen.*

Back upstairs, Elmo jumped up on the adjoining double bed and smooshed his face into the pillows. It was his reward for being pent up during the day. I crawled into bed, leaving the TV off, and waited silently. Callie slid in beside me and wrapped her arms around my waist, pressing her cheek against my back and cupping my breasts with her hands. I felt a great sadness wash over me. *What if this is it? What if I can't have this for the rest of my life? Or worse, what if I can have Callie Rivers at some superficial level and then, below that layer is something saved for someone else?* My chest hurt, as if a piece of my heart was being slowly torn away from the whole.

"What are you thinking?" Her voice was soft and quiet in the darkness.

"Just business," I lied, and a burning anger began to kick in to mask the pain. "I checked on the show that Elliot Traugh said he was late for when he dashed out of Karla's house. There was no show at that time, or any time for the next five hours, so Elliot lied—like everyone else in this town. Must be catching."

Callie let go of me, turned over, and moved to the other side of the bed. It was the second time I'd called her a liar.

CHAPTER EIGHTEEN

"Teague, regardless of what you feel or don't feel for me, don't let Rose get killed over it."

"Very dramatic," I said scornfully, locking my suitcase in preparation for loading the Jeep.

"Please." She placed her small hands on my wrists, closed her eyes, and breathed deeply, diminishing my anger. "I'm asking you as a personal favor—don't leave me here alone."

Unfair, I thought. *If anything happens to her now I'm responsible because she asked me to stay and not leave her alone. Does she really believe something will happen? Or is she using me again?* She looked up into my eyes, and with that look of innocence and pleading, Callie Rivers talked me into staying to help finish the case, without ever saying another word. *It's her way of getting me to stay in hopes that my anger will die down and we'll get back together. How can I ever trust her? I've seen her with someone else with my own eyes!* Besides, Callie Rivers was dangerous. She could look at me and get me to do things. Like a horse whisperer, she was able to mentally connect with me and make me move toward her without ever speaking my name. Her look said, "you know you love me, don't leave me." Looks are more dangerous than words. Callie had the ability to control me with a look. I bolted for the door, terrified of being owned in that way, wanting to put distance between the two of us. Not wanting her to—look at me.

❖

Elmo and I spent the day walking the Strip alone. I was thinking about Callie and I was sure he was thinking his legs were way too short for this kind of exercise. "Elmo, I know you love her too but I just don't see how it can work. If she will flirt with a man in a public place, she'll do other things right in front of me and deny she's doing them. That has to be a sign of, at best, a pathological liar. How could someone like me, who has been trained to read people, be so wrong about her? My heart got in the way. That's all I can say for myself. My heart did me in."

Elmo made a series of short, grunting sounds I'd never heard before that sounded a lot like blah, blah, blah. I stared at him. "Are you making fun of me?" He rolled his eyes and went silent, walking more slowly. "Okay, we're both tired," I said less defensively.

❖

We returned from our walk still saddened. Callie barely registered a nod as we came into the room. "Have a good day?" she asked, clearly put out by our having been gone.

"Fine, thanks," I said sullenly. Elmo's dragging ears signaled that he felt the drain on our energies, and he plopped down, pleading for dinner. I started to order room service but decided maybe Callie was right on this one, so instead I reached up on the top shelf of the closet to retrieve the extra cans of Elmo's dog food I had brought with me. My reaching only pushed them farther back onto the shelf, and I had to pull the desk chair over and stand on it to retrieve the elusive chow. That's when I saw the thin black wire and dime-sized lens embedded back in the closet wall. I stood on my toes and leaned into the shelf. I was looking into the back of a pinhole surveillance camera—the lens focused on room 1250.

"Thank you, Ms. Loomis," I said quietly. "This room does have a better view."

"What did you say?" Callie asked.

"Ms. Loomis is trying to tell us something. Take a look. It's like a nanny-cam. Receiver could be a hundred yards away and linked to a box where it could be recorded."

Callie climbed up to have a look. "So who monitors and where are they?"

We both went silent, contemplating that. I finally said, "Just about anybody."

❖

That night, Callie and I went to the theater together. We spoke very little, walking side by side almost like two strangers. I could barely stand to be with her because it reminded me of what I couldn't have. I tried to focus my thoughts away from her and onto the scenery.

With the house lights up full, I could see the theater in all its gay-guy grandeur festooned in red velvet drapes and large gold sconces and lots of paintings on the side walls of young Greek boys in compromising positions. Callie and I took a seat down front, and I ordered a drink. Callie changed my order, whispering to the waiter, "She'll have bottled water." Looking at me she said, "Safer. Who knows where the water comes from and who's touched it?"

"Your regular water will be just fine," I said, letting the waiter know that his orders came from me and letting Callie know that I didn't really care what she thought anymore, and letting myself know that if the regular water killed me that would be just fine. I felt half dead anyway.

The waiter gave it one more beat and said, "Bring you one of each, on the house," and spun in a diplomatic exit, no doubt to tell his friends in the kitchen that there was a dyke fight in row one.

We were extremely early, not sure what to do with ourselves since we were now estranged lovers—I couldn't yet bear the term "ex-lovers." I suggested we go backstage to the dressing rooms and check on Rose Ross. It was as if I thought by locating her often enough we could prevent something bad from happening to her. We inched our way between the tables and up the side steps onto the wings of the stage and down an equipment-littered path along the massive concrete walls.

Twenty feet farther on, I took a wrong turn, headed behind a parallel set of scenery flats, and ended up in a jumble of lighting, ropes, and other stage debris. As I turned around to lead us out, I caught sight of Rose in silhouette. She was apparently rehearsing her entrance, which involved standing on two ropes that hung from the sky. One arm was wrapped around each of the thickly braided colorful ropes and her feet were planted firmly in the clear plastic footholds that jutted from the ropes, creating an unsteady pair of rope stilts that held her a few feet off the ground. Sophia stood slightly below her, giving her guidance and positioning her feet. She smoothed Rose's pale pink leotard, pressing the wrinkles up the leg toward the body of the costume. When their eyes met, Sophia's hands moved quickly down and away, coming to rest on Rose's ankles, and both women froze in a trembling tableau of erotic realization. They slowly came to life when Sophia once again caressed Rose's calves and knees and thighs, then lifted her skirt, and through the thin pink leotard used her thumbs to massage between Rose's legs and rested her cheek on the girl in just that spot to smell her and feel her.

"Now that takes balance," I whispered. We were voyeurs, afraid to move and let them know we were present, and unable not to look—the girl dangling there like a doll in the wind and the older woman having what she could of her. Rose had her head back as Sophia transported her to a place from which she could no longer concentrate, much less stand, and she threatened to faint and fall. Sophia held her with one strong arm around her small thighs as Rose fully understood in that moment that, most likely, she was gay.

Footsteps approached. I panicked on behalf of the lovers, who were oblivious to the sounds of anything but their own soft moaning. I moved to cut off the approaching intruders, and Callie moved toward the lovers to warn them. It was Marlena rounding the corner in her soft slippers.

She looked surprised to see us. "Where are Sophia and Rose? They need to take their places for the curtain. And what are you two doing back here?"

"Wrong turn in trying to get to the greenroom." I shrugged.

Marlena spotted the two women, who by now had begun to realize that they were the center of a gathering.

"She fell," Sophia said with unwavering aplomb, cradling Rose on the floor. "She's a little dizzy, that's all. We'll be there."

"Dizzy wouldn't begin to cover it," I said softly, shooting Callie a look.

Marlena spun on her heel and left, leaving a trail of captivating cologne.

Sophia gave me a look of lasting gratitude. I spun Callie around by her shoulders and retraced our steps back down the littered backstage area, guiding her through the maze of potential mishaps, down the dim corridor, and out into the mezzanine section.

"Odd positions seem to be an aphrodisiac in the theater world," I remarked.

"Walls can be an aphrodisiac too, as I recall from personal experience," Callie said, and I pretended not to hear her.

We took our seats as the small orchestra took up its position and struck up the overture. On the final crescendo and sustain, the chorus line of dozens of men—in black pants, shirts, and ties, looking like male models—dance-kicked out from stage right, arms locked, crossed in front of the footlights, and exited stage left, returning from the wings stage right in an unbroken chain, only this time the men were now women in black jodhpurs, white shirts, and beautifully made-up faces. The audience broke into wild applause and speculated in whispers about how they had managed to make the gender transition in less than thirty seconds while moving. It was quite an opener.

The show's theme was *Things Are Not Always What They Seem,* and in truth, they were not. It was easy to see how Elliot Traugh became the headliner for the show—perhaps not the female good looks, or the long graceful body, but Elliot Traugh had real talent. He was a masterful performer, morphing into characters. He turned his profile to us, facing stage right, a handsome John F. Kennedy embracing a gorgeous woman. As he spun to profile us, facing stage left, we saw that he himself was the beautiful woman and that woman was Marilyn Monroe. When he took his final bow facing the audience, his costume was half and half, and the audience went wild. The illusion was beautifully staged, timed, and executed. Callie and I giggled and oohed and aahed with the rest of the tourists over the show's brilliance. Just as soon as the audience felt comfortable that all the women were in fact men, the real women let them know they'd been fooled again. Gender-bender entertainment was always great when well done, and the *Boy Review* was among the best I'd seen.

After the show, Callie and I made our way backstage to see the performers, as we had promised Elliot Traugh we would. While the makeup room was crowded and noisy, the tone was more businesslike than joyous. An inexplicable pall hung over the air. Sophia was there along with two other biological females who were part of the illusion.

A drag queen wearing a bouffant wig yanked it off her head and ran her hands through her hair, the heavy makeup accenting her voluptuous lips and large brown eyes in stark contrast to her boyish haircut. We recognized her immediately as Marlena.

"You were wonderful," Callie said from the doorway, and Marlena caught sight of us through the large lighted makeup mirror in front of her and did not bother to turn around.

"Thank you," she said like someone used to compliments, while giving us the cold shoulder.

I caught sight of Elliot Traugh and told him what an amazing job he'd done. He arched an eyebrow and smiled at us, as if to say that perhaps we finally understood his importance. He was no mere drag queen.

"I miss Joanie," Marlena said suddenly, lowering her head into her hands, her shoulders shaking slightly as she cried. "She was wonderful!"

"We went to see Joanie. She had bruises on her neck, the kinds of bruises that occur when someone has you by the throat just before you 'slip and fall.' Someone must know what really happened. We need your help," I pleaded.

"This is a private dressing room. Show them out," Elliot ordered, and Sophia jumped to her feet and herded us out of the dressing area.

She followed us for several yards, then leaned in and whispered, "I warned you!" She ran her fingers along the strange symbols dangling from the strands of her necklace and then quickly moved on. I felt strongly that her warning went beyond this moment.

Several other theatergoers had made their way backstage and were hugging and congratulating the cast.

"What's up with the bug necklace? Sophia fingered it like a rosary," I said.

"Scorpions. She had a Stellium in Scorpio around her neck. She's saying she's the one who put the Stellium chart in your suitcase and the article under the lamp and she's the one trying to unravel what's going on," Callie said with great certainty. "Sophia is the Plutonian energy threatening to destroy this secret world."

Chapter Nineteen

I grasped the large brass door knocker in the shape of a cherub's backside and banged its cherubic cheeks up against Karla's front door. As far as I was concerned, we were here to get to the heart of the matter—the hotel's sanctioning a boy porn ring.

An intercom clicked on and Karla's voice asked who was at her door. I apologized for not calling in advance. The door swung open immediately,

"Gio's crying over that fag." Karla grimaced, already steeped in gin. "And I am once again alone. Come in, come in."

I had lost all sympathy for Karla in light of her handling of the sex video, so I canned the small talk, telling Karla we wanted to talk to her about the young boy in our hotel whom we'd rescued. As I described him and the incident, Karla still managed to stay a step ahead of me. "Must be the kid they found near the hotel half dead," she said.

I told her it couldn't be the same kid, although I didn't know whether it was or wasn't; I just didn't want it to be. Karla turned on the TV to a news channel and said the story had been broadcast all day. In minutes, there he was: Joey Winters, the young boy we'd rescued from Sterling Hackett's room. He'd been beaten to a pulp and scooped up off the pavement like roadkill. Callie and I were both in shock. Callie asked Karla if she could use her connections to help find the perpetrator, referencing her unspoken mob ties.

She waved her hand to dismiss us. "Too many kids and too much trouble. I ain't Mothah Teresa. They don't have to, if they don't want to, and they get paid to, don't they?" Karla said and took another shot of her gin and tonic. "Look, honey, sex with young boys has been happenin' since before the Greeks. How do ya think they came up with the Greek position, ya know? Boys are horny little bastards; if they weren't doin' it with some ole guy, they'd be doin' it with each other."

"You know," I said, mentally editing entire paragraphs from my reply in order to avoid shouting at her, "somebody at the hotel told me that there was a sex ring going on." Normally, I didn't shout unsubstantiated evidence at potential criminals, but Karla was pushing all my psychological buttons.

"Listen, chickie, it wasn't my deal. Big shots would fly in and want special services. Mo would get somebody to provide. Pretty soon word got around that if you wanted the hottest young hoofers, stop by the Desert Star Casino. I don't think they had any idea what people would pay. Ya know, Mo and Gio was mob guys, and hookers was hookers, and they didn't bring that much, but here these kids was bringin' a shitload. It got really big, and then some pervert offed one of the boys."

That's what the old newspaper article said. That's what Sophia was trying to tell us. Callie and I exchanged looks.

"Made the papers. Of course, not like it really came down, but cleaned up for citizen consumption, as Mo used to say. After that, I tried to stop it, but Mo wouldn't hear of it. He said the mob would kill him if he tried to break it up. After Mo died it all stopped. Those was the old days. Today, if Hackett had some kid in his room, his own people set it up. What's goin' on now is just the leftovers, ya know? Few clients probably still show up. Most of 'em probably can't get it up. What's a blow job for ten thousand bucks?" She shrugged. "Done it myself."

There was no point in arguing with Karla. Her background led her mind to its present position. She walked over to the bar and poured herself another drink.

"The ring isn't leftover; it's in full swing! Guys come up to a dealer—a dealer with a special ring on his finger—and they put 10K down and give him a number; it's always a number under seventeen, and a boy that age is taken up to the man's room." I paused, breathless, having blurted out my thoughts without editing them.

She turned and stared at us for a long moment and then abruptly laughed. "Now that'd be a trick, wouldn't it? Does the dealer stop dealin' right there and say, 'Sure, number seventeen, right away, sir. Would ya like a pizza with that?'" Karla could not have been more derisive, trying to embarrass me out of the notion of a porn ring happening out in the open, but I was convinced that was why it worked—because it did happen out in the open.

"That's just how they place the order. The delivery time is woven into small talk, stuff like, 'Front desk is so busy, I'll be lucky to get checked in by one a.m.,' or 'Think I'll hit the sack now and call it a day.' The dealer changes shifts right after the order and passes the word to someone in the hotel. We haven't figured out who that is yet," Callie said.

"Well, tell you what, Sherlock, you keep at it and you let me know. 'Cuz the minute I know, they'll be lucky to be fired instead of fired upon." She downed her drink, locked eyes with me, eyes that said she meant every word she was saying. "You think I don't get it. Well, I get it. I've tried to clean up this place from day one; constant battle since Mo died. It ain't worth it to me. Fucked-up boys, dead boys. Those are my choices. I'm done with it. So you have at it."

"And who do you think causes their deaths?" Callie asked.

"The cosmos." She smirked at Callie, and suddenly, the other Karla surfaced, the one who wasn't happy to see anyone, the one who wanted us to get the hell out now. We were on the street in no time.

"She talks in circles. How'd she know it was Hackett who had Joey in his room?"

"Because she owns the hotel?" I asked.

"So, someone at the hotel told Karla that Joey got sent to Hackett's room. Joey was in the same kind of trouble the kid in that old newspaper article was probably in. It makes sense. If the old energy is back, then it brings with it the same old issues," Callie said.

"But it didn't make the papers—that's what was written on our article—yet she said it *did* make the papers." I thought about that. "I guess a cleaned-up version for 'citizen consumption' got printed."

"She also said it was ten thousand for a blow job. How would she know that unless she's seeing the profits from a porn ring?" Callie wrinkled her nose in distaste.

"Like the lady said, done it herself."

❖

Callie insisted we head for the hospital. We might have gotten Joey into a situation that caused him to be beaten. After all, he'd left Hackett's room, but only after the fake vice squad presumably appeared.

How would anyone have seen or known that? There was no one in the hallway, no one in that linen room.

Once we'd made our way to the ICU, I adopted a calm but concerned demeanor with the nursing station.

"We're his aunts from Pittsburgh," I told the nurse.

"He's very ill. Only one of you at a time," the nurse said.

"You go," Callie said, unable to bear looking at him.

A nurse sat beside Joey. He had tubes in him and his face was blackened nearly beyond recognition.

"I'm his aunt," I said to the nurse at this bedside.

"He can't talk," she said.

One look at Joey, and it wasn't hard to pretend to be grieving over him. This kid had been done in, and from the looks of him, who knew if he'd ever get out of this hospital alive.

"Joey, who in the world did this to you, baby?" I exclaimed.

"The police came but he couldn't talk any," the nurse reiterated.

I looked into Joey's eyes and I knew Joey wasn't trying to communicate, because he didn't trust anyone. His eyes connected with mine. I gave him a slow, knowing wink.

"Joey and I have always had a special communication, haven't we, honey? I wish I knew who did this to you. I would box their head for them!" I said like a kindly old aunt.

Joey raised his small, frail hand and brought two fingers together against his thumb, once, then twice and then dropped his hand to the bed, unable to exert any more energy.

"I think he's saying good-bye. He's tired," the nurse said.

"Joey, remember what your other aunt Callie told you. By the time you're eighteen, you're going to meet someone special and your whole life will change for the better, which means, young man, that you will be alive and well at eighteen. So you'd better get out of here." I kissed him on the forehead and left the room.

I stopped by the waiting room and got Callie, who was squirming over the dark energy in the hospital. "People die and don't move on. They wander the corridors, and it just leaves you open to walk-ins and attachments." I apparently gave her an odd look because she added, "Walk-ins and attachments easily access weakened energy fields… that's why drunks and drug addicts and even the terminally ill can have someone take over their bodies."

I raised my hand in the air to signify that I couldn't take any more.

She'd have to save some of her way-out-ness for later. I was depressed over something more tangible—Joey Winters.

"How is he?" she finally brought herself to ask.

"I think we got him beaten up. He talked to us and someone knew," I said.

"Who knew we were talking to Joey?" Callie seemed to be asking the cosmos.

"Maybe the room is bugged," I said. "But then how much more bugged can you get than people videotaping you? Besides, Joey was never in our room."

"Maybe we talked about him after we got back to our room."

"I feel like my freakin' underwear is bugged! Everybody seems to know everything we say or do. Let's go back to the room and take the place apart just to make sure we haven't missed anything."

We drove back across town to the hotel in a depressed state and went up to our room. We clicked open the hotel door and said nothing to Elmo, but merely patted his head. Whoever was listening might think it was merely a maid entering to clean. Carefully, we began looking in drawers, under beds, along window ledges, inside phones, overhead in vents, and finally in the pockets of the clothes we were wearing the night we'd talked to Joey. Elmo watched us with intent interest. We sat down on the edge of the bed, our eyes scanning the room for anything that might have been moved or added, anything we'd missed, any place where a microphone could be concealed.

Elmo sobbed and clawed at his collar, as if scratching at a flea, and suddenly Callie knew. She grabbed a piece of paper and wrote a note to me: *Elmo! They had Elmo for several hours downstairs, and he was with us in the linen closet with Joey!* We both knelt beside him and felt his body everywhere, and then Callie unbuckled his collar. Right where all the dog tags hung and the collar got bulky, someone had sewn on a small directional microphone. I took scissors and started to cut it off but then stopped. I went over to the door and opened it loudly, then closed it as if we were entering and greeted Elmo.

"You know what?" I said out loud. "This hound of mine is starting to have a doggie odor. I think he could use a bath."

"Don't think the spa offers that service," Callie said.

"The tub. He'll love it! Come on, Elmo. Let me take your collar off. It's wet; did you put your head in the shower? I'm going to put it over here to dry." I wrapped the collar up in towels to muffle the sound. I looked at Callie, anger in my eyes, as I dragged the three of us into the bathroom and turned on the shower. "Okay, buddy, we're going to scrub you up and then let you air dry. That should only take a couple of hours with this thick coat." I closed the bathroom door loudly.

"What have we said in front of Elmo since we got him back from the manager's office?"

"Everything! I can't imagine anything we haven't talked about in this room," Callie said. "And if we haven't talked about it here, we've talked about it while we were walking him."

"A directional mike can pick up more than a hundred feet away if it's line of sight," I said.

"Wouldn't his jangling collar and his breathing drown out any conversation?" Callie asked.

"Elmo rests a lot so they've undoubtedly gotten plenty of conversation. They probably have people staked out with gear throughout the hotel, which means someone in Valet Park probably is in on it and they put the receiver into our car so they can hear us around town."

"Could they hear us on the road trip to L.A.?" Callie asked.

"We'd be out of range after about a mile. We'd better check on Rose. Our conversations have probably put her in the same kind of danger Joey encountered," I said.

Callie rang Rose's number. No answer. She rang the theater, and they said she'd taken a few days off and her understudy would be performing tonight.

"So did she take a few days off, or are they going to off her in a few days? That's what we don't know and we've got to find out," I said darkly. "I think we have to use their own surveillance equipment to set a trap for them. We'll need to think about how that trap might work. We can leave that mike muffled for about twenty-four hours and get away with it. They'll think his collar's drying and we just forgot to put it back on him, but after that we'd better have a damned good plan or we're in real trouble and so is Rose Ross."

CHAPTER TWENTY

I should have remembered this," Callie said, slamming shut the book titled *Rules of Rulership*. "The Eighth House includes death and legacies of the grandfather of a woman." She examined the chart again. "But what woman? And who is the grandfather? We need to go see the last place Mo was before he was killed." And with that, Callie took us back to the theater. I'd been in the theater so many times I was starting to get the itch to play a role.

"How do you know that he died in this theater?"

"Randall Ross told me. He said he died of asphyxiation. Some sort of carbon monoxide accident. Of course, the rumor was that he turned the gas on himself."

"How the hell do you get asphyxiated in a room the size of this theater?"

"I don't know," Callie said, looking around the room. Suddenly a small blue light appeared on the theater wall at the farthest point from the stage where we were standing. I glanced up at the projection booth to see if someone was inside, but it was dark. The light moved down the wall and then swung across the room, landing on the opposite wall. Callie's eyes followed it and she took a few steps toward it. Then the light traveled down the wall to the floor and came to rest at the edge of the circular stage next to the metal disk at our feet, as if someone were secretly watching and trying to point something out to us.

"Who the hell's doing this?" I asked.

Callie focused on the light. She sat down suddenly on the polished stage floor and watched the light as one would watch a movie. It flickered and then finally went out.

"He died right here," Callie said and then added, "But that just doesn't feel right."

I looked up at the booth again but couldn't see who the operator was. "We're sitting ducks out here. Let's get going," I whispered, but Callie looked up at me, offered her hand, and pulled me down beside her with exceptional strength. My eyes connected with hers. *Life is short. Why can't she be mine—just mine?*

"I think if Mo were here he'd say that he's haunted by what's going on at his hotel and it has to stop," Callie said.

"Why didn't he stop it when Karla asked him to?"

"I don't know. I'm being told to come back here and see the *Boy Review*," Callie said.

I didn't mention to her that we'd already seen the show once. I just let it ride.

Out of the corner of my eye, I caught sight of a man who looked familiar. I focused on him. He was a short, muscular man in a business suit, a buttoned-up employee crossing the theater aisle apparently on a mission: perhaps checking up on the cleaning crew or checking on supplies for the greenroom or maybe just taking a shortcut somewhere, and then I noticed the lifts. Lifts like the shoes worn by the man who delivered Joey to Sterling Hackett's hotel room. He turned in profile and it was Paco man. Images collided in my brain as if a projector light had illuminated my head: Opening night, Paco in the bar, cut to tight shot of "my friend Paco" bobbing inside the silk pants and grabbing my flesh with his thumb and forefinger. Cut to the same man coming at Callie near the slot machines, Paco in his pocket, his thumb and forefinger nipping at her leg, but this time in his pocket was a knife. Cut to Joey in the hospital, his small, frail hand, thumb and forefinger coming together like—Paco! I jumped up and sprinted toward the man.

"Hey, you!" I shouted. The man turned and looked at the stage, focusing on us for the first time and registering a decidedly startled look. "You know Joey Winters?" I asked and I saw the slightest tensing around his eyes. "Hold it, just a second!" But the man turned and ran. I pursued him as if spring-loaded.

"You beat that kid, didn't you, you sorry-assed sonofabitch!" I tackled him and we both fell to the floor. I rolled him over, pushed his chin skyward with my left hand, and slammed my fist into his Adam's apple with my right. "I should slit your damned throat!"

Callie was standing over us. "Tell us who you work for!" she shouted at him.

He struggled to reach his gun, visible now in its shoulder holster hidden beneath his suit coat. He was strong, and I only had him down due to the element of surprise. I squeezed his jugular vein and cut off blood flow to his brain. "Who hired you to beat up the kid?" I squeezed more tightly and he began to lose consciousness. "Shit!" I jumped up off the guy. "I shouldn't have done that," I said, straightening my clothes and feeling suddenly uneasy about how quickly I could turn violent.

"Why should he wake up feeling fine? Joey doesn't," she said, bitterly cold. Callie's cosmic attitude was apparently put on ice.

"Plus, he ripped your suit." I took a deep breath and tried to make light of it.

I rang Security Guard Roy, the front desk, and the LVPD. Roy arrived first and quickly explained that the man was a longtime lounge performer, beloved by the patrons, and that his behavior was due to having lost his wife. To which I replied, "Bullshit!" The woman from the front desk was none other than the lady who'd tried to comprehend homo-fucking, so I realized my current dilemma was several stratospheres above her comprehension. Her presence actually made me look forward to meeting the Las Vegas police, who arrived within minutes and began asking questions and taking notes. I went through the preliminaries and explained that the man before them had taken a young boy up to a room for sex. That boy was now in the hospital—Joey Winters. One of the officers, a tall, somber fellow, asked if I had evidence or a motive or something that could tie him to the case.

"Get a photo of this guy," I said under my breath to the officer, "and show it to the kid in the hospital. He'll ID him, I'd bet my life on it."

The officer said they'd look into it and after more conversation took Paco man with them. "Call me jaded"—I sagged into a chair—"but they'll prosecute that guy when pigs fly. For all I know those two weren't even cops, or they're cops that Karla has in her pocket." I watched Roy departing and started to laugh. "There's your guy with the headset! Roy! Why didn't I think of that before. Roy is in on it just like Ted and every other security person in this hotel, which means everyone who's guarding us is not only listening but is out to do us in!"

"Good to have clarity," Callie said and almost made me laugh.

❖

That night, we returned to the theater again. This time for the show, because according to Callie, Mo wanted us to see it. There were a lot of remarks I could have made about that, but I chose to remain silent. I wasn't feeling too talkative, much less funny.

The *Boy Review* was one of the few places I could be perfectly comfortable kissing Callie, and now I was no longer kissing Callie, because I still hurt, my feelings were on ice. *Why in hell do I care if she's snuggling up to some old fart at a bar, if she's chosen me to make love with? Why can't I just enjoy the moment and take from it what there is to take? Because I'm hard-wired for fidelity, because I flunked sharing, because she's either all mine or she can go screw whoever she wants and get the hell away from me! I have to shut this out of my mind before I go nuts.*

We were midway through the show, beyond all the high kicks and Marilyn Monroe impressions, and into the full acrobatic review that came just before intermission. It was quite an extravaganza designed to have us heading out to the lobby in a wild, enthusiastic buzz. Boys in tights dangling from high wires, cyclists on wires overhead, acrobats leaping into the air. It was a virtual *Gay du Soleil* and exceptionally well done, cut in time to rhythmic rock music, the strobe lights fluttered disco style, and with each strobe effect, all the men onstage turned into women and back again.

By the time we hit the famous first half finale, the stage was a feast of feathered flight. Graceful birdlike men slashing across the skies, their wings outspread, sending a massive breeze across the audience, choreographed to celestial music that gave everyone chills. It was awe-inspiring. Suddenly, Callie gasped and stiffened in her chair, staring center stage. "Do you see Rose?"

"Rose isn't even on the stage," I said. "She's out of town, remember?"

"We've got to find Rose!" Callie was out of her seat and heading for the lobby. I hurried out after her, catching up with her just past the massive theater doors and into the bright lights on the other side where I worked to get her to find a spot and plant her feet so we could talk.

"Rose Ross was caught in the rope hanging from the scaffolding in the back of the set."

"Rose Ross was caught in a rope onstage?"

"Yes, I saw her," Callie panted.

"Like you saw the other two?"

"Yes, I finally get it," Callie said.

"Well, help me out, because I don't. Start with the guy in the bathtub. Was he real?" I asked.

"He was real, but he was alive at the time that we saw him in the bathtub. He wasn't in the bathtub at that point. It was Mo putting that image, that form there, a man lying in the tub demonstrating that Bruce Singleton was about to drown in water."

"Mo's dead, you told me!"

"Mo was showing me that a man who looks like this is about to die. Of course, I didn't get it, so hours later the guy is found dead. Then the woman at the party who cracked her skull on the terrazzo, I looked for help, and no one seemed to even care. Well, that's because they couldn't see her—Joanie Burr in full costume! It was Mo putting the form of Joanie there, saying someone who physically looks like this, wearing this, is going to die. Sure enough next day, Joanie Burr is dead from having hit her head on the patio, and I didn't get it."

"Mo is talking to you from the grave?"

"Tonight, Mo showed me Rose Ross hanging dead before my eyes. He's saying she's in trouble, big trouble, Teague, and we've got to find her. Within twenty-four hours of my seeing the other two, they were dead."

"Did he give you any clues? She's hanging by a rope, right? From a scaffolding. Maybe there's a big construction site?"

"I'm trying to tune in, but I'm not getting anything."

We went back to our room to determine our battle plan. Elmo was barking at the phone, having discovered that when we picked it up and talked into it, food came to the door.

"Sorry, Elmo, we made a pact not to eat food from room service… too dangerous," I said. As if by magic, there was a knock at the door. We froze. I looked through the peephole. "Room service," I whispered to Callie and stared at Elmo as if he had mentally ordered it up. I opened the door and a waiter sailed in with a tray. "We didn't order anything," I said.

"Compliments of the hotel manager," he said. The tray smelled of hamburgers, and Elmo was already nudging the silver domed cover off to get to them.

"I know you. You're the guy from backstage…" I said.

"Yeah, the one with no name tag. Only now I have it on," he said.

"Rob! How did you get this duty?" Callie asked.

"They switch us around when we first come here so we learn different areas," he said.

"Well, I'd ask for a transfer out of this gig," I said and tipped him.

He'd barely closed the door when Elmo put his paws up on the table in an uncharacteristic show of bad manners.

"Hey, hold on. One day you might meet a nice lady basset, and you don't want to have the manners of a warthog," I warned him.

I pulled the lid off. "Don't they normally put the flowers in a vase beside the plate?"

Callie stared down at the burgers with the single flower lying beside it. "A dead rose," Callie said. "We have to find her right away!"

"Look!" There was a plastic card under the rose. It was a security clearance card. I couldn't believe my eyes. "Why would someone give us that?"

"Someone gave us that to get us through the cashiers' room. So they're either helping us or setting us up," Callie said. "They could have someone waiting there for us to say we stole the card to break into the cashiers' cage. Imagine trying to explain how we got the card."

"Yeah, it arrived with a hamburger we didn't order and was under a dead rose." I sighed.

Elmo dove on the burgers before Callie could get them away from him. I hooked up Elmo as he gulped the last bite.

"Come on, buddy, we'd better take a quick walk. This could be a long night."

I stopped at the front desk because the room service order with the dead rose was presumably compliments of "the manager."

"Is Ms. Loomis in?" I asked.

"Ms. Loomis is gone," the golden woman said and went back to her computer screen.

My body froze. "Gone? For the day, for the week, forever?"

The woman shrugged and gave me a sweet smile.

Joanie was killed after we asked if she would talk to us. Joey Winters was beaten nearly to death for talking to us, and now Rose is missing for talking to us. Have they gotten to Loomis too? And who the hell are these bastards?

CHAPTER TWENTY-ONE

I took my gun on the walk with Callie and Elmo, looping Elmo's long leash around his neck to substitute for his collar. I knew things were heating up. I might not have a sixth sense about much, but I have it about dangerous situations. It was an uneasy feeling, and Elmo seemed to have it too. He glanced up at me, gauging my tension, then hit the bushes fast, aware that we were in a time crunch. The three of us went inside and crossed the casino, where I caught sight of Dealer Brownlee who was there the night the man he called Mr. Emerson bet ten thousand dollars on number fourteen.

"I think we need to talk to that guy. I just think he knows something." Callie nodded toward Brownlee.

One thing was for sure, I couldn't get his face out of my mind, the way it looked when the man bet on number fourteen, like somehow he disapproved or that it was the wrong number. The expression on his face had stuck with me. The number of players around the table was sparse. I pulled some money out of my pocket.

"This gig is costing me a fortune. Every time I want to talk to a dealer, I lose about twenty bucks!" I slid onto the black tufted leather bar stool in front of his table and fooled around in my wallet to delay the transaction.

"Too bad about that young kid that got beaten up out here," I said. The dealer didn't respond, but the woman next to me did.

"Terrible! There's a rumor that he came to the hotel as a male hooker!" the woman said. *I just got lucky. A perfect stranger saying all the things I need said.*

"Can you imagine?" she said in indignation. "And he was only fourteen!"

I looked straight into Brownlee's eyes. *Fourteen, he was only fourteen! I was right! The man bet ten thousand on fourteen. Brownlee knew Mr. Emerson well and most likely got his boys to him in short order, but maybe not that young. Maybe fourteen turned even Brownlee's stomach.* The woman lost her money, cooed over Elmo, and left like an angel, having been planted there to help me.

"So Mr. Emerson and even the famous Sterling Hackett get their chicken from you?" I glanced down at the bird on his pinkie ring. "But this time the chicken was a little too tender even for your taste," I said flatly. "But, of course, you went ahead and sent Joey Winters up there anyway, because business is business, right, Mr. Brownlee?"

"I'll call security," he said.

"And I will turn you over to the FBI so fucking fast it will make your Gambler Boy Name Tag pop off your three-dollar tux! Tell me right now, who has Rose Ross?"

He blinked at the sound of Rose's name.

I put my money down and he slid some chips across the table, putting them on red. The house took my money, and I didn't care. I bet again as he spoke, his lips barely moving. "Get away from my table and don't come back," he threatened.

"Where is Rose Ross?"

"Don't know her."

Another dealer relieved Brownlee on a shift change, allowing Brownlee to escape out through the back of the casino. I was certain there was a camera, or a button, that had allowed him to signal someone and get the brilliantly timed change of dealers just as I was boring in on him. I signaled Callie to follow me, and we tracked Brownlee to the backside of the casino and into an alcove where he was on his cell phone.

"They're asking questions," he told the person on the other end of the phone.

I stepped into his line of sight and pulled my gun and placed it under his chin.

"Hang up," I said quietly, and he made an excuse for having to go.

"That was so fucking stupid. Now I have to do something really unpleasant to you," I said, and he began to beg. "And why should I save you? You were willing to get Joey killed; you're willing to have someone kill Rose Ross; why is it killers are such cowards? All I want to do to you is maybe blow off your hand so you can't work..." and I put the gun into his palm.

"Please, please, listen. You don't know what you're dealing with," he said in an unintentional play on words.

"Who runs the ring?" I demanded.

"People say Mo Black still runs it from the grave. The money from the transactions goes into a small vault in the back of the casino through the tunnel." *So there is a tunnel; Callie was right!* "Everybody says it's the ghost who takes it out. Look, I won't tell anyone about you."

"But you just did. Who was on the phone with you?" I grabbed his cell phone and hit redial, wanting to know who he'd talk to about us. A voice answered saying, "Welcome to the Desert Star Casino. How may I direct your call?'"

"Brownlee wants to talk to her again," I said quickly, taking a fifty-fifty chance it was a her, and I was right. There was a click, and hold, and then Ms. Loomis came on the line. I hung up. "So Loomis is here, on duty, in the hotel and hiding from me, or someone wants me to think she's gone," I said to Brownlee.

"Please just get away from me and leave me out of this. I'm just trying to make a living. Traugh. He knows everything. The Rose girl, she knows too much, is all I hear."

"Who's got her?" I asked.

But Brownlee either didn't know or wasn't telling. Despite my gun pointed at him, he yanked free and ran, apparently having decided that being head-shot was preferable to what awaited someone who squealed on the ring. Elmo growled and lunged after him, but I held the fearless basset in check.

With Elmo in tow, we headed for the theater to find Elliot Traugh.

"I know your legs hurt, Elmo, but we don't have time to take you back to the room," Callie told the hapless hound, and I could have sworn he groaned. We proceeded down the long corridor under the arches and to the theater door. It was unlocked and no one was inside. The stage was empty. I looped Elmo's leash lightly over a stair rail and asked him to wait for us; it was dark in the theater, and I didn't want to trip over him. Callie and I worked our way down the long aisle. A man's voice rang out over the PA system, asking us if he could help us. Callie informed him that we were looking for Elliot Traugh.

"Right here," he said and a single light bulb came on overhead, illuminating an A-frame ladder and Elliot Traugh standing beside it in what I thought was a very clever and dramatic entrance. "My theater wannabe friends," Elliot lightly mocked us.

"Brownlee said you know everything, and I don't think he's referring to the meaning of life."

"You're beginning to bore me," Elliot said.

"How boring would it be if I told you that rumor has it that you killed Joanie Burr?" I said, cutting through his B.S.

"That's the problem with rumors. They're so…rumor-ish."

"Stellium in Scorpio is this hotel's chart," Callie interjected. "A Stellium in Scorpio has great intensity, and the potential for extreme good or evil."

"So which is it?" he asked, and then answered his own question. "Depends on which side of the sod you're on, I suppose. If you're dead, you probably think this place has great potential for evil. Mo Black most likely thinks so."

"Mo committed suicide?" Callie's voice was a question mark.

"That's what Karla told you, didn't she? The truth is that Mo Black and Giovanni were partners in this boy business, and Gio tried to shut it down. Mo threatened to blackmail Gio—not good to be a macho, Italian mafia type who likes boys better than hookers. So, in retaliation, Mo…committed suicide? That doesn't sound right." He paused for dramatic effect. "Or was it that Gio murdered Mo? Or was it that Karla killed Mo? You see the dilemma. Of course, the police could never prove anything. The police in Las Vegas don't try to prove much related to the mafia."

"And why are you telling us all this?" I asked.

"Because like me, the ghost has got you, the ghost has hung you… isn't that what they chant at the ghoul pool gathering?"

"I wouldn't know. I haven't been there," I said.

"Well, to the precise point, Gio and I were lovers once. Then he decided he liked his boys younger and queerer." Traugh looked off in another dark direction of the theater, as if delivering his lines to a different audience, and he raised his voice as if playing to the balcony.

"So, he has them now. Of course, they're dying on him at a great rate, but he has them nonetheless."

"Where's Rose Ross, Elliot?" Callie asked.

"I'm afraid she's offended everyone by befriending someone who's been sharing our little secrets. Sometimes one of the boys can get away with that. All they have to do is fuck their way back into someone's good graces. Unfortunately for girls, there's no road back home. Your friend is in trouble," Traugh said, "and if I were you, I would pray for her." He reached up, clicked his fingers, and disappeared into blackness.

"Where'd he go?"

"Someone else is here," Callie said.

I grabbed her by the arm, swooped up Elmo by his leash, and dragged them both from the theater through a side door into the alley, not wanting to find out who, if anyone, was in the theater besides Elliot. Although as I left, I smelled cologne I recognized but couldn't place.

People on the street were going about their business oblivious to our fears. I suddenly realized, what a brilliant place for a murder. Orchestral tympani, explosives, every sound imaginable could be heard on these stages. Why would anyone think it was anything more than a rehearsal going on?

"He said pray for her. I feel that means she's at the chapel," Callie said.

Still clutching Callie and Elmo, I headed for our car. Outside, leaning up against the wall of the theater, Sophia was apparently awaiting our arrival, because she ran toward us the moment we hit the cement.

"Rose is missing, and I've got to find her. She left me a note saying she was going to meet Gio at the chapel. He wanted her to help him with a fundraiser there, but I phoned and there was no fundraiser, and she didn't come back. That was yesterday."

The three of us circled around to the parking lot and got into the car without exchanging another word. Elmo hunkered down in the backseat, staying firmly on his side of the car, refusing to cuddle up to the distraught stranger beside him. He let out a couple of short, high squeaks, which he only did under extreme stress, clearly indicating to me that he felt things were completely out of control.

"It'll be okay, buddy," I tried to reassure him, but he squeaked again, clearly not believing it.

As we drove, I quizzed Sophia. I was long past the elementary interrogation and was zeroing in on details.

"Who did Joanie Burr say attacked her?" I asked.

"She was dead when I got there," Sophia said.

"Who told you we were in the theater just now?"

"The theater community is pretty tight knit and cautious. We look out for each other—"

"Who?" I demanded tersely.

"I got a call on my cell phone saying you were in the theater," she answered me.

"From who?" I dragged the word out to illustrate my impatience and there was a long pause.

"Elliot," she finally replied.

Callie shot me a look that indicated that it couldn't be Elliot. From the moment he knew we were in the theater, we'd seen his every move—a fact that Sophia could not have known.

"Hey, everybody's fingering Elliot Traugh. Must be an unpopular guy," I said.

"Loomis," she came clean. "Loomis called me."

"Why?" I asked, but Sophia was silent, the wheels in her head turning.

Why would Loomis warn Sophia about anything? Sophia is just an insignificant showgirl, a little fish in a very dangerous big pond.

"How did you know about the Stellium in Scorpio chart and that it was supposed to be sent to Callie if the hotel was in trouble?"

There was a long pause. "Talk or walk," I said, suddenly slamming on the brakes.

"I knew Mo Black's daughter years ago. She gave it to me and she told me what it meant."

Of course! The photo of Mo and his first wife on Karla's mantel. She mentioned he had children from his first marriage.

"So you must have known the daughter pretty well," I probed. Sophia clamped her jaw tightly shut. Conversation over. Even I knew that.

CHAPTER TWENTY-TWO

We pulled the car onto the hilltop road that curved around the bell tower, ending in the dirt parking lot of the chapel. It was dark now and there was no one around. The wind swirled the dirt into the air of the courtyard and snapped the bell rope in strict warning to the penitent. There was no one visible: no priest, no parishioners, and no maintenance people. It was as if God had left for the holidays, leaving the doors open and no one at home. I cracked the car window a quarter of an inch and locked Elmo inside, telling him we'd be back and to stay quiet.

Leading the way into the darkened chapel, I found a light switch and turned on the overhead lights, waiting expectantly for someone to enter from the side doors behind the altar and ask what we needed. No one appeared. We walked to the front of the chapel and I crossed myself out of habit as I passed the crucifix.

"Never cross yourself. That's why the world is so burdened. A Grand Cross in astrology is the intersection of four squares, and people with that in their chart feel crucified and—" Callie lectured.

"Not in front of the children," I said in reference to Sophia.

"Are you an astrologer?" Sophia asked. "Are you able to tell if two people are meant for each other?" she added, without waiting for an answer.

"Apparently not," I said snidely in reference to Callie and me.

"There are compatibility charts," Callie replied.

"Okay, let's put the stars on hold a minute." I signaled them to be quiet as I gently slid the vestry door open. Inside, the long table with its green and gold embroidered cloth was bare, the chalice having been washed and stored. A large Bible rested on one end, next to the tall cabinet doors that housed the priests' vestments. As Callie walked across the room to examine a picture of an older priest in red vestments, she tripped on the long oriental runner that ran the length of the room. I caught her and bent over to pull the rug back into place. Under the rug was a circular design with smaller concentric circles. The smallest circle appeared to contain only a beautiful inlaid pattern, but on closer inspection that inlay was an embedded handle so perfectly carved that it lay as flat as the wood surface of the floor. I wondered aloud what it could be as I lifted it slowly and turned it to the right. From behind me, the wall with the priest's portrait slid back like a pocket door, revealing a narrow opening. So beautifully crafted was the seam that concealed the door, no one would ever, in a million years, have suspected the paneling of parting.

I made the decision that Callie and I would investigate while Sophia stood guard. If we didn't return in twenty minutes, she was to call the police. If anyone appeared, she was to shout for us. I commanded her to leave the wall open and not to move the floor handle at all. I didn't want to chance her not being able to figure out how to get us out.

Leaving her as the guard was a calculated risk. She could be one of them, whoever "them" was, but unguarded, the door could be closed by anyone wanting to entomb us. A voice in me said it would be safer to leave Callie guarding the door and take Sophia with me, but I'd let Callie go to her apartment without me after we first met, and she was kidnapped. I had decided then and there that she would always stay with me. *The irony is that after this investigation is over, she won't be with me anyway.*

I pushed that thought out of my mind and took Callie's hand and pulled her behind me into the darkened space. I stood still for a moment smelling the musty, but not unpleasant, odor of damp earth, and I thought perhaps a hint of wine, or maybe my mind wanted to believe I was in an old wine cellar rather than something more insidious. Our eyes were growing accustomed to the dark. Ahead of us, the walls seemed to narrow down the long passageway, making the journey feel claustrophobic from the outset. We walked nervously, having no flashlight, only our hands to run along the earth-packed walls that ended who knew where. Fifty feet farther, an earthen wall rose up in front of us—the end of whatever tunnel someone had dug and then abandoned.

Maybe it had been an unfinished escape route for someone years before. Maybe it had been a hiding place for people being pursued. Maybe they had intended to line the walls and use it for storage. Whatever the intent, work was aborted and there was nothing there.

"Are you sure?" Callie whispered. "I just feel like there's more."

I was on my knees rubbing my hands across the dirt floor and up the side of the walls. Aside from the uneven earth, packed hard over centuries, this place held nothing. Fifteen minutes later, I led Callie back out, arriving in no time at the entrance to the vestry room. To my great relief the door was still open, and we walked out into the brightly lit room blinking like Punxsutawney Phil in search of his shadow. I whispered Sophia's name, but there was no answer. I spoke her name in a more normal voice. No response. We quickly exited into the chapel and called to her. Nothing. I was beginning to panic. Had someone taken her too? We walked briskly to the courtyard heading to our car. Under the windshield wiper was a note written on church stationery that said, *Got a call and had to leave. I'll be in touch.*

"What did she mean she had to leave? Did she spread wings and fly? There's no way out of here unless she drove, and we've got the car. Unless someone picked her up. Maybe she called someone and they came and got her. That would be fairly rude, since we were depending on her to make sure that we didn't end up locked in that tunnel," I said.

"Where would she get church stationery?" Callie examined the note. "I didn't see any church offices open."

I took a look at Elmo. His hackles were up and he was panting and drooling a little. "Judging from Elmo's condition, someone took her," I said. "Maybe she heard them coming and maybe she led them away from us before they took her. Otherwise, they would have enclosed us in that tunnel and let us rot."

"You're right." Callie looked at Elmo. "Who was it, Elmo?" she asked him, only unlike other people, she expected an answer.

"He says a big woman came and took her," Callie said.

"Elmo is talking to you?"

"The way animals talk—with mental pictures."

"A big woman? All women are big to a dog with four-inch legs," I said.

"He says he doesn't talk to you much, that you do most of the talking."

"Yeah, well, maybe that's because he can't talk with his mouth full—"

"Unkind," she said to me. "She doesn't mean it, Elmo," she assured my hound.

I pulled out my gun and told Callie to stay close. We walked around the grounds checking to see if there was another entrance to the building or a cellar or any place where Rose Ross and Sophia might be.

My cell phone rang and we jumped reflexively. I grabbed it as if to choke it into silence on this eerie night. It was Wade, in Tulsa, and he spoke loudly as if he thought I were deaf. "You still alive out there? Can you hear me? Listen, Tee, tell beautiful hello for me. She still with you or did she dump you?"

"Would you get to it, Wade?" I said irritably, since he'd pressed my Callie breakup hot button.

"Excuse meee, I'm bein' paid so much for this, I almost forgot to mind my own business. I got some info for you, hotshot. Mo Black, the dead guy? Well, his kid works at the hotel." My mind raced as Wade filled me in on the details. "That all mean somethin'?" Wade finally asked.

"Thanks, Wade, I'll get back to you," I said, and hung up as he was saying, "Tell me what the hell it means."

"He said Sophia did get the Stellium in Scorpio from Mo Black's daughter, Barbara Black, who married a guy named Loomis."

"So Manager Barbara Loomis is Mo Black's daughter!" Callie said.

"Loomis was married for a couple of years when she was younger, to a guy who worked at the newspaper, name of Pappagallo. Loomis's daughter is Sophia Pappagallo, which makes Sophia Mo Black's granddaughter," I said.

"She's either in the middle of what's going on, or someone has her *because* of what's going on. I would guess she knows something she shouldn't," Callie said.

"So that's why Loomis is calling Sophia; she's calling her daughter," I said.

"A woman in the middle of things…like the chart said. Sophia put the Stellium in Scorpio in your luggage, which meant to our mysterious surveillance squad that she was talking, and someone wants to put an end to that. You remember when I told you there's a Sabian Symbol for every degree of the zodiac on the Ascendant? In this case, the Sabian Symbol said 'an exotic bird listening and then talking.' Sophia's overheard something, listening, maybe to her grandfather, or her mother, and now she's talking, and that has put her in danger."

"How do you know the Sabian Symbol is talking about Sophia?"

"The Sabian Symbol is an exotic bird—*pappagallo* is Italian for 'parrot,'" Callie said.

The church bell rang, and I whirled around to see a young acolyte in his white tunic pulling slowly on the rope. I asked him if he'd seen a young woman moments before near our car.

"No, señora, no ha pasado nadie por acá."

A few cars were kicking up dust on the road and several Hispanic women were walking toward the compound over the hill. I checked my watch. It was time for evening Mass.

It was at that moment that a soft, kind voice spoke from behind us. "Welcome to Saint Hidalgo. I am Father Ramon. You must be new to the area or perhaps you are just visiting." His English was laced with just the hint of a Spanish accent.

"Just visiting." I smiled at the young priest as Callie backed away from him, much as if he were a snake oil salesman.

"Come in, welcome. Mass will be taking place in only a few minutes."

"We have to—" I began my excuses to avoid putting Callie in a traditional church, but she interrupted me to say that we'd be delighted to attend. I looked at her as if she were possessed, as she walked toward the chapel doors.

"We're searching for a missing girl. Two missing girls, Father. Rose Ross and Sophia Pappagallo. Sophia comes here to Mass," I said, looking for a reaction.

"How long have they been missing?" he asked.

"One for several days, the other more recently," I said.

"Come inside. We will pray for their safe return." He looked saddened.

"Thank you," Callie said.

"You getting religion?" I said under my breath.

"Prayer is always good," she said. "The priest…there's something familiar about him…his mannerisms. I know him."

"Well, he's too young to have been here when the hotel was built, so you must know him from another lifetime," I goaded her.

❖

Mass began with the traditional prayers. *Glória Patri, et Filio, et Spiritui Sancto* rang throughout the chapel as the young priest adhered to a lot of the old Latin, apparently ignoring the Vatican II dictates. It reminded me of my childhood as I accompanied my grandmother to Mass each Sunday and dutifully learned to pronounce the Latin words that I didn't understand, loving the way my leather-bound missal felt in my hands and admiring the gold leafing on the page edges and the colorful ribbons that hung from the top of the book, allowing me to mark various pages: the place for my name in the front, and information about my family. It made religion personal and beautiful, and I liked shaking hands with the priest at the door afterward.

The priest gave a five-minute homily on the importance of tithing, which felt a lot like a fundraiser telethon and took a little more away from my spiritual experience, but he did interject a short but heartfelt prayer for the safe return of Rose and Sophia. Then, we were at the point of communion. In theory, I couldn't take communion, being officially Episcopalian now and not Roman Catholic, but for my money, God didn't care, and I decided I would line up at the altar rail. Callie saw me rise and tried to pull me back onto the pew. The idea of my drinking wine from a chalice from which twenty strangers had drunk was enough to send her head into a Linda Blair spin. I could read it in her eyes without ever getting the dialogue from her lips. I almost giggled at the frantic look. I leaned over and whispered, "I won't drink the wine; don't worry. But you're not kissing me anymore, so what do you care?"

"I care about your health," she said.

I got in line behind a man bent over in prayer as he proceeded to the altar rail. I knelt and gazed up at the crucifix, saying a prayer for the world, and my family, and especially Callie and for myself. The priest came by with the bread and placed it in my hand, making the sign of the cross. I closed my eyes and said another prayer as the acolyte rang the bell. Moments later the priest came down the row again, this time with the chalice, and I crossed my arms over my chest, signaling that I would not drink, but would take only the blessing. As he raised his right hand to bless me, I glanced up. The light caught the ring on his pinkie finger and I saw the bird, as clearly as a brand put there by the heavens, a rooster—a cock! I stared into his face, trying to conceal my shock at the horrible revelation. *The priest has the ring! The same ring the dealers at the hotel have! What in the world is he doing with that ring on?*

I hurried back to the pew and slid in beside Callie as she whispered her disapproval. I interrupted, "The priest is wearing the ring!"

She turned fully toward me in shock. "Are you sure?"

"I'm absolutely positive," I said. "Get in line at the door and shake his hand. You'll see it."

❖

The greetings at the door didn't take long. We were fifth in line. He took my right hand in his and then folded his left hand over the top of mine in a warm and comforting gesture. I bowed my head as if in respect when, in fact, I was getting one more look at the ring and giving Callie a chance to see it too.

As we walked slowly toward the car, like any normal churchgoers, Callie breathed, "The priest is in on it."

"Can't be," I said.

"Why not?" she replied.

I wanted to say because priests were good, and they were men of God, and they were carefully selected, and they were trained, and they were the men I trusted from my childhood, but I knew that was the idealist, the child, the Believer in me rationalizing.

"There just has to be another answer," I said.

"You'd better find it, then," Callie said sadly. "The ring is the marker. You said it yourself. It's how they know who can order the boys for them. Who would know more young boys than a priest? Brownlee goes through Loomis, so she'll know what room they go to; that's what I'm getting. Then Loomis has to contact someone who knows the boys."

"She gets them from the theater. She doesn't call the priest, for God's sake. Jesus, I don't want her to be calling the priest!" I said like some disillusioned child.

Chapter Twenty-three

Callie and I wandered across the lobby of the Desert Star, deep in thought. I was still troubled over the sight of a priest wearing that ring. I was also fixated on the money that Giovanni said went to the ghost.

Suddenly Callie stopped as if something had beamed in on her at that exact second. "The bogus cop who handed us the ticket said ring the vault. But we don't know which ring. I doubt they all have rings that open the vault. Then you said that Sophia was fingering her Scorpion necklace like a rosary, like she was in church. The Eighth House is the house of death. The cemetery is where they place the dead. Maybe she was trying to tell us that the priest's ring is the one that matters. It's the one that opens the vault," she said.

"Okay, how can you deduce that from that?" I stared at her.

"I don't know, I just do. I didn't say I was right."

"The priest comes to the casino?" I asked, incredulous.

"No, the vault is in the church," Callie said with surety.

"The church spooks me out. I don't want to go there until you have something more concrete than a crazy string of deductions."

We walked across the lobby toward the elevators. To my left through the arches I could see Karla sitting at a table in the bar. I pointed her out to Callie, and we headed in that direction. An older, attractive woman was leaning over, bracing herself with her hands on the edge of the table, and whispering in Karla's ear, making her laugh. On closer inspection, the woman was none other than Manager Barbara Loomis. Karla was having a private chat with her stepdaughter, and Loomis seemed to be in an excellent mood for a woman whose daughter was missing—but then, maybe she didn't know it yet. Upon spotting us, Ms. Loomis waved. "Mr. Elmo!" she said jovially. "Are you enjoying the Strip?"

"If the Strip were a sirloin, he'd love it," I joked. "Good to see you again, Karla!"

She raised her glass in an exaggerated but mute hello.

"The front desk told us you no longer work here," I said to Loomis.

Loomis looked at Karla and registered mock surprise. "Is there something you haven't told me?" she asked Karla, who made a derisive sound that dismissed the entire staff as uninformed.

"Well, good. Now that I know I still have a job, I will go do it and leave you to talk to the guests," Loomis crooned.

"And what questions do you have for me today?" Karla tilted her head like a large bird. "Because you never come just to talk; you always have questions."

"We're writers," I said. "Nosy by nature, inquisitive by occupation."

"You might be a writer, but you're also an ex-cop," Karla said smoothly and then turned to Callie. "And you're the psychic who did the hotel ceiling. I knew it from the first day I met you. You two don't think I've stayed alive in this town by bein' stupid, do you? I got more people feedin' me information than NASA. Don't forget that, huh?" She gave me a penetrating stare and held her empty glass in the air.

A waiter nearly vaulted over the top of the bar to get to her as quickly as possible. It was obvious that as the deceased boss's main squeeze, she held sway.

Callie leaned in and spoke softly. "Karla, Rose Ross is missing, and now, her friend Sophia is missing too. Who would know something about that?"

"How the hell would I know?"

"You know every important person in this town, and you know who is most likely to have taken those girls," Callie said.

"Listen, cutie." Karla's voice was cutting. "This is a town of high stakes. You come here, you roll the dice. You get in the way of the game, and somebody removes you from play. It's a big boy's town. The women know that, the ones who make it."

"What if someone were so naïve that she didn't know she was

causing trouble, or getting in the way of the game, wouldn't there be room to save that person?" Callie asked.

"The only person I care about savin' is me." Karla laughed. There was a brief moment when I thought she might say something more, but instead she rose from her chair unsteadily. I moved to help her, but she jerked her arm away as if she wanted nothing more to do with us either mentally or physically. We watched her, drink in hand, stagger across the lobby, acknowledging employees with a nod or a wave, like royalty, heading for her waiting limo.

As Karla's limo pulled away, Callie approached the front desk and leaned over to talk discreetly to Loomis.

❖

"What did you say to her?" I asked when Callie rejoined me and we headed for the elevators.

"I told her that we know that Mo Black is her father and that Sophia is her daughter and that Sophia is missing. I told her we can't help unless she points us in the right direction, that we need some serious guidance. We don't know who to trust."

"What did she say?"

"She couldn't have said less if she were a figure in the wax museum," Callie said and sounded discouraged.

Callie, Elmo, and I entered our room and all three of us plopped into bed. I missed touching Callie more than I missed anything I could ever remember. I cuddled up to her, wrapping my arms around her soft middle, trying to forget that we had no future together beyond this trip. I missed her too much to care. Callie hesitated a moment and then embraced me. We both felt the electricity between us, but we tried to act as if nothing unusual was happening.

"Feels like a dead end," Callie said.

"Us or the case?" I asked and she ignored my remark. "Maybe it's just a momentary pause. Let's entertain ourselves." I produced the DVD I'd taken from her suitcase. "I think we should look on the bright side—we would never have a sex video of ourselves otherwise."

"You can't be serious." Callie was shocked.

"Aren't you just a little bit curious? It could be sexy, interesting, educational."

"When I think about it, I think of someone invading our privacy, violating us. I don't see it as sexy."

"We should see it, if for no other reason than everyone else in this city has seen it."

"No, we shouldn't. Our lovemaking will just be reduced to those images, the way the camera caught us, not the way the cosmos sees us."

"But now that we're not lovers, we don't have to worry about the way the cosmos sees us, do we?" I verbally jabbed at her. *Besides, how can I not look at it! How will we know how badly we've been violated unless we see what half the hotel and the entire Vegas police force have seen?*

She crossed her arms and stared at me.

"If you care for me at all, you won't look at it, and you will destroy it," Callie said emphatically, interrupting my mental monologue. "It's negative energy. It's the product of someone's sick, stalking mind. Why would you ever want to see it? It's not sexy. No one captures our love but us," she said. That last sentence was a window opening, a small crack through which we might reach out to one another again. I stared at Callie Rivers knowing this DVD represented a leap from the fork of a twenty-foot tree into the arms of a lover, a lover's fire walk, a blindfolded trip over hot coals, the consummate moment of trust, and I could tell I only had seconds to make the decision.

"Have you ever seen those wedding rings, where the bride's half fits exactly into the groom's half, making a whole?" I asked, and then suddenly, I snapped the DVD in two over my knee and handed her half. "I think I'll have my half framed." I grinned.

She stared at me for a long moment. "You're wonderful," she said, and pulled me down onto the bed and kissed me so passionately that I knew for certain I'd made a brilliant split-second decision. "You're an odd combination, Ms. Richfield the honorable vigilante."

"Vigilante's a good word," I said.

"Is that what happened, you were a vigilante?" Her tone made me believe she already knew what had happened when I was a cop but wanted to hear it from me.

"It wasn't so much what happened, it's what I knew could happen," I said.

Callie watched my body tense and my mind race. "Say it out loud," she urged.

"Two men kidnapped a woman to rape her at knifepoint. She jumped out of a car doing eighty miles an hour to save herself and hit the road face first. The highway tore most of her face off. In court, her attackers got off because they hadn't yet raped her, and the judge said it was her decision to jump. A woman was cut up so badly that she looked like hamburger meat from the waist down, and she begged paramedics to let her die. She did die and her murderer got twenty years, paroled in six. When men invented the scales of justice, they tilted them in their favor. I would kill someone rather than waste taxpayer dollars on a system that sucks. If justice is random and one guy gets three years for raping, torturing, and murdering a young girl, and another guy gets twenty-three years for having marijuana in his possession, then my justice is just as valid as theirs. And my justice would come quick and early and would most likely land me in jail. So that's why I quit. So there you are. You don't know everything about me either."

Callie tightened her arms around me. "Yes, I do."

"I'm too angry to be a good cop. For all my joking around, Callie, I'm pretty angry."

"Really?" she said. I ducked my head. "Stop being angry," Callie said sweetly with her mouth curled into a slight smile, and she slid her hands up under my shirt and held my breasts. "I'm going to help you wipe away that anger."

"It might take more than one session," I said darkly.

"I anticipate that," she said, kissing me and watching the tension fall from my shoulders and the anger dissolve into lust.

At that moment, I decided to trust again. The silver-haired man weighed on me. The image of him so close to Callie tormented me, but one thing I knew: I could choose to trust, or I could choose to distrust. The choice was entirely mine. The feelings would be entirely mine. The experience would be mine. I would not let it take away my love for her.

This time our lovemaking was evenly paced. We were savoring one another like a pleasure too long withheld. Her kisses were slow and warm and full. I let myself go, completely dissolving into her, not caring if there was a moment's breath after this moment, so long as I had her now. I marveled at how quickly she turned me into a river of wanting and seemed only to want to swim endlessly in me. When I was so wet I thought I would drift away, we slid into that mutual number that is so intimate that there's no deeper intimacy one can ask. With eyes closed and every other pleasure point pulsing and open, we were in one another simultaneously, not knowing up from down, inside from outside, where I began and she ended. We brought each other to climax and lay bathed in each other's sweet smells and wet longings.

"I can't live without you," I confessed.

"What made you decide to trust me?" she asked, stroking my hair.

"Maybe I just wanted great, impermanent sex with you and chose to ignore the other," I said, trying to recover my bravado after such an unguarded statement about loving her.

"I don't think so. You couldn't make love with that kind of emotion if you were reserving a piece of yourself. You trusted me," Callie said.

"I know." I put my head on her chest. "I just want to so much. I love you."

"I love you too, Teague. In fact, I'm *in* love with you, which is far more serious," she whispered and kissed me.

Did I hear that? I thought beneath the sensual warmth of her mouth. *Did she really say she was in love with me? What does that mean? Does it mean the same for Callie Rivers as it means for regular people? Does it mean she's mine in an ordinary sense or just in some cosmic mumbo-jumbo sense?*

"It means whatever you want it to mean," she said, smiling at me.

CHAPTER TWENTY-FOUR

I don't know what awakened me. I think it was the sobbing sound Elmo made. I glanced at him, and the hair on his back was standing up. I looked across the room to see what he was upset about and there at the foot of the bed was a man, the silver-haired man from the bar. I gasped so loudly that I almost choked, and I grabbed Callie's hand, but she was already sitting straight up in bed, having apparently seen him first. How long he was there, I don't know, but it felt like minutes. *Is he going to rob us or kill us? I've got to get my gun.* I reached for it on the bedside table, but Callie's grip on my arm steadied me; it seemed to be telling me not to move and we would be fine. She never took her eyes off him. His eyes bored into hers as if some form of silent communication was passing between them, and then he slowly faded away before our eyes.

"Jessuzzzchrist!" I shouted, once he was gone. "Did you see that? Did you fucking see that? What was that? Omigod, what was that?"

"Just energy from the other side. He came to deliver a message," she said.

Elmo let out a long, sustained, violin-like shriek, and the ridge of hair that ran all the way up his long back stood up even taller in a terrified salute.

"Well, I don't like messages brought to my room like that!" I sank back in mental and physical exhaustion, my heart pounding. "What the hell was it?"

"Mo Black," Callie said.

"This is freaking me out! He's dead!"

"He's trying to tell me something but I haven't gotten it yet."

"So does that mean he'll keep coming back?"

"I don't know. I'm always so pleased when good spirits try to help," she said.

"Oh, me too," I said with shaky sarcasm. "So, this was the man in the bar…the energy you were trying to feel?"

"Yes," she replied. "This is what I couldn't explain, because you wouldn't believe me."

"You've got that right. I'm not even sure I believe it now! The only thing I like is knowing he's not someone you're coming on to," I said. "So from that perspective, I'm wild about him."

"Randall Ross was as terrified as you—probably more so when Mo Black appeared to him."

"Why didn't you tell me the whole story up front?" I complained.

"That I was hired by a man who saw Mo Black's ghost and wanted me to follow up on the ghost's message about someone trying to murder his daughter and—"

"Okay, you make a good point," I said. "I can't stay in this room right now!" I flipped on all the lights and threw on some sweatpants. Callie followed suit. I grabbed my wallet and my room keys, then took a look at Elmo, who had shoved his head under the pillow and was sobbing.

"Come on, buddy, I won't leave you here alone. You're coming with us." Elmo leapt off the bed, obviously anxious to get the hell out of Dodge. Callie stopped me at the door long enough to give me a comforting kiss and to remind me that she loved me. I was still in shock.

"So do you see these…apparitions all the time?"

"No, only when I really need information badly. You're surprised that I see ghosts, but you saw him too."

"Holy shit, you're right! I don't want to see ghosts!"

"Then you won't. You'll subconsciously block their energy. If you're not open to them, they won't appear."

"I'm closed. Totally closed," I said. "When did you figure out that you could talk to them?"

"Everyone can talk to them, but most everyone gets freaked like you, and when you're freaked, you can't talk to the people you know here on earth, much less to them. I learned not to be afraid of them when I was young. There was a spiritualists' church in this little town where I grew up. It was a bakery really, but behind the bakery, there was a big room, and that's where the owner, a wild-haired lady with a wonderful face, held her meetings. People would speak in tongues, and sing, and levitate—or at least try. Most of the time they couldn't." Callie laughed. "Mom would go and she'd sit for hours and listen. I'd get bored and slip into the bakery to see if there were any buns left. One night, while I was in there, I saw a lot of flour had been left on one of the big cutting boards. I heard this kind of shuffling sound like a hand brushing off a countertop, or maybe shoes brushing across the floor, and then the flour on the cutting board parted, as if a finger were drawing in it, and it wrote, 'Hello.' I couldn't believe my eyes. I was so young. I gasped in delight, and then giggled. So it wrote 'Hello, Callie!' "

"Are you kidding?"

"I swear. I was hooked. I couldn't wait to go to the meetings and slip back into the bakery and wait to hear from this spirit. Sometimes it didn't write, and then I would think it wasn't there, but it was teaching me to be attuned to the cold rush of air, the sounds, even the smells sometimes. It was teaching me to know when someone from the other side was present."

"You're creeping me out," I admitted.

Callie laughed. "Sometimes it just did tricks, like knocking a pan off the counter to make a big noise and get me into trouble. Someone would pop in from the chapel and tell me to be quiet because I was disturbing the spirits. I wanted to say the spirits are disturbing me! Anyway, one day, this spirit materialized, and it was very faint, but I recognized her as my grandmother. Of course, I didn't ever know my grandmother, so how did I know her…but I did. Then she wrote 'Bye' in the flour, and I didn't feel she was there anymore. I guess my lessons were over or she was needed elsewhere."

I had no doubt Callie was telling me the truth. It was simply that her truth was so far afield from what I had been taught growing up and what I had experienced in my life, that I could not have felt more off balance emotionally. One day I was going about my business writing screenplays, and the next I'd met this amazingly gorgeous, psychic woman, about whom I was crazy, and while I was trying to sort out our relationship, I learned that she saw ghosts—routinely, since childhood—and thought nothing of it! The good news, however, was that she wasn't kissing silver-haired guys in hotel bars. As if she knew what I was thinking, Callie whispered, "I'll never lie to you, Teague."

"Thank you," I said and then thought about the ghost again. "What does he want?"

"He wants us to go to the chapel."

"In the middle of the night?" I fretted, and Elmo moaned, but Callie was already headed out the door.

❖

The doorman watched us leave, and I suspected him of calling someone and having us followed. Frankly, I suspected everyone in this hotel of something. It was a full moon, and Sheik Skippy brought the car around in just minutes. I gave it the once-over to make sure whoever had bugged Elmo's collar hadn't done a similar job on our car. Then I hopped in on the driver's side, tipped Skip, dodging his hat with the four-foot plume, and drove us out of the circular drive toward the mountains. I watched the doorman in my rearview mirror opening another car door, waggling his large purple feather aside, and offering his hand to assist the passenger from the car. *Why is it that we decide exactly in which location it's okay to wear a four-foot feather on your hat?* I thought to myself. *It's okay at the circus, it's okay at the royal palace, it's okay at the entrance to the Desert Star Casino, but it's not okay at the Pentagon, the symphony, or church.*

"You think about social customs a lot, don't you?" Callie said out of the blue, as if wired into my head.

"Yeah, I guess so. Everything seems so arbitrary."

"Like?"

"It's like that tribe, let's say they're in New Guinea, where their culture demands that a young boy lose his virginity to his uncle as a matter of custom. If the uncle doesn't sleep with his nephew, well then, he hasn't done his duty. So you don't sleep with your nephew in New Guinea and you get ostracized, and then you do sleep with your nephew in New Mexico and you get jailed. I'm not taking a moral stance here, I'm just saying…"

"What are you saying?"

"I'm saying it all makes no sense. I'm wondering if, in a thousand years, a man and woman sleeping together will be an absolutely shocking event because the world will be run by lesbians who've obtained their children through cloning that dates back to some DNA-

Sourdough-Starter-Kit. Then with my luck, I'll come back as one of the guys, and I'll still be on the wrong side of the fence."

"Do you wish you were straight?"

I took her small hand in mine. "Not unless you like straight men."

"We've been all through that," she said.

❖

We pulled slowly into the empty chapel parking area. The night was still, the wind still; the cacophony of distant automobile horns drifted past us in that hollow way the night air carries sound. I shut the lights off and rolled to a stop, leaving the car very near the chapel doors in case we needed to make a quick exit. I told Elmo to stay inside, keep the doors locked, and not to make a sound, we'd be right back. I took my gun out of the console and tucked it into the waistband of my jeans.

"Take it out of your pants!" Callie ordered. "Just carry it. I don't want you to blow your ass off," she added, her stress starting to show.

"Saving it for you." I grinned.

We got out of the car and pushed the chapel door open, letting our eyes grow accustomed to the dark. I made no move to turn the lights on. After a few moments, hand in hand, we made our way down the dark aisle to the vestry door. It too was open as if this church were the most trusting place on earth. We looked around; no one seemed to be within earshot of us. The wall was ajar. I gave Callie a look that said "someone must be here." I peeked inside into total darkness. If someone was here, they were taking the same dead-end path we had taken before.

We moved slowly and quietly down the long dirt corridor, feeling our way again and instinctively knowing not to make a sound. As I felt we were about to see the wall before us, something fluttered in the distance ahead of us, the edge of something, maybe the wing of a large bat. I put my hand up as a signal to stop and stay back against the wall. There it was: a man. A man in a brown cape and a skullcap, blending into the earthen walls. *A priest, of course,* I thought. *But doing what?* The priest reached to his right at a spot on the wall about shoulder height and pressed his palm against it. The wall slid back slightly, revealing another wall with a box in it. The priest slid the ring off his little finger and placed the flat bas-relief side of it onto a reverse engraving that was apparently created to interlock with the ring. He slid his forefinger into the ring, using it like a ratchet, and turned the ring ninety degrees to the left. A small door swung open, the size of a safe deposit drawer. The priest reached in and removed a stack of cash, put it in his robe, shut the door, and reset the combination on the lock with his ring, then put the ring back on his pinkie finger. It dawned on me that the tunnel was in the direction of the hotel and that the hotel probably connected uphill and underground with the church.

"Didn't know it was the church's money, Father," I said, startling the priest and upsetting Callie, who'd been pulling on my arm, trying desperately to get me to exit this place, but there was something about a priest slipping around in the dead of night taking money from some unknown source that made me lose common sense.

"Who dares enter here?" he whispered, fearful, I was certain, that he had been discovered. "How dare you desecrate the house of God? Be gone!"

Without waiting for an answer, he swung back his cape and pulled a knife from his cassock, lunging at us. I couldn't see well enough to shoot. Plus I was fearful the dirt walls might be covering rock, and a bullet could ricochet, hitting us.

I pushed Callie back and swung my arms wildly, trying to make myself an erratic target. He used his cape like a matador, gracefully swinging it and twirling the edge in front of me, concealing momentarily the knife's blade and then allowing it suddenly to slice out at me. The priest was deadly graceful, ducking and turning and swirling, but I managed to snag the end of his cape as it whipped by my eyes, and I circled it over his arm as it came at me again, binding him up in his own cloth. I bit into his wrist, holding his other arm at bay. The knife clattered to the floor, and Callie scrambled for it as the priest threw me to the dirt and put his hands around my neck. My mind flashed to Joanie Burr and the marks on her neck. Had the priest killed her too? *Not the priest,* I prayed.

"Come near me, and I will choke the life from her!" he shouted at Callie, who now had the knife firmly in hand. I was gasping and weakening, knowing I had only seconds to do something. Overcoming the instinct to push him away from me, I tucked my chin to my chest as tightly as I could, trying not to panic as it made my breathing even harder. I reached behind my head with my right hand, grasped the fingers of his left hand, pulled them backward as far as I could, pinning his left forearm with mine while I broke his fingers. The sound of the bones snapping was a relief. He howled and let go. Callie ran forward and drove the knife into his side, not hesitating, as I might have, to attack the Cloth. As he lay on the floor, I knocked him unconscious with a kick to the head and pulled the ring from the little finger of his right hand, and we both ran back to the end of the corridor. He roused himself, recovering quickly. The small space ahead of us was already beginning to close. I pushed Callie through and nearly crawled over her in my attempt to avoid the slamming wall that caught the heel of my shoe.

"That was close!" I panted as we ran to the car and made our escape.

Neither of us spoke. I was in shock over what had just happened. As we sped away, I dialed Wade and asked him to check with the diocese on a Father Ramon, a priest who had just tried to kill us. After I hung up, I just sat and caught my breath for a moment.

"We've got to create a story that will turn them against each other and bring them all to one place, so we can finally see who the hell is behind this," I said.

"There's too many of them for that, but maybe you'll get the ringleader," Callie said quietly.

Chapter Twenty-five

Back in the relative safety of our room, I uncovered Elmo's dog collar with the hidden microphone still attached. "Here you go, buddy. You're all nice and clean and I forgot to put your collar back on! There." I slipped his collar over his head and gave him a pat. I glanced at Callie as if to say this was the moment for setting the trap.

"Why in hell did that priest try to kill us?" I asked.

"I have no idea. Maybe he's the one hiding Mo. Priests have kept secrets for centuries and have often hidden fugitives around the world."

"I just can't believe it. You're psychic. How come you didn't know?" I asked.

"Mixed signals, I guess. Randall telling me he was dead, then Karla saying he was dead. She could be in on it, double-crossing her partners."

"Well, if this note is for real, then Mo Black's not dead and he's been playing everyone for a sucker for years. He's getting most of the cash and maybe splitting it with someone who fronts for him, and he makes everyone else believe he's dead. So someone in this group of players has betrayed all the rest of them."

"Let me see the letter." Callie leaned over my shoulder for timing purposes to stare at nothing. "It could be a trap. I mean, maybe this letter was written by hotel employees who are in on this thing, and we'd be walking into an ambush if we head down that tunnel."

"Only one way to find out. I'm guessing the tunnel is on the other side of the cashiers' cage. We've got to get through there first. We need uniforms like the employees."

❖

Thirty minutes later, with Elmo safely in his cage, we left the room and headed for the hotel laundry where I told the supervisor I was picking up dry cleaning for Brownlee. The laundry supervisor made a quick call while I held my breath, then almost instantly he received permission to give us two white shirts, a vest, and pants. As he disappeared back into the laundry to retrieve the items, Callie told me not to worry about getting her a complete outfit because it would look terrible and she wasn't wearing anyone's clothing.

"They never get sweat out of clothes," she fretted. "It's sweat that grows bacteria. You're just wearing someone else's disease. I would never wear it. If you put a blue light on those pants, you would jump out a window before you'd put them on," she continued.

"Thanks for sharing," I whispered. "This whole deal is too easy. Way too easy."

"Someone's helping us get where they want us to go," Callie said in a chipper tone as if we were about to attend a family reunion. "We just have to believe we have higher protection than they do."

"Yeah, well, you might want to give your highest contact up there a little heads up that we're gonna need all they've got."

Back in our room, I put the outfit on and asked Callie to cover her blond hair with a hat. In any other location, a person might stand out in a hat, but Vegas was full of people wearing odd gear. Before leaving, I tossed Elmo a large chew bone and I gave Callie her final instructions, aware that people were probably listening via Elmo's mike. "Okay, the secret to success is in boldly acting and looking like we belong. Never slink or creep or slip around. Walk like you own the place and that it's your God-given right to go back to the cashiers' cage and open the door and walk through it. People are like animals; they sense when you're feeling like you're doing something you shouldn't be doing. Take big direct strides. Focus on the cashiers' cage door."

We left Elmo and the microphone behind as we headed out the door.

"So they should know exactly where we're headed now," Callie said, out of earshot of the microphone.

"Right," I replied. "If they want to meet us, this will do it. I didn't bring my gun. I was afraid it would set off metal detectors or something in the cash room and everything would come to a halt. So we're unarmed."

"Well, let's put it more positively," Callie said. "We don't have conventional weapons."

❖

Out on the casino floor, Callie followed close behind me as if she were my invited guest. I knew there were cameras trained on us, but I never looked up or made any attempt to shield myself from them, because that too would have drawn attention. I used the security clearance card on the electronic eye next to the cashiers' cage door and it let us in without a hitch. We moved through the cashiers' room, without looking or pausing, and exited through a smaller back door, which opened onto a paved concrete tunnel that stretched out long and dark before us. Hotel golf carts were parked to our right, and I jumped in. Callie got in beside me. I cranked the key, aware that there was no turning back now. I drove into the darkness, a slight glow from ground lights illuminating the road. After more than a mile, the road turned right, then left, and then rose steadily. I warned Callie to hang on to the overhead bar. After a few minutes, we started up an incline that rose several hundred feet in the air.

"Stop!" Callie ordered. I stopped abruptly and set the brake. Ahead, in the wall of the tunnel, was a polished metal door with an entrance key pad beside it.

"This could be a service entrance; we're not at the end of the tunnel yet," I warned.

"This is where we're supposed to go," she said.

"How do you know—" But my words were broken by the blue iridescent light I'd seen on the theater wall that now hovered above the floor next to the door. I didn't have time to ask Callie who or what the light was; in fact, I didn't really want to know. If we were being followed by friendly spirits, fine. I just hoped they were armed.

We got out of the cart and walked up to the entrance, aware of the eerie echo our feet made on the cold cement. No sound emanated from the other side of the door. The flat electronic key pad turned out to be something more complex. In the center was a tiny image of a bird with its clawed foot raised in the air. From my pocket, I took the priest's ring, its gold surface as hard as painted steel. Placing the bas-relief bird image against the wall plate's identical reverse image, I put my index finger through the ring to use my hand as a ratchet. The doors swooshed open rapidly, startling us. We forced ourselves to step forward rather than back, and the doors swished shut behind us. We were standing inside a small theater in the round, where perhaps a hundred people could gather. It was awe-inspiring in its attention to detail, which was visible even in the dim light, almost a replica of the large theater used in the *Boy Review,* but this theater felt private, personal, and secretive—a magician's room, where one could become intimate with trickery. In the center was a forty-foot polished silver disk made up of circles within circles. It appeared to be a brilliantly engineered stage upon which countless breathtaking illusions had been performed. So dramatic was the stage's design that I nearly missed the young woman standing in a corner, a rope around her neck, looking terrified and exhausted—Rose exactly as Mo had depicted her. I made a move to free her as a voice emerged from the eerie darkness.

"And so it happens exactly as we planned." Karla stepped toward us out of the darkness, surprising us. "I don't know what your game is, but Mo Black is dead. I buried him myself," she said without a trace of her gun moll façade.

"You've lost your accent," I remarked.

"It's a town of loss: lost innocence, lost virginity, lost lives. An accent is a small thing to lose," she said, and despite fearing what was in store for us, for a fleeting second, I pitied her because she saw the world in terms of losses and not gains.

"Why do you want us here?" Callie asked bravely.

"It ties up loose ends." Karla smiled at Rose. "I have to get rid of Sophia, who has a pathetic plan to avenge her grandfather's death and clean up his hotel. We tried to warn her by threatening her little girlfriend, but then Rose had already involved you, and unfortunately, the two of you don't know when to mind your own business."

Suddenly the door behind her opened and Giovanni came into the room. He looked sleepy and drugged and not sure why he'd been summoned. He seemed confused when he saw all of us standing there.

"How did they get in here?" he asked.

"I led them here! I even instructed the laundry to give them a uniform to wear so they would think it was difficult and that they were clever. You're in my world, not yours," Karla said. "We have to clean up our mess, Gio. It's gone on long enough."

"Does that mean killing your own grandchild, Karla?" I asked.

"Step-grandchild. Hardly a relative at all," Karla said. "It's Loomis I hate to upset, but we'll all mourn together and then perhaps name our new restaurant the Sophia in her honor."

"So you control the porn ring through the hotel, and Gio controls the ring of men who finger the boys and get them to the rooms—"

"I make certain that the money is there for the ghost," Giovanni interrupted, blinking into the dim light.

"There is no ghost in this instance, Giovanni," I corrected gently.

"The Holy Ghost," he said. "I get money to the Holy Ghost, and I atone."

"For what do you atone, Giovanni?" Callie asked.

Giovanni looked like a man who had left his body, his spirit in too much pain to stay confined in the flesh. "I speak to God about many things, and I help God build his church, and his school, and his hospital, and I pay for the children to have a place to play, and God forgives me when I have to do certain things." He looked at Rose, who trembled. Tears filled his eyes. "Mo wanted to stop the ring." Giovanni broke down in tears. "But you killed him," he said almost inaudibly.

All heads turned to behold Karla, gun in hand, staring at Giovanni, her demeanor cool as ice.

"You're such a pussy," she said. "We've talked about that. You'd rather be with boys than girls. Now for me, that's a little distasteful, because I was supposed to be your girlfriend. My price for being your lover without the loving is that the boy ring and the money from the ring continue. I don't care how many perverts come here to do whatever they want to do, as long as no one tells and everyone pays. Ahh, but someone told, didn't you, Rose? And now I have to go behind everyone and clean up the mess, as usual."

Suddenly the door on the opposite side of the small theater opened and standing before us was Father Ramon, his pants and shirt recognizable but the rest of his garb removed. His side was bleeding through the bandages where Callie had stabbed him, and his broken fingers were swollen.

"Father, why are you here? You must leave! What's happened to your hand? You're injured!" Giovanni said. "Please, Father, leave here now."

"You silly fool!" Karla laughed.

"I absolve you of all your sins, dear Giovanni." Father Ramon made the sign of the cross over Giovanni and then he put his hand to his priestly face and pulled the skin away, stretching it from his head like the loose skin of a chicken. The edges began to tear at his cheekbones and separate from his skull, and the rubbery material fell to the floor. "Tah-dah!" he shrieked with theatrical flourish.

I drew back, shaken by the totality of the illusion. I had knelt before Father Ramon and looked up into his dark brown eyes and had no idea I was staring at Elliot Traugh. It was a chilling transformation. The *Boy Review* quick-change master had played his greatest role. Giovanni looked like he might pass out, and he doubled over racked in sobs.

"There, there, poor Gio. The lover you spurned has had the last laugh. But you mustn't blame yourself for being duped." Elliot spoke with mock sympathy. "I studied to be a priest for several years. I just found the role too limiting. But my knowledge of the character made it easy to convince the old priest before he died that I'd been sent to train under him."

Karla put her arm around Elliot, apparently proud of her dear friend.

"The day you dashed out of Karla's house to get to your performance, you weren't going to the theater, you were going to Mass where you perform as a priest," I said. "So you, Karla, force your step-daughter, Loomis, to contact you when a client hits the casino floor, and Gio procures the young boys for them. But Sophia found out about the boy porn ring from her mother and some of her theater pals, and she encouraged Joanie Burr to go with her to the police because younger and younger boys were being hurt. To keep Sophia in line, and Joanie quiet, Rose was placed on the ghoul pool list and Joanie Burr was killed," I said.

"You're such a busy little bee." Karla smacked me with the butt of her gun, splitting the side of my head right above the temple. I screamed and Callie winced, sending me a look that said "stop talking," but I refused to shut up.

"Elliot had a lot to protect: the theater that made millions each year and was a nice source of young boys that the hotel needed for the boy porn ring, which in turn was the source of the cash that flowed to the church and its pseudopriest. If the theater, the hotel, or the church was threatened, one of you would step in. Bruce was using Karla to get control of the theater so you, Elliot, had to arrange that fatal dip in the desert, since I doubt even Karla would have had the heart to off yet another lover."

"Karla has always put business before pleasure. The two of us like money. We call our spending a result of the 'fuck fund,' which is far more reliable in its returns than the stock market, since the dick goes up more often than the Dow." Elliot Traugh smiled at his clever remark and then quickly changed his expression to one of regret. "But, Karla, my dear, I'm afraid our fun has come to an end."

Marlena stepped out from the darkness and into view, dragging Sophia at gunpoint. Rose gasped and begged Marlena to let her go. Marlena replied in her rich, deep voice, "I don't think so, sweetie. Drop the gun, Karla."

"Do something, Elliot!" Karla pleaded as she let the weapon slip from her hand. Elliot did. He gave Marlena a long kiss on her even longer neck.

I was trying to stay focused on getting us out of this mess, but I couldn't help but be amazed.

"Surprised?" Marlena asked the room at large. "Certainly you don't think I wanted that corpulent old queen over there as my lover?"

This was apparently sad news for Giovanni, who, having been betrayed by his priest and now by his lover, begged Marlena not to say those things.

"You son of a bitch!" Karla screamed and charged Elliot, but Marlena knocked her backward with one blow of her long, gloved hand. That movement sent Marlena's distinctive cologne wafting across the room, and I knew it was she who had been in the theater with Elliot, plotting and planning.

"Everyone seems so out of sorts!" Marlena said. "We have paid the ultimate price for ownership of this theater and control of the church coffers: me having to go down on an old Italian goat, and Elliot having to kiss up to a viper. The theater is going to be signed over to us in a document dated a year ago. Gio will continue to help us operate the hotel, and I will run the theater, and Elliot will run the church, so the only purely expendable member of our disparate band is…you, Karla."

"No, please!" Giovanni begged. "Marlena, you mustn't do this!"

"I think we're going to have a carbon monoxide accident, much like Mo's. These crazy backup generators just weren't vented properly, and sometimes when you try to create a fog effect the vent hose just"—with a gloved hand, Marlena yanked the hose loose from the side of the wall—"comes loose!" And I now understood how Mo could have been killed in a theater by carbon monoxide gas. He was killed in this very small and private theater.

"I think the police will discover that all of you were in the private theater asking Gio to demonstrate how the special effects work, and because poor, dear Gio was self-medicating and couldn't operate the controls, he asked Karla to do it! And instead of hitting the fog controls, Karla accidentally hit the generator start button." Elliot yanked Karla viciously by the hair toward the control box, grabbed her hand, and used it to punch the button on the wall, breaking the button's plastic seal and Karla's hand simultaneously. The generator and Karla roared in unison; I suspected Karla's pain was not in her hand but in her heart. She had been betrayed yet again, and one had only to look at her hardened expression to know this was a woman who despised betrayal.

Elliot tossed Marlena a knife and ordered her to cut the rope binding Rose. He instructed Rose and Sophia to lie beside the large silver disk that formed the stage as it began to rotate slowly and fog seeped out from under the disk. Generator exhaust fumes containing carbon monoxide began to fill the room. I knew we had only a few minutes, and I looked over at Callie to determine who to attack first when Sophia flung her body onto Rose, crying that she loved her and distracting everyone for an instant. That was our break. Elliot pushed Karla down to the floor alongside the girls, but Karla, fueled by anger and regret, got a grip on Elliot's leg with her good hand and toppled him to the floor. Sophia and Rose attacked him as Marlena took aim at them. Giovanni shouted a warning that Marlena was going to kill them, and Callie and I tackled her. Callie got the knife out of Marlena's hand while I wrestled Marlena for the gun, attempting to keep the barrel pointed away from everyone and up at the ceiling.

So many bodies slammed up against one another and wrestled for control of weapons that it looked like a World Wrestling Federation SmackDown. I caught a glimpse of Sophia giving Elliot a decidedly vicious whack to the head just as Marlena overpowered me and got control of the gun. She pointed it at Callie. "Everyone, attention! Stop!" On her face was a wild, triumphant smile.

She turned to Elliot. "Are you all right, my darling?"

He jumped to his feet and grabbed me by the throat. It appeared that in seconds, all of us would die, if not from a gun or knife, then surely from the carbon monoxide that was already making the air toxic.

Out of the corner of my eye, I saw Callie focus on the disk, squinting, her hands out to her sides as if she were saying one final prayer.

And then, as if by magic, the disk began to turn even faster and spin hypnotically. A thicker fog seeped out from under it, and the center of the disk separated from its outer edge and pushed up from the underworld to reveal a figure beneath it. A smoky, amorphous image.

"Look!" Callie said loudly.

"What the hell?" Elliot breathed and loosened his grip on my throat.

The substance began to take form, as if the smoke were being coalesced and poured into the shape of a person: a silver-haired man wearing expensive black pants and a black suit jacket and a black fedora. He stood there staring at us.

"Holy Mary Mother of God, it's Mo!" Giovanni gasped.

"Mo!" Karla said quietly.

Marlena stared at him and shook from her shoulders to her shoes, and her gun clattered to the floor. Mo stared at all of us, and then he vanished in the same way he'd appeared…into thin air. Karla retrieved Marlena's gun, took aim with her one good hand, and fired at Elliot Traugh, killing him on the spot.

It was a showstopper. Elliot Traugh, master of disguise, performer extraordinaire, a star of the *Boy Review,* appeared to be dead at the hands of his friend and confidante. The enormity of the event even took its toll on Karla, as she let the gun dangle from her hand. She looked defeated and lonely and betrayed. Giovanni put his arm around her as Callie turned off the generator and opened the theater doors.

Sophia was up and dialing the police, and her mom, and the few employees whom she knew to be on the right side of the hotel's business. Before I knew it, the stage was covered in crime tape and cops, hotel staffers, and hospital paramedics.

"Who's who?" the cop shouted.

"Arrest her," Sophia ordered, pointing to Marlena, who was sobbing over Elliot Traugh's body. "And I have an entire list of hotel staff you'll need to arrest: look for Brownlee, the security team—"

"And who are you?" the officer interrupted.

"I'm Mo Black's granddaughter. This is my hotel." Sophia sent Karla a look that clearly said this was the new deal if she and Giovanni didn't want to end up in jail.

"That true?" The cop looked at Karla.

"Family arrangement," Karla said, and the cop focused on what Sophia wanted done.

"Sophia was afraid that if she told you what was going on…well, exactly what just happened would happen," Rose said.

"Drew it to her," I said to Callie.

Barbara Loomis burst into the theater and flung herself on Sophia and hugged Rose, showing emotion for the first time since I'd met her, telling the two girls how frightened she'd been and how they would no longer have to look over their shoulder in fear every minute. Loomis caught sight of us and came over with the girls to thank us for stepping in and saving their lives. It was a veritable love-fest as each of them kissed us and thanked us. We watched them retreat, arms around each other in a grateful group hug, joyful their travails were over.

"So you think Rose will live with Sophia?" I asked.

"Maybe. There seems to be a cosmic connection," she said.

"Did you actually summon Mo?"

"Did it blow your mind?" Callie grinned.

"Hell, yes."

"Well, sorry to disappoint you, but despite all my beliefs, I still haven't mastered the summoning of spirits on cue."

"So he just showed up?" I asked and Callie smiled.

Across the room, Sophia was looking up at the dark technical booth. "The theater has always had the ability to present holographic imagery. The walls were painted black at one time," she explained to the police officer. "Mo, my grandfather, bought the laser equipment years ago. Let's see, the light source must have come from in here, because there's nothing down on the stage." She led the police officer up the steps to the booth. “Frankly, I didn’t know there was any holographic film of my grandfather.”

“So who do you think ran the equipment?” the cop asked.

Sophia stood perfectly still, staring at the empty room. “There is no equipment,” she said.

“Then how does this hologram thing happen?” he asked.

“It doesn’t,” she said softly.

❖

I turned back to Callie. “Is this one of those ‘body-in-the-bathtub, there but not there, the bakery with your grandmother writing in the flour, the dead are creating illusions’ kind of thing?”

“Maybe death is an illusion,” Callie said quietly and I shook my head like Elmo when he doesn’t want to think about something too hard.

I could see the Las Vegas police putting crime tape across the stage and beginning their interviews. I was certain they’d be in a quandary as to how to book Mo Black’s widow and Giovanni, one of the richest mafia types in town. *They’ll be searching the books, and their collective shorts, for misdemeanors and extenuating circumstances,* I thought to myself and grinned. Off to one side of the theater, Rose had joined Sophia and was kissing her with a passion born of relief and wanting. Callie and I stood back and watched the entire scene as everyone busied themselves unraveling the story.

“Stellium in Scorpio…it unearthed everything and brought it into the open. On the negative side, the hidden secrets and lies, on the positive side, hidden love, and in this case, it was all for the good. Energy retrieved,” Callie said, quite pleased with the way things had turned out, and she took my hand and kissed me.

CHAPTER TWENTY-SIX

That night in our room, Callie and I breathed a sigh of relief. For the first time, I felt like we were alone, not being watched by anyone but each other—and Elmo, who had watched us nonstop until he was certain we were safe. He was now lying on his back about to go to sleep.

"So you don't think I listen," I said to the exhausted basset. "Well, I'm sorry. Go ahead and tell me something. I'm all ears, just like you." I smirked and paused, dutifully waiting for an answer.

Elmo sniffed loudly and Callie giggled. "What?" I asked.

"He said you're still talking—not listening." I must have looked hurt because Callie added, "It's okay. I told him that you just aren't able to hear him yet, but that you will."

"How do you know I will?"

"Because you don't know it, but you're getting more in tune with things around you."

"Speaking of things around me," I said, "I want you around me. I want to live with you."

"Remind me again why we need to settle this right now?" She cuddled up to me.

"For a very practical reason. You've made me afraid of the dark. I don't want weird guys materializing on me in the middle of the night, and you not there to tell them to hit the road. Elmo absolutely chatters if I don't let him sleep with a pillow over his head now. He hates spooks."

I rolled her over playfully and jumped on her, rumpling her and wrestling her and ultimately diving into lovemaking with her. I was relaxed now. I felt the auditioning was over. I had admitted I was wild about her and she had, in an unguarded moment, told me she was in love with me. There was nothing left to be said, only things left to be done. She needed to be with me. Why she couldn't get to that point was beyond me.

"I'll make you a deal." I spoke calmly to her as if we were having coffee rather than having sex, and I slipped my hand between her legs.

"What kind of deal?" she said, barely able to focus on my conversation.

"Well…" I kissed her and then pulled back in favor of massaging her shoulders and down her back. "I will make love to you…"

"Really?" she said as if my tone meant I was doing her a favor.

"Yes, I will…" I kissed her again, slightly longer this time, massaging her thighs and letting my hand drift across her belly and then sliding my fingers down between her legs once more. Finally lifting my lips from hers, I said, "If I satisfy you…" Her hips were moving slightly against me, her mouth was searching urgently for mine. "Then…" I drew the words out. "*If* I satisfy you…" Her moves were more intense and deliberate as her body begged me to stop delaying the pleasure. "…*then* you have to live with me," I whispered with the final thrust of her hips as she climaxed into me.

"Well, looks like that's settled," I said as she wrapped her arms around me.

"Very funny. Very cocky," she said, breathing hard. "And very good."

The phone rang. I reached across her and answered it. It was Barrett Silvers. I listened to Barrett's quick patter on the other end of the line, barely able to focus my thoughts.

"That's great. Perfect. No, I'm very excited," I said into the phone while looking at Callie. "Callie's excited too," I said, giving Callie a sly grin.

"Your voice sounds like you're having a better time than I am." Barrett lingered a moment on the phone.

I ignored the remark and said, "I'll call you later." I hung up and smiled at Callie. "They're going to let me write the script. I can either work from L.A., or Barrett has a cabin in Sedona that she'll loan me. It's very pretty there, more peaceful. I think the cabin would be great."

"Where will Barrett be?"

"In L.A. working, I assume…unless she's planning on taking time off."

"When will you be going to Sedona?"

"I thought Elmo and I would go home and take care of a few things. Transfer mail and calls and then plan on being in Sedona in two weeks. I'll have Jeremy's notes on the treatment by then, and I'll have eight weeks to do the first draft."

"Sedona is an extremely mystical place for psychics," she said.

"No kidding?" I feigned ignorance.

"I was thinking that maybe I should join you. I could get your place ready, do the shopping and run errands, take care of Elmo while you write. After all, this is a pretty big deal."

"That would be absolutely fabulous. Do you mean it?" I kissed her warmly.

"Uh-huh, I do," she sighed. "I know a great place there, down by the creek, a beautiful place. I'll make the arrangements. We won't need Barrett's cabin." She smiled, letting me know how she felt about anyone encroaching upon what just might be her territory.

"Okay then. I'll let Barrett know." I smiled.

"I'll let her know." She smiled back and then pulled me back onto her and kissed me into next week.

Things are definitely looking up, I thought, marveling, yet again, that timing is everything.

About the Authors

Andrews & Austin live on their ranch in the Central Plains. They were a screenwriting duo in L.A. for years before becoming writers of lesbian fiction. Their fast-paced, humorous style, strong characters, and great storytelling have roots in their motion picture backgrounds. When they take a break from writing, Andrews & Austin can be found riding their horses or working with their other animals on their ranch.

For more information visit www.andrewsaustin.com.

Books Available From Bold Strokes Books

Punk and Zen by JD Glass. Angst, sex, love, rock. Trace, Candace, Francesca...Samantha. Losing control—and finding the truth within. BSB Victory Editions. (1-933110-66-X)

Stellium in Scorpio by Andrews & Austin. The passionate reuniting of two powerful women on the glitzy Las Vegas Strip, where everything is an illusion and love is a gamble. (1-933110-65-1)

When Dreams Tremble by Radclyffe. Two women whose lives turned out far differently than they'd once imagined discover that sometimes the shape of the future can only be found in the past. (1-933110-64-3)

Fresh Tracks by Georgia Beers. Seven women, seven days. A lot can happen when old friends, lovers, and a new girl in town get together in the mountains. (1-933110-63-5)

The Empress and the Acolyte by Jane Fletcher. Jemeryl and Tevi fight to protect the very fabric of their world…time. Lyremouth Chronicles Book Three (1-933110-60-0)

First Instinct by JLee Meyer. When high-stakes security fraud leads to murder, one woman flees for her life while another risks her heart to protect her. (1-933110-59-7)

Erotic Interludes 4: Extreme Passions. Thirty of today's hottest erotica writers set the pages aflame with love, lust, and steamy liaisons. (1-933110-58-9)

Storms of Change by Radclyffe. In the continuing saga of the Provincetown Tales, duty and love are at odds as Reese and Tory face their greatest challenge. (1-933110-57-0)

Unexpected Ties by Gina L. Dartt. With death before dessert, Kate Shannon and Nikki Harris are swept up in another tale of danger and romance. (1-933110-56-2)

Sleep of Reason by Rose Beecham. Nothing is as it seems when Detective Jude Devine finds herself caught up in a small-town soap opera. And her rocky relationship with forensic pathologist Dr. Mercy Westmoreland just got a lot harder. (1-933110-53-8)

Passion's Bright Fury by Radclyffe. When a trauma surgeon and a filmmaker become reluctant allies on the battleground between life and death, passion strikes without warning. (1-933110-54-6)

Broken Wings by L-J Baker. When Rye Woods, a fairy, meets the beautiful dryad Flora Withe, her libido, as squashed and hidden as her wings, reawakens along with her heart. (1-933110-55-4)

Combust the Sun by Andrews & Austin. A Richfield and Rivers mystery set in L.A. Murder among the stars. (1-933110-52-X)

Of Drag Kings and the Wheel of Fate by Susan Smith. A blind date in a drag club leads to an unlikely romance. (1-933110-51-1)

Tristaine Rises by Cate Culpepper. Brenna, Jesstin, and the Amazons of Tristaine face their greatest challenge for survival. (1-933110-50-3)

Too Close to Touch by Georgia Beers. Kylie O'Brien believes in true love and is willing to wait for it. It doesn't matter one damn bit that Gretchen, her new and off-limits boss, has a voice as rich and smooth as melted chocolate. It absolutely doesn't... (1-933110-47-3)

100th Generation by Justine Saracen. Ancient curses, modern-day villains, and a most intriguing woman who keeps appearing when least expected lead archeologist Valerie Foret on the adventure of her life. (1-933110-48-1)

Battle for Tristaine by Cate Culpepper. While Brenna struggles to find her place in the clan and the love between her and Jess grows, Tristaine is threatened with destruction. Second in the Tristaine series. (1-933110-49-X)

The Traitor and the Chalice by Jane Fletcher. Without allies to help them, Tevi and Jemeryl will have to risk all in the race to uncover the traitor and retrieve the chalice. The Lyremouth Chronicles Book Two. (1-933110-43-0)

Promising Hearts by Radclyffe. Dr. Vance Phelps lost everything in the War Between the States and arrives in New Hope, Montana, with no hope of happiness and no desire for anything except forgetting—until she meets Mae, a frontier madam. (1-933110-44-9)

Carly's Sound by Ali Vali. Poppy Valente and Julia Johnson form a bond of friendship that lays the foundation for something more, until Poppy's past comes back to haunt her—literally. A poignant romance about love and renewal. (1-933110-45-7)

Unexpected Sparks by Gina L. Dartt. Falling in love is challenging enough without adding murder to the mix. Kate Shannon's growing feelings for much younger Nikki Harris are complicated enough without the mystery of a fatal fire that Kate can't ignore. (1-933110-46-5)

Whitewater Rendezvous by Kim Baldwin. Two women on a wilderness kayak adventure—Chaz Herrick, a laid-back outdoorswoman, and Megan Maxwell, a workaholic news executive—discover that true love may be nothing at all like they imagined. (1-933110-38-4)

Erotic Interludes 3: Lessons in Love ed. by Radclyffe and Stacia Seaman. Sign on for a class in love...the best lesbian erotica writers take us to "school." (1-9331100-39-2)

Punk Like Me by JD Glass. Twenty-one-year-old Nina writes lyrics and plays guitar in the rock band Adam's Rib, and she doesn't always play by the rules. And oh yeah—she has a way with the girls. (1-933110-40-6)

Coffee Sonata by Gun Brooke. Four women whose lives unexpectedly intersect in a small town by the sea share one thing in common—they all have secrets. (1-933110-41-4)

The Clinic: Tristaine Book One by Cate Culpepper. Brenna, a prison medic, finds herself deeply conflicted by her growing feelings for her patient, Jesstin, a wild and rebellious warrior reputed to be descended from ancient Amazons. (1-933110-42-2)

Forever Found by JLee Meyer. Can time, tragedy, and shattered trust destroy a love that seemed destined? When chance reunites two childhood friends separated by tragedy, the past resurfaces to determine the shape of their future. (1-933110-37-6)

Sword of the Guardian by Merry Shannon. Princess Shasta's bold new bodyguard has a secret that could change both of their lives. *He* is actually a *she*. A passionate romance filled with courtly intrigue, chivalry, and devotion. (1-933110-36-8)

Wild Abandon by Ronica Black. From their first tumultuous meeting, Dr. Chandler Brogan and Officer Sarah Monroe are drawn together by their common obsessions—sex, speed, and danger. (1-933110-35-X)

Turn Back Time by Radclyffe. Pearce Rifkin and Wynter Thompson have nothing in common but a shared passion for surgery. They clash at every opportunity, especially when matters of the heart are suddenly at stake. (1-933110-34-1)

Chance by Grace Lennox. At twenty-six, Chance Delaney decides her life isn't working so she swaps it for a different one. What follows is the sexy, funny, touching story of two women who, in finding themselves, also find one another. (1-933110-31-7)

The Exile and the Sorcerer by Jane Fletcher. First in the Lyremouth Chronicles. Tevi, wounded and adrift, arrives in the courtyard of a shy young sorcerer. Together they face monsters, magic, and the challenge of loving despite their differences. (1-933110-32-5)

A Matter of Trust by Radclyffe. JT Sloan is a cybersleuth who doesn't like attachments. Michael Lassiter is leaving her husband, and she needs Sloan's expertise to safeguard her company. It should just be business—but it turns into much more. (1-933110-33-3)

Sweet Creek by Lee Lynch. A celebration of the enduring nature of love, friendship, and community in the quirky, heart-warming lesbian community of Waterfall Falls. (1-933110-29-5)

The Devil Inside by Ali Vali. Derby Cain Casey, head of a New Orleans crime organization, runs the family business with guts and grit, and no one crosses her. No one, that is, until Emma Verde claims her heart and turns her world upside down. (1-933110-30-9)

Grave Silence by Rose Beecham. Detective Jude Devine's investigation of a series of ritual murders is complicated by her torrid affair with the golden girl of Southwestern forensic pathology, Dr. Mercy Westmoreland. (1-933110-25-2)

Honor Reclaimed by Radclyffe. In the aftermath of 9/11, Secret Service Agent Cameron Roberts and Blair Powell close ranks with a trusted few to find the would-be assassins who nearly claimed Blair's life. (1-933110-18-X)

Honor Bound by Radclyffe. Secret Service Agent Cameron Roberts and Blair Powell face political intrigue, a clandestine threat to Blair's safety, and the seemingly irreconcilable personal differences that force them ever farther apart. (1-933110-20-1)

Innocent Hearts by Radclyffe. In a wild and unforgiving land, two women learn about love, passion, and the wonders of the heart. (1-933110-21-X)

The Temple at Landfall by Jane Fletcher. An imprinter, one of Celaeno's most revered servants of the Goddess, is also a prisoner to the faith—until a Ranger frees her by claiming her heart. The Celaeno series. (1-933110-27-9)

Protector of the Realm: Supreme Constellations Book One by Gun Brooke. A space adventure filled with suspense and a daring intergalactic romance featuring Commodore Rae Jacelon and the stunning, but decidedly lethal, Kellen O'Dal. (1-933110-26-0)

Force of Nature by Kim Baldwin. From tornados to forest fires, the forces of nature conspire to bring Gable McCoy and Erin Richards close to danger, and closer to each other. (1-933110-23-6)

In Too Deep by Ronica Black. Undercover homicide cop Erin McKenzie tracks a femme fatale who just might be a real killer…with love and danger hot on her heels. (1-933110-17-1)

Stolen Moments: Erotic Interludes 2 by Stacia Seaman and Radclyffe, eds. Love on the run, in the office, in the shadows…Fast, furious, and almost too hot to handle. (1-933110-16-3)

Course of Action by Gun Brooke. Actress Carolyn Black desperately wants the starring role in an upcoming film produced by Annelie Peterson. Just how far will she go for the dream part of a lifetime? (1-933110-22-8)

Rangers at Roadsend by Jane Fletcher. Sergeant Chip Coppelli has learned to spot trouble coming, and that is exactly what she sees in her new recruit, Katryn Nagata. The Celaeno series. (1-933110-28-7)

Justice Served by Radclyffe. Lieutenant Rebecca Frye and her lover, Dr. Catherine Rawlings, embark on a deadly game of hide-and-seek with an underworld kingpin who traffics in human souls. (1-933110-15-5)

Distant Shores, Silent Thunder by Radclyffe. Dr. Tory King—along with the women who love her—is forced to examine the boundaries of love, friendship, and the ties that transcend time. (1-933110-08-2)

Hunter's Pursuit by Kim Baldwin. A raging blizzard, a mountain hideaway, and a killer-for-hire set a scene for disaster—or desire—when Katarzyna Demetrious rescues a beautiful stranger. (1-933110-09-0)

The Walls of Westernfort by Jane Fletcher. All Temple Guard Natasha Ionadis wants is to serve the Goddess—until she falls in love with one of the rebels she is sworn to destroy. The Celaeno series. (1-933110-24-4)

Change Of Pace: *Erotic Interludes* by Radclyffe. Twenty-five hot-wired encounters guaranteed to spark more than just your imagination. Erotica as you've always dreamed of it. (1-933110-07-4)

Honor Guards by Radclyffe. In a wild flight for their lives, the president's daughter and those who are sworn to protect her wage a desperate struggle for survival. (1-933110-01-5)

Fated Love by Radclyffe. Amidst the chaos and drama of a busy emergency room, two women must contend not only with the fragile nature of life, but also with the irresistible forces of fate. (1-933110-05-8)

Justice in the Shadows by Radclyffe. In a shadow world of secrets and lies, Detective Sergeant Rebecca Frye and her lover, Dr. Catherine Rawlings, join forces in the elusive search for justice.
(1-933110-03-1)

shadowland by Radclyffe. In a world on the far edge of desire, two women are drawn together by power, passion, and dark pleasures. An erotic romance. (1-933110-11-2)

Love's Masquerade by Radclyffe. Plunged into the indistinguishable realms of fiction, fantasy, and hidden desires, Auden Frost is forced to question all she believes about the nature of love. (1-933110-14-7)

Love & Honor by Radclyffe. The president's daughter and her lover are faced with difficult choices as they battle a tangled web of Washington intrigue for...love and honor. (1-933110-10-4)

Beyond the Breakwater by Radclyffe. One Provincetown summer, three women learn the true meaning of love, friendship, and family. (1-933110-06-6)

Tomorrow's Promise by Radclyffe. One timeless summer, two very different women discover the power of passion to heal and the promise of hope that only love can bestow. (1-933110-12-0)

Love's Tender Warriors by Radclyffe. Two women who have accepted loneliness as a way of life learn that love is worth fighting for and a battle they cannot afford to lose. (1-933110-02-3)

Love's Melody Lost by Radclyffe. A secretive artist with a haunted past and a young woman escaping a life that has proved to be a lie find their destinies entwined. (1-933110-00-7)

Safe Harbor by Radclyffe. A mysterious newcomer, a reclusive doctor, and a troubled gay teenager learn about love, friendship, and trust during one tumultuous summer in Provincetown. (1-933110-13-9)

Above All, Honor by Radclyffe. Secret Service Agent Cameron Roberts fights her desire for the one woman she can't have—Blair Powell, the daughter of the president of the United States. (1-933110-04-X)

BOLD
STROKES
BOOKS